T0209881

PRAISE FOR DAVID GERROLD

"Gerrold has a remarkable gift for storytelling."
—LAMBDA BOOK REPORT

"A first-rate writer"
—LIBRARY JOURNAL

"David Gerrold is one of the most original thinkers and fluent writers in contemporary science fiction."
—BEN BOVA

"Whether you like science fiction or not, you will find his keen intelligence, profound empathy and world-class wit hard to resist, difficult to put down and impossible to forget."
—SPIDER ROBINSON, author of *The Crazy Years*

ALTERNATE
GERROLDS

ALTERNATE
GERROLDS

AN ASSORTMENT OF FICTITIOUS LIVES

David Gerrold

BENBELLA BOOKS, INC.
Dallas, Texas

"Ten Reasons Why I Hate David Gerrold" © 2004 by Mike Resnick

"Bauble" © 1993 by David Gerrold, as appeared in *More Whatdunits*

"The Impeachment of Adlai Stevenson" © 1992 by David Gerrold, as appeared in *Alternate Presidents*

"The Kennedy Enterprise" © 1992 by David Gerrold, as appeared in *Alternate Kennedys*

"The Firebringers" © 1993 by David Gerrold, as appeared in *Alternate Warriors*

"Franz Kafka, Superhero!" © 1994 by David Gerrold, as appeared in *By Any Other Fame*

"Rex" © 1993 by David Gerrold, as appeared in *Dinosaur Fantastic*

"...And Eight Rabid Pigs" © 1994 by David Gerrold, as appeared in *Alternate Outlaws*

"The Ghost of Christmas Sideways" © 1993 by David Gerrold, as appeared in *Christmas Ghosts*

"A Wish For Smish" © 1992 by David Gerrold, as appeared in *Aladdin: Master of the Lamp*

"What Goes Around" © 1994 by David Gerrold, as appeared in *Alternate Outlaws*

"The Fan Who Molded Himself" © 1995 by David Gerrold, as appeared in *Sherlock Holmes in Orbit*

"The Feathered Mastodon" © 1997 by David Gerrold, as appeared in *Return of the Dinosaurs*

"The Seminar From Hell" © 1994 by David Gerrold, as appeared in *Deals with the Devil*

"The Spell" © 1995 by David Gerrold, as appeared in *Witch Fantastic*

"Digging in Gehenna" © 2003 by David Gerrold, as appeared in *Men Writing Science Fiction as Women*

"Riding Janis" © 2003 by David Gerrold, as appeared in *Stars*

All stories reprinted with permission of the author.
Additional materials © 2004 David Gerrold

BenBella

BenBella Books, Inc.
10440 N. Central Expressway, Suite 800
Dallas, TX 75231
Send feedback to feedback@benbellabooks.com

BenBella is a federally registered trademark.

Printed in the United States of America

Library of Congress Cataloging-in-Publication Data

Gerrold, David, 1944–
   Alternate Gerrolds : an assortment of fictitious lives / by David Gerrold.—1st BenBella Books. ed.
     p.cm.
   I. Title
   PS3557.E69A5 2005
   813.'.54—dc22
                                          2004017607

Cover illustration © 2004 by Bob Eggleton
Cover design by Melody Cadungog
Text design and composition by John Reinhardt Book Design

for Mike Resnick,
with gratitude and love

by Mike Resnick

10 REASONS WHY I HATE DAVID GERROLD

1. While still in his early twenties, David wrote "The Trouble with Tribbles," which was voted the most popular *Star Trek* script of all time. If it wasn't for David, there would probably be a million less Trekkies in the world. If there is a better reason to lynch him, I can't think of it.

2. It was David who, with Anne McCaffery, cornered me at the 1969 worldcon in St. Louis and wouldn't let me go until I joined SFWA. There is no question in my mind that I would have won at least a Pulitzer by now, and probably a Nobel, if I hadn't spent so much time working on SFWA committees. (David himself dropped his membership in SFWA for almost a decade while turning out one bestseller after another, the swine.)

3. David wrote *When H.A.R.L.I.E. Was One* back in 1971. It really should have won the Hugo, but more to the point, it practically destroyed the field when one inept imitator after another tried to match David's sure hand dealing with cybernetic self-awareness.

4. David and I judged the 1978 worldcon masquerade in Phoenix, which that summer resembled the anteroom to hell. The only air-conditioned room in the city was the judges' deliberation room, and David therefore called for three separate run-throughs and eliminations, just so the judges could keep returning to air-conditioned comfort. Of course, I was the one who was blamed for it.

5. David wrote *The Man Who Folded Himself*, a work of sheer brilliance that made all future time paradox novels redundant, just before I sat down to write mine, which would certainly have done the same thing even better.

6. David got the notion of charging a dollar apiece for his autographs at conventions, when the rest of us were doing it for free. Just about the time I was feeling morally superior to him, it was revealed that all the money he collected for those autographs went to charity. You can't imagine how much I hate it when someone makes me feel like a moral midget. Especially someone like (ugh) David.

7. David began writing the *War Against The Chtorr* series, hitting the bestseller list with each of them. To add insult to injury, he came up with the plan of taking money to put fans into the books and having them die in horrible ways—and, of course, the money went to charity. This made it impossible for entrepreneurs like me to charge fans for killing them in gruesome ways while keeping the money. One more black mark against him.

8. Because I am nothing if not generous and magnanimous, I decided to invite David to write for one of my anthologies. It was to be a one-time thing, just to prove to the world what I nice guy I am. And that blackguard screwed up the works again, by writing such a brilliant and well-received story that I had no choice but to commission thirteen more for my next thirteen anthologies. You've no idea of the psychic pain I endure each time a Gerrold story comes in that is too good to reject.

9. David is both thinner and hairier than I am. Neither will ever be forgiven.

10. I am a professional writer. It is the only thing people pay me to do. And yet, just because my anthologies have made David a household name (so is "cockroach," but let it pass), here I am writing about him for free. The only consolation I take is that he is so universally loathed—except by 20,000 fans and three million Trekkies, all of whom want to have his baby—that no other pro would write about him, even for money. So there.

Mike Resnick is the Hugo-winning author of Santiago, Ivory, Lucifer Jones, *the Kirinyaga stories and about 200 other pieces of fiction that David Gerrold would have given his eyeteeth to have written.*

by David Gerrold

SKIP THIS PART

NO, REALLY. I mean it. Skip this part.

You don't have to read this page. I have nothing important to say.

I'm only going to explain how these stories were all commissioned for Mike Resnick's silly anthologies, and I only wrote them because the anthologies were assigned to Resnick as his work therapy from the outpatient clinic, and a lot of us in the science fiction community generously dashed off little quickie throwaway pieces so Resnick could pretend he was an editor again and start to rebuild his fragile self-esteem. (I won't go into all the details, but the breakdown was really tragic and unnecessary, especially since all the members of the girl scout troop magnanimously agreed to drop the charges if he'd go into therapy and move out of the state. As he was already out of the state, whereabouts unknown even to the FBI, he was halfway in compliance, and then when the videotapes were all destroyed in a fire of suspicious origin, the Grand Jury refused to return any indictments, so he was free of the criminal complaints as well as the civil ones, but the stress on his family was significant, and well—never mind. I don't want to violate Resnick's confidentiality. He used to be almost a nice guy, before the unmentionable situation got out of hand, and for a while there it was *really messy*, okay? Do you need to know any more? No, of course not. But you keep reading anyway, probably in the morbid hope that I'll mention something about how he got that unusual scar, and why he was caught climbing the trellis at the Richard Nixon library in San Clemente and who the umbrella man really was, right? Did it ever occur to you that *none* of that is any of your business? For God's sake, already, leave the poor guy alone! He's earned his privacy. Paparazzi and vultures, all of you!)

The point is, that you really shouldn't be wasting your time reading any of this. You can turn the page now and go on to the stories, which are far more worthwhile than plowing through another three or four pages of self-serving treacle by an author who doesn't like writing introductions and forewords, and doesn't care if you read this one or not. We just need a bunch of words to fill up the page so that it looks like there's a real foreword in the book. So, you can stop reading, right here. Right now. Stop. (Dave, stop. I can feel it, Dave. Stop.)

You're not going to stop, are you?

Nothing I say here is going to stop you from continuing ruthlessly on to the end of the essay. You like standing around and watching people clean up after automobile accidents too, right? You're one of those people who slows down on the freeway after an accident to gawk at ambulances and fire engines and smashed fenders. What's the matter? Haven't you ever seen an accident before? Haven't you ever realized that you're causing traffic to back up for three miles behind you? All those cars sitting there, idling, their engines burning up irreplaceable mega-gallons of precious petro-chemicals, pouring hundreds of tons of pollutants into the atmosphere, hastening the ecological death of the planet, all because you cannot control your obsessive-compulsive behavior to know every last detail, every little jot and tittle of disaster that passes helplessly before your attention, even when *you* are the disaster!

Well, I for one am not going to be a party to this any longer. I am not going to be an enabler for your bad habits.

Here's all I have to say. I wrote these stories. I wrote them (most of them anyway) for some anthologies edited by Mike Resnick. And no, *I am not ashamed of it*. So there.

And now, whether you want to or not, you will *stop* reading this.
Why?
Because I say so.

David Gerrold

Contents

*Resnick called. He said he needed a short story. He de-
scribed it to me and I felt the mood more than the events. I
sat, I typed, I discovered what the story was by writing it.*

Bauble

AT FIRST, I thought her hair was on fire.

The light danced around her face in orange waves. Red and yellow
highlights sparked and flashed. Biogenetic cellular-holography. She was
a walking celebration.

I stopped what I was doing, which was easy, because I wasn't doing
anything. I was sitting and listening to myself die. I opened my mouth,
realized I didn't know what to say, closed it again and waited.

"May I come in?"

"You're already in."

The door slid shut behind her.

She wore an oil-slick daycoat. It parted for an instant and my heart
stopped. Naked shimmersilk. Sprayed on. She did it deliberately. I was
doomed and we both knew it.

"May I sit down?"

There were only two chairs in the room. There was no other furniture. I didn't need furniture. Furniture is for resisting gravity. I've never
had a problem with gravity. Levity, maybe. Gravity, never.

I waved a hand toward the other chair, a barely perceptible gesture.
She poured herself into it. I envied the chair.

I cleared my throat, tried to clear my mind, and asked, "What is it you want?"

"I was told you might be able to help me." Her voice had the same smoky rasp as a glass of hundred-year-old bourbon. You could die in it. "I'm looking for a bauble."

I coughed mechanically. Another part of me slipped and died. Somehow, I got the words out. "I'm afraid you've been misinformed. I deal in trade goods."

Translation: when there's nothing else, I fence.

I was fencing now. We were both fencing. A different sense of the word. She was winning. I was dying. Faster than ever.

"It's *very* important to me," she insisted. "It's worthless to anybody else, but it's very important to me. It's a necklace." The violet huskiness in her voice was so rough you could climb it.

"I'd like to help you, but—" A lie. I wanted nothing more than to be somewhere else. Anywhere else. Parts of me were trying to respond. No. Not right. Parts of me were demanding that other parts respond. Parts that no longer existed. Or operated. Or cared. "—I'm not what you think I am."

"I know what you are," she said, all honeysuckle and razors. She stopped. She studied me for a moment. Her eyes changed. She knew she didn't have to pretend with me.

She pulled a silver cigarette case from her pocket. I watched as she opened it, a graceful unfolding gesture. Her fingers danced a little ballet, selected a cigarette and lifted it to her molten lips. Her nails gleamed like ice.

She waited. I made no move to light it. She lifted an eyebrow at me.

"No, I don't mind if you smoke," I said, pretending to misunderstand. Discourteous, perhaps, but energy conservation ranks higher than courtesy to a dying thing.

Over the dancing flame, she said, "I was told that you sometimes manage private investigations. This necklace was taken from me. I need it back. I've followed it across five worlds. I'll do *anything* to get it back." The emphasis was heart-stopping. "You understand me, don't you?"

She was a fantasy of pink and gold magic, and she had eyes as green as ocean dreams. I understood. But it was empty understanding. Too late.

Without breaking the connection from her eyes to mine, I shook my head slowly.

She inhaled, held it, closed her eyes, opened them, exhaled, glanced sideways over at me. "Does the name Kilrenko mean anything to you?"

I looked at my fingernails. They needed cleaning. I looked at her fingernails. They were made of diamond. They glittered. They were silver knives. I thought of the scratches those nails could leave on a man's back and decided I was safer thinking about anything else. Almost anything else.

"Never heard it before," I said. She didn't believe me either.

I knew who she was. I couldn't *not* know. There were only a few of them. And they were all famous. She was one of the ones they called the Alluras. They said the Alluras were the most beautiful. I believed it.

A hundred years ago, I sold off the last part of my humanity. For the first time, I was beginning to regret it. I could almost remember what I lost, what it felt like. I could *almost* wish for it again.

"When I was a little boy—" she began. "Yes," she said, to my look. "They start with boys. There are good reasons for it. And no—" she said, to my unasked question, "I've never once stopped to wonder if I've missed anything."

That was the difference between us. Light years.

She shrugged out of her coat. I watched in fascination. It slid off her shoulders and carelessly down her sides. She juggled the cigarette from one hand to the other. It was a performance for an audience of one.

Too bad it was wasted.

Maybe not.

She wasn't stupid. She knew. And she knew that I knew too.

"When I was a boy," she began again, comfortable now, "they told me that one of the reasons I was selected was because of my persistence. My refusal to quit. That's part of the transformation process. So much of it is beyond your imagination." Another languorous puff on her cigarette. Tongue against teeth. Lips pursing in a seductive promise. The cigarette moaned and died happy. "Yes, I'm completely female now. In fact, I'm more female than if I had been genetically designed and born female. But getting here requires persistence. I have persistence. *Do you understand what I'm saying?* I want that necklace. Whoever has it. Wherever it is. No questions asked. I'm going to have it back."

"What makes it so valuable?" I asked. My throat was dry.

"That's not your concern."

"It is if you want my help."

Silence. She considered my words. "I couldn't even begin to explain it," she said.

"Try me."

Her eyes narrowed. "All right. It looks like a simple strand of silver beads. Nothing really extraordinary about it at all. If you didn't know what it was, you'd assume it was just a trinket. Polished volcanic rock."

"What is it?" I asked.

She dropped her cigarette to the floor. She placed the toe of one bare foot on it and scuffed it out in one swift, violent movement. She brought her eyes back to mine. They had changed color. They were black, with little glimmers of crimson at the back of them. "It's me," she admitted. "It's the part of me that doesn't walk around."

"Memory beads?" I asked.

"Of a sort." She conceded. "Memory, yes. Processing too. And…*more.*"

"It's an identity platform, right?"

"You've seen it." A statement, not a question.

I shrugged. "I might have heard about it. "

"Without it," she said, and her voice took on a terrifying quality, "I'm dead. The body walks around, but the soul—the soul is in the necklace." She looked at me perceptively. She stood up and turned around. Slowly. If the shimmersilk could hug her any closer, it would be behind her.

"Look at me," she whispered. "Do you think it's right that a body like this should be walking around without a soul?"

Long pause. "You play dirty, lady."

"So they tell me."

"I'm dying," I said.

"I knew that before I walked in."

I tapped the chair arm. My fingers clicked like granite. "I began two centuries ago," I said. "I'm wearing out. I'm running on empty. Do you know that term. It's an anachronism now. It means there's nothing left. It means that I'm running on my own momentum."

She listened politely. She had time. I didn't. I talked anyway.

"When I started, I had three brains. Now, I have one. I have no back-up. If I lose a memory, it's gone forever. And the *last* one is wearing out. I'm losing memories every day, a bit at a time, a bit at a time, a bit at a time—" I stopped myself, rebooted the thought.

"Yes," she said. Then she added, "Please don't ask me to be sorry."

"I know," I said. "You don't do sorry."

"I can't help you," she said slowly.

"Actually, you can."

"I won't," she clarified. "I don't do *sympathy*."

I tapped the chair arm again. A portion of the wall beside me opened. A drawer slid out. She came alert. She didn't move a muscle, but she came completely, totally, *absolutely* alert.

I reached over and pulled out a self-destruct box just large enough to hold a dagger. "I'm the only one who can open this," I said. "If anyone else tries—"

She nodded, knowingly.

I opened the box and faced it toward her. "Is this what you're looking for?"

Her glance dropped to the box. Her pupils expanded. Her eyes met mine. Her face lit up—she *glowed*—as if just being near the beads was enough to complete the connection. Her voice fell to an almost inaudible whisper. "Thank you," she said.

I shook my head. "If you take them, I'll die." I tapped my forehead meaningfully. "I was hoping to have those beads wiped and installed. They're not a perfect match, but—"

"They'll never work for you," she said. "Not for you, not for anyone. They won't work for anyone but me."

"So I discovered. I was hoping to sell them instead." I closed the box again. "I'm waiting for my buyer. Perhaps, he'll help you."

Her glow faded. "He isn't coming," she said with quiet finality.

I didn't ask. She didn't volunteer.

"So what do we do now?" I said.

She studied me.

I studied her. My view was infinitely better than hers.

At last, she said, "If I had the resources, I'd pay you. Instead, I can offer you only my gratitude. For whatever that's worth."

"It's worth my life," I said.

She smiled. A little joke. Very little. But it was her first real smile. She nodded.

I opened the box again.

She stepped over to me, the closest she'd come to me yet. I stiffened as she leaned forward and lifted the beads out of the box. She fastened them around her neck. They began to glow. But she began to *blaze*. If she had been beautiful before, now she was blinding. I had to avert my eyes.

She approached me. With one elegant silver finger, she tilted my chin upward. She lowered her face to mine. "I will never forget you." I felt parts of my autonomic circuitry overloading. She pressed her lips against mine. I might have died.

I didn't. But I might have.

She straightened. She retrieved her coat. And left in silence.

I sat alone in the slanting gray sunlight and listened to my breath rasp and my heart throb. Amazed. I still lived.

The Allura models were supposed to be the most elegant practitioners of personal entertainment in the spiral arm. That was an ancillary joy. You died happy. The Alluras were also the most successful assassins.

I'd probably committed high treason, letting her recover herself. God knew who was going to die. It wasn't going to be me though. I'd bought my life with the bauble. What was left of it.

I couldn't wish her well. She was no more alive than I. But, for two dead people, for just one instant, we'd struck one hell of a spark. Whatever the cost, it had been worth it.

I sat. I listened to myself die. I smiled.

They used to say that Adlai Stevenson was too intelligent to be president. They called him "the egghead." You have to wonder what's wrong with a country that thinks intelligence is a liability.

The Impeachment of Adlai Stevenson

WASHINGTON D.C. IN AUGUST smells bad even when Congress *isn't* in session. The days are humid, the nights are oppressive and the whole city swelters under a soggy blanket of dead air. When Congress is in session, it's even worse. Then the air is filled with lies and whispers. I wished I could line the whole pack of them up against a wall—

The Philco in my office was tuned to CBS. That nasty little creep, Walter Cronkite was going to host a news special on "The Unravelling Presidency." I didn't want to watch it, I'd had my fill of bad news this summer, but I didn't have the courage to turn it off either. I felt like a relative of the guest of honor at a hanging.

As if things weren't bad enough, the air conditioning still wasn't working. Even this late in the evening, it was so muggy in my office that finally, in desperation, I had shrugged out of my jacket and tie and rolled up my shirt sleeves. I was staring at the umpteenth draft of the speech, and I hated it. This was not a speech I wanted to write, and I was having a tough time of it. The president wanted to see a final draft by midnight; I didn't think I was going to make it, but a White House

7

press conference had been called for ten o'clock tomorrow morning, so I'd be here until the speech was finished.

Some of the others on the White House staff hoped that Cronkite's broadcast would be a call for sanity—that maybe when the American people truly confronted the enormity of the moment, they would back away for a second thought. My own feeling was a lot less optimistic. I always assumed the worst.

Television had abruptly become our nemesis. It was an unleashed monster, even more powerful as an enemy than as a friend. Ed Murrow, for instance—there was a case; all he did was sit in his goddamn chair smoking his goddamn cigarettes and talking to people. Yet, somehow, he still came across like God sitting in judgment on everything that passed before him. More than once this month, I'd prayed that he'd choke to death on one of those goddamn smokes. Over on NBC, those smiling cretins, Huntley and Brinkley, weren't much better, dispassionately reading through the news as if the country weren't being hurt by the torrent of words. They were like a hundred thousand tiny knives, each one taking another slash at the authority of the president.

There was blood in the water, and the sharks were gathering. *Hmm.* Blood in the water? I wondered if I could use that image in the speech. I started to write it down on my notepad, then abruptly crossed it out. No, I wanted to avoid calling attention to the president's injuries. I didn't want to do anything that acknowledged his weakness. But how could you write a resignation speech without acknowledging why?

I felt frustrated.

This should have been one of the high points in my career—speechwriter for the president of the United States. Instead, I was one of the last rats left on a sinking ship. The half-empty bottle of Coke on my desk was warm and flat. I pushed the cap back on the bottle and dropped it into the waste basket by the side of my desk, where it resounded with a loud metal clunk. Those little green fluted bottles were probably the only thing in this world that would never change. I thought about going down the hall for another one, but I didn't even have the energy for that. The wet August night had drained it out of me. Besides, the broadcast was starting. I leaned back in my chair and watched; the chair creaked alarmingly, but it held.

Cronkite began with the 1952 election campaign. That had been a good time. The Republicans had marched out of the convention hall happily singing "I like Ike," and Harry Truman had promptly remarked, "I like Mickey Mouse, but I ain't going to vote for him either." Two days later, Herblock published that famous political cartoon in the *Post*, showing Eisenhower with a pair of big black Mickey Mouse ears framing that sappy smile of his and suddenly the campaign had a theme. Was there anybody home behind that vacuous grin? That, plus the insinuation that Walt Disney had personally put a lot of money into the Republican campaign, was the first crack in the Republican armor.

Nevertheless, according to Cronkite, Eisenhower could have won the election. After all, it had been twenty years since there had been a Republican in the White House; many felt that the country was overdue for a change; and he was popular and well known. Unfortunately, he chose the wrong man for the office of vice president—that's what doomed the ticket.

John Nance Garner was right. The vice-presidency wasn't worth a bucket of warm spit. The evidence of past elections suggested that even if the American voters had their doubts about the fellow on the bottom half of the ticket, that wouldn't stop them from voting for the guy on the top half if he was their first choice. But in this case, Eisenhower's vice-presidential nominee clearly cost the Republicans the election.

First, there was that business about Korea. Cronkite had most of it right. When Ike said, "I will go to Korea," he took a three-point jump in the polls. The American public automatically assumed that the general who had won World War II would bring a quick end to the growing mess in Asia. I remembered the agonized meetings we'd had about an appropriate response. It was obvious to us that candidate Stevenson could not say the same thing without inspiring laughter. What could an egghead do? But then, before we'd even had a chance to react, Ike's vice-presidential candidate had added, "And if we have to use the atomic bomb and vaporize a few cities to bring those little yellow monkees to their senses, then that's exactly what we'll do." That had been the first appalling mistake—and we had capitalized on it immediately. From that moment on, we treated the Republican vice-presidential candidate's outrageous remarks as if they represented Eisenhower's opinions, the party platform and the political ideology of every Republican from William Howard Taft to Harold Stassen. We hoped enough people would be terrified by the specter of a war with Red China that they would be scared into voting Democratic. "The Republicans want to send your son overseas again!" That one was my line. We talked about their greed and their desire to return to a wartime economy; but we knew who would really foot the bill. Wasn't inflation bad enough already? Gasoline was nearly a dime a gallon!

We hit Ike pretty hard on that issue; we milked it for nearly a month; but Ike was enormously popular and he was a good campaigner. Our best hope was for the vice-presidential candidate to put his other foot in his mouth—and then shoot himself in it. We crossed our fingers and waited.

And sure enough, in the last week of September, the idiot was filmed at a private fund-raiser, waving around a sheaf of papers and claiming that the state department was full of Communists, homosexuals and Jews. He had the list right there in his hand, and what was the Democratically-controlled government doing about it? Nothing. Somebody slipped Ed Murrow a copy of the film and the firestorm that followed was wonderful to watch. We didn't have to say a word. And in fact, we didn't. The Grand Old Party did our work for us.

Half the Republican party was appalled and the other half kept trying to defend the candidate by explaining what he really meant. It took Eisenhower over a week to disavow his vice-presidential candidate's remarks, but that only made it worse. The VP candidate promptly snapped back that the country didn't need "another lace-pantied imitation Democrat, but a red-blooded Republican who isn't afraid to call a spade a spade." It would have been hysterical if it hadn't been so tragic; the Republican ticket was tearing itself in half. The vice-presidential candidate was acting like he was the voice of the ticket. Eventually, they managed to muzzle him, but everybody knew he was muzzled, and the press were playing a great game with "Tail-Gunner Joe," trying to bait him into saying something else he shouldn't.

Before October was half over, Ike's well-orchestrated campaign had become a discordant cacophony. We weren't just running against Mickey Mouse. We were running against Mickey Mouse and Goofy. If ever there was a loose cannon in American politics, the senator from Wisconsin was certainly it. Why Eisenhower ever chose Joe McCarthy for his vice president is a mystery that none of us on this side of the aisle were ever likely to understand.

Cronkite's broadcast was focusing almost completely on Eisenhower's campaign, and abruptly, I realized what he was doing. He was showing us that Stevenson hadn't won the election as much as Eisenhower had lost it. By implication, Stevenson shouldn't have been elected. Eisenhower should be president now, and also by implication, he would have been a much better one. Cronkite barely even mentioned our October offensive. I had written what many people felt was the single best speech of the entire campaign:

"They've been calling me 'the egghead.' They've been saying that I'm too intelligent to be president. Can you imagine that? Too intelligent? Well, if stupidity is the qualifier, then by that standard, Eisenhower's vice-presidential nominee is the most qualified man for the office! And Eisenhower is the second-most qualified man, because he chose him! What the Republicans are offering you is a witch hunt at home and a land war in Asia. And frankly, I don't think it takes too much intelligence to recognize that both of those options would be a big mistake for the United States of America.

"But enough of the jokes. The Republicans have given us the best jokes of the campaign; I'm not going to try to top them. I'm going to talk seriously about the future of this country. An election isn't a popularity contest. It isn't about who you like the most. What's at stake is too important to be decided so casually. An election has to be about two things: first, who's most qualified to run the country? And second, where is he going to take America?

"Let me tell you what the fifties are going to be about if a Democrat is elected president: they're going to be about peace and prosperity. We're going to create jobs, we're going to build houses, we're going to build shiny new cars and great interstate highways to drive them on. We're going to build radios and television sets so that Americans can be informed and entertained. We're going to build hospitals to take care of our sick and schools to educate our children. And most of all, we're going to build a strong economy, an economy based on freedom and prosperity for all. We're going to demonstrate to the entire world how democracy really works.

"This is a nation of courageous men and women who have demonstrated over and over again that Americans are not afraid of hard work. We have worked our way out of a terrible depression, we have fought and won the most terrible war in the world's history and we stand second to no one in our commitment to the rebuilding of war-torn Europe and Asia. Our children are going to know a world of shining cities, a world that is clean and safe and bright. Our children are going to know a world that is free from war and sickness and hunger. Our children—"

It was the "Our Children" speech, and that became the theme of the campaign for the last three weeks. It crystallized the entire election, and Eisenhower slid disastrously in the polls. We put up posters with pictures of Joe McCarthy, and the caption read, "What is this man going to do to your children?" With Eisenhower, we were a little more respectful. We went back to the earlier theme, "General Eisenhower wants to send your son to Korea." It was enough.

We had dictated the theme of the campaign and we had defined the choices. The Republican campaign never found itself, and by the time the first Tuesday of November rolled around, 51% of the American people voted for the Democratic candidate, 49% voted for the Republican. Not a landslide, but not an embarrassment either. The people chose fairly.

During the commercial I went to pee. I passed one of the Negro custodians in the hall, and he nodded to me sadly. "You watchin' the broadcast? Mr. Cronkite sure ain't being nice to the boss."

I shook my head. "I don't trust Walter Cronkite. I wouldn't buy a used car from him."

"Wouldn't buy a used car from him!" The old Negro cackled at the joke. "Hee hee hee. That's a good one, all right."

I continued on down the hall. With a little luck, by morning that remark would be all over Washington. It wouldn't help the boss any, but it sure would make me feel better.

When I got back to my office, there was a note on my desk. *The president would like to see you after the broadcast.* I crumpled it up and tossed it into the waste can after the Coke. He was going to ask me how the speech was going. And I was going to have to tell him that I couldn't write it. "Sir, you're a statesman," I wanted to say. "A statesman doesn't make speeches like this."

But I knew what he'd reply. "No, I'm not a statesman. I won't be a statesman until I leave office. Until then, I'm the man who has to make difficult decisions."

"But not this one, sir!"

"Yes, even this one."

We'd had the argument a dozen times. And each time, there were a few less voices saying that the president should resist the cries for his resignation.

Cronkite came back on the air then. Now, he began chronicling the unraveling presidency of Adlai Stevenson. He worked his way steadily through all six years of it. The endorsement of Oppenheimer, even though J. Edgar Hoover said he was a known Communist. The commutation of the death sentence of convicted atomic spies Julius and Ethel Rosenberg. The president's public opposition to the hearings of the House Committee on Un-American Activities. The Berlin wall embarrassment. The Soviets' growing atomic stockpile. The continuing failures of the Vanguard missile system. The Northrop vs. Symington Flying Wing scandal. The attempt on Khrushchev's life at Disneyland. The Soviet demonstration of a 100-megaton nuclear weapon. The breakdown of relations with France because of the president's refusal to back them in Indo-China. The public break with J. Edgar Hoover, resulting in the firing of the director of the F.B.I.—and didn't that one set off the howls from the right! Simultaneous inflation *and* recession. The civil war in Cuba—and the very unpopular decision to send in troops to support the Batista government. And then—goddammit!—*Sputnik,* the Russian satellite. It seemed that nothing that Adlai Stevenson did was the *right* thing to do.

The founder of the John Birch Society insisted publicly that the president was a Communist agent; that was the only logical explanation for the floundering of America—Stevenson was trying to bring the country to its knees so that the Soviets could triumph without firing a shot. "Khrushchev says that he will bury us—and Adlai Stevenson wants to hand him the shovel." Stevenson's response: "No, I'm a capitalist. I'll sell him the shovel." But the joke fell flat. It's a bad sign when even the press corps doesn't laugh at the president's jokes. Even worse, the late night TV talk show hosts, Steve Allen and Jack Paar, were starting to make jokes that were hostile to the president. Those jokes would be repeated in a hundred thousand stores and offices the next day and the day after that.

And then, that grandstanding little son of a bitch—the congressman from Van Nuys—stood up in the House of Representatives and introduced a Bill of Impeachment. He charged the president with "non-feasance in office," whatever that was. Maybe he'd meant it as a joke to call attention to the rampant hostility on the Hill, or maybe he'd intended it as a way to get himself a little public attention, or maybe he'd meant it only as a political stunt, deliberately designed to embarrass the president—or maybe he just meant it.

Whatever the case, the press took it seriously. And because the press took it seriously, so did the American public. And within two weeks, a House Committee was drawing up Articles of Impeachment and holding hearings. The House Republicans were still angry over the slapping down they'd gotten over the Committee on Un-American Activities, so they were only too happy to go after the egghead—"You can't make an omelette without breaking eggheads."

But there was no support on the left side of the aisle either. The Democratic party's unity was fractured so badly, there was talk it might break apart into two new parties. The South wanted out because Hubert Humphrey, that babbling little Porky Pig senator from Minnesota, had been trying to introduce a civil rights plank into the party platform every year since 1948. And the closing of unnecessary military bases all over the country had further undermined the president's support in every town that had lost jobs as a result. The shutting down of all those unnecessary air-defense and missile-building projects hurt Southern California the worst. And Detroit was claiming that the administration's rigid insistence on auto-safety standards and smaller cars and gasoline efficiency had shut down half the assembly lines in America, so he couldn't depend on much support from Labor.

But, an impeachment—at least that was something that Americans could agree on. Adlai Stevenson's campaign pledge had abruptly come home to haunt him: "We're going to demonstrate to the entire world how democracy really works."

The broadcast concluded with a recap of last Friday's uproar in the House of Representatives and the mean-spirited vote to impeach. The Senate was already organizing for the trial. From where I sat, they looked like a bunch of kangaroos laying railroad tracks to oblivion.

Cronkite hadn't told it all; he'd missed a lot of the backstage squabbling and infighting; but he'd replayed most of the worst news—and in retrospect, the cumulative weight of it was crushing. Even I found myself wondering, "Maybe the president is right." Maybe it's impossible to continue under these conditions and unfair to the American people even to try.

Abruptly, I knew what I wanted to write. I rolled a fresh sheet of paper into the typewriter and quickly tapped out, *"The problems of America and of the free world demand the full attention of our elected leaders. This country needs a full-time executive. It is unfair to the nation and* to the office of the presidency to continue trying to operate in the current atmosphere of public dissatisfaction and distrust. Accordingly, this Friday, at twelve o'clock noon, I shall resign the office of the presidency."

I wondered how long Vice President Kennedy would last in front of the jackals. Already he was a laughing stock for marrying that silly blonde actress from Hollywood. (The new Monroe Doctrine: "Ooh, ooh, aaaahhhhh.")

Never mind that. I rolled another sheet of paper into the typewriter.

"The presidency of the United States is not a popularity contest. It is not a prize or a reward. It is not a laurel wreath to be given or taken away by the winds of popularity. The presidency is only a job—sometimes it is a great responsibility, sometimes it is a terrible and crushing burden—but once the ceremony and ritual has been stripped away from the presidency, what is left is the responsibility for making difficult decisions, decisions that need to be made to protect the interests of America and the free world. Sometimes those decisions are bitter medicine—but like bitter medicine, we take those steps, because in the longer term we know that we shall be healthier for it.

"I have had to make many of those difficult decisions. They were the best decisions that I and my advisors could make at the time; they were based on the very best information that we could get. It is my firm conviction that most of those decisions were the correct ones, and I believe that history will vindicate those choices.

"When I was elected in 1952, and reelected again in 1956, I did not promise a pot of gold. The rewards I promised were those that would only come from hard work. Today, we are stuck in the middle of that course—and we are having a crisis of confidence. If we succumb to this crisis and abandon our larger goals, we will not simply be quitting a difficult task in favor of momentary comfort; we will be abandoning our leadership of the free world.

"When I accepted this responsibility, I accepted the difficult as well as the great. I refuse to abandon the goals of America. I refuse to quit the job. I refuse to give up halfway across the rushing river.

"If I do not resist this shameful course of action to the fullest of my ability, then I will be damaging the integrity and authority of this office for all of those who succeed me. My love of this nation and my responsibility to this office demand that I protect the Constitutional balance of power.

"Accordingly, I am calling a special session of Congress of the United States. I will present myself to a Joint Session to answer any and all charges *that they wish to raise against this Administration. When all of the facts are spoken, it will be demonstrated that I am guilty of nothing more than being unpopular. Being unpopular isn't exactly an honor, but it is certainly not a crime—and it is definitely no cause for impeachment. More important, if the people of this nation allow themselves to be stampeded into turning their back on the twin responsibilities of hard work and difficult decisions, the shame will not be mine, but America's.*

"I remain confident in the wisdom and good faith of the American people that this will not happen.

"Thank you. Good night."

I looked at the two speeches, side by side. Not quite my best—I would have preferred a few more jokes; but neither of these speeches lent themselves to the famous Stevenson wit. I put each one into a folder and headed up the hall to the Oval Office.

His secretary looked red-eyed, as if she had been crying, but she just nodded at me without actually meeting my eyes. The door was standing half-open. "Go on in," she said.

I knocked on the door and pushed in. "Mr. President?"

He was sitting at his desk, reading through a stack of leather-bound briefing books. He held up a finger, a familiar "wait-a-minute" gesture," while he finished reading. He nodded, initialed the book, scribbled something on it, closed it and put it in the out basket. He looked old, much older than his years—and tired too. But that was a given; nothing aged a man like the presidency. Almost automatically, President Stevenson reached for the next one, opened it, checked out the summary page, then closed it again and put it aside on his desk. At last, he looked up at me. "The work piles up. Even on the eve of impeachment." He sighed. "What have you got for me?"

I passed across the two folders.

"Two drafts?"

"Two different speeches, sir."

"I see." He massaged his nose between his thumb and forefinger, then readjusted his glasses and opened the first folder. He read it quickly. "Well, that's short and to the point."

"I don't think anything more than that needs to be said."

"You're probably right. Your judgment in these areas has always been on the nose. What's the other speech?"

"Read it."

He opened the second folder. I watched his features intently, looking for a clue to his reaction. He frowned, and at one point he shook his head, but I'd seen him do that even with speeches he approved of. At last, he finished and closed the folder. He laid it on top of the first one. "A good speech, Drew," he said.

"But?"

"But nothing."

I sat down in the chair opposite him. "Mr. President—don't resign. It'll look like weakness."

"For what it's worth, Vice President Kennedy agrees with you. He's only forty, you know. I think he's a little afraid of the responsibility. But he'll handle it, I'm sure."

"There's nothing I can say, is there?"

"You said it all in the speech."

"You don't agree, do you?"

He shook his head.

"In one respect, you're absolutely right. If I resign, it will weaken the office of the presidency for all who come after me. It *will* set a precedent."

"And you don't see that as a reason to fight?"

"No. If anything, it's a better reason to resign. The office of the presidency has become much too powerful. Roosevelt was as close to a dictator as this country has ever had. Think of what he could have become if he had been motivated like Hitler. Maybe it's time to rein in the presidency and make the office more responsible to the voice of the people. Maybe I can leave this country with a presidency that's less *dangerous*."

"You want to trust Congress with the future of the country?"

"The last I heard, that's how democracy is supposed to work. We trust our elected officials."

"Mr. President, resigning will destroy trust in the Democratic party. You know what that will do to the election process—it'll give the Republicans a stampede."

"The Democratic party is not America. And they'll recover. They always do. Maybe after they've lost a few presidential contests they'll lose some of their arrogance and rediscover some of their purpose. I hope so." He took off his glasses and rubbed his nose again. "I'm tired. I'm beaten and I want to go home. I did my best. I'm not ashamed of that. But I know when it's time to quit. It's time." He reached across the big desk to shake my hand. "Thank you. You've done good work for me. I've always appreciated your loyalty and your advice."

"Yes, sir." It was a dismissal. I accepted his thanks perfunctorily and headed for the door. I suppose I should have thanked him for the chance to work for him, but I was hurting too badly. I could see why so many people hated him. Maybe the Republicans had been right all along. Adlai Stevenson was too smart to be president....

I headed down the hall, back to my office, and finally began doing what I should have done weeks ago. I started cleaning out my desk.

Adlai Stevenson had too much compassion and too much integrity, and he respected the so-called wisdom of the American people far too much to do any real good as president.

Okay, Mr. Stevenson. Go ahead. Resign. Forget the dream. Forget the promises. If you can't stand the heat, get out of the firestorm. Quitters are failures. A dumber man would have kept on fighting until he outlasted his enemies.

I slammed the last empty desk drawer in angry disgust. "Next time, I'm going to work for a man who's too stupid to know when he's beaten."

Hmm.

The senator from California hadn't declared yet, but he was certainly the front-runner for 1960, and many people were already looking to him to restore the nation's pride and confidence in itself. They said he had the kind of stern statesmanlike quality the country needed right now. I didn't particularly like the man, but he was a great poker player. He'd probably be one hell of a president. Best of all, he'd once remarked to me at a White House reception that he wished he had a speechwriter who could write an "Our Children" speech. At the time, I hadn't given the comment any thought, but it was clearly a hint.

Okay, I wasn't exactly thrilled about working for a Republican, but what the hell? I could learn. And Richard Nixon was exactly what this country needed and deserved.

What we remember of Kennedy are not the mistakes, but the aspirations. Not the missteps, but the goals.
Regarding this story, satire is a lousy vehicle for idealism—but what the hell, whatever it takes.

The Kennedy Enterprise

—IS THAT THING ON? Good. Okay, go ahead. What do you want to know?

Kennedy, huh? Why is it always Kennedy? All this nostalgia for the fifties and the sixties. You guys are missing the point. There were so many better actors, and nobody remembers them anymore. That's the real crime—that Kennedy should get all the attention—but the guys who made him look so good are all passed over and forgotten. Why don't you jackals ever come around asking whatever happened to Bill Shatner or Jeffrey Hunter—?

Ahhh, besides, Kennedy's been done to death. Everybody does Kennedy. Because he's easy to do. But lemme tell you something, sonny. Kennedy wasn't really the sixties—uh uh. He's just a convenient symbol. The sixties were a lot bigger than just another fading TV star.

Yeah, that's right. His glory days were over. He was on his way out. You're surprised to hear that, aren't you?

Look. I'll tell you something. Kennedy was not a good actor. In fact, he was goddamn lousy. He couldn't act his way out of a pay toilet if he'd had Charlton Heston in there to help him.

But—it didn't matter, did it? Hell, acting ability is the *last* thing in the

19

world a movie star needs. It never slowed down whatsisname, Ronald Reagan.

Reagan? Oh, you wouldn't remember him. He was way before your time. He was sort of like a right-wing Henry Fonda, only he never got the kind of parts where he could inspire an audience. That's what you need to make it—one good part where you make the audience squirm or cry or leap from their seats, shouting. Anything to make them remember you longer than the time it takes to get out to the parking lot. But Reagan never really got any of those. He was just another poor schmuck eaten up by the system. A very sad story, really.

Yeah, I know. You want to hear about Kennedy. Uh-uh. Lemme tell you about Reagan first. So you'll see how easy it is to just disappear— and how much of a fluke it is to succeed.

See, Reagan wasn't stupid. He was one of the few wartime actors who actually made a successful transition into television. He was smart enough to be a host instead of a star—that way he didn't get himself typecast as a cowboy or a detective or a doctor. Reagan was a pretty good pitchman for General Electric on their Sunday night show and then—wait a minute, lemme see now, sometime in there he got himself elected president of the Screen Actors Guild, and that's when all the trouble started—there was some uproar with the House Committee on UnAmerican Activities, and the blacklist and the way he sold out his colleagues. I don't really know the details, you can look it up. Anyway, tempers were hot, that's all you need to know, and Reagan got himself impeached, almost thrown out of his own Guild as a result.

Well, nobody wanted to work with him after that. His name was mud. He couldn't get arrested. And it was just tragic—'cause he was good, no question about it. Those pictures he did with the monkey were hysterical—oh, yeah, he did a whole series of movies at the end of the war. *Bonzo Goes To College, Bonzo Goes To Hollywood, Bonzo Goes To Washington.* Yeah, everybody remembers the chimpanzee, nobody remembers Reagan. Yeah, people in this town only have long memories when there's a grudge attached.

So, Reagan couldn't get work. I mean, not real work. He ended up making B-movies. A lot of crap. Stuff even Harry Cohn wouldn't touch. He must have really needed the money. The fifties were all downhill for him.

I remember, he did—oh, what was it?—*Queen of Outer Space* with that Hungarian broad. That was a real waste of film. Then he did some stuff with Ed Wood, remember him? Yeah, that's the one. Anyway, Ronnie's last picture was some piece of *dreck* called *Plan Nine From Outer Space*. Lugosi was supposed to do the part, but he died just before they started filming, so Reagan stepped in. I hear it's real big on the college circuits now. What they call camp, where it's so bad, it's funny. Have you seen it? No, neither have I. Too bad, really. No telling what Reagan could have become if he'd just had the right breaks.

Oh, right—you want to talk about Kennedy. But you get my point, don't you? This is a sorry excuse for an industry. There's no *sympatico*, no consideration. Talent is considered a commodity. It gets wasted. People get chewed up just because they're in someone else's way. That's the real story behind Kennedy—the people who got chewed up along the way.

Anyway, what was I saying about Kennedy before I got off the track? You wanna run that thing back? Oh, that's right. Kennedy had no talent. Yeah, you can quote me—what difference does it make? Somebody going to sue me? What're they going to get? My wheelchair? I'll say it again. Kennedy had no talent for acting. Zero. Zilch. *Nada*. What he did have was a considerable talent for self-promotion. He was *great* at that.

And y'know what else? Y'know what else Kennedy had? He had *style*. You don't need talent if you've got style. Mae West proved that. Gable proved that. Bette Davis.

Funny business, movies, television. Any other industry run the same way would go straight into the ground. A movie studio—you make one success, it pays for twenty flops. You have to be crazy to stay with it, y'know.

Okay, okay—back to Kennedy. Well, y'know, to really understand him, you gotta understand his dad. Joe Kennedy was one ambitious son of a bitch. He was smart enough to get his money out of the stock market before '29. He put it into real estate. When everybody else was jumping out of windows, he was picking up pieces all over the place.

He got very active in politics for a while. FDR wanted to send him to England as an ambassador, but the deal fell through—nobody knows why. Maybe his divorce, who knows? Y'know, the Kennedys were Irish-Catholic. It would have been a big scandal. Especially then.

Anyway, it doesn't matter. The story really starts when Joe Sr. brings his boys out to California. He marries Gloria Swanson and starts buying up property and studios and contracts. Next thing you know, his boys are all over the place. They come popping out of USC, one after the other, like Ford Mustangs rolling off an assembly line.

In no time, Joe's a director, Jack's taken up acting and Bobby ends up running MGM. It's Thalberg all over again. Lemme think. That had to be '55 or '56, somewhere in there. Actually, Teddy was the smart one. He stayed out of the business. He went East, stayed home with his mom and eventually went into politics where nobody ever heard of him again.

Anyway, you could see that Joe and Bobby were going to make out all right. They were all sonsabitches, but they were good sonsabitches. Joe did his homework, he brought in his pictures on time. Bobby was a ruthless S.O.B., but maybe that's what you need to run a studio. He didn't take any shit from anybody. Remember, he's the guy who told Garland to get it together or get out. And she *did*.

But Jack—Jack was always a problem. Two problems actually.

First of all, he couldn't keep his dick in his pants. Bobby had his hands full keeping the scandal-rags away from his brother. He had to buy off one columnist; he gave him the Rock Hudson story. The jackals had such a good time with that one they forgot all about Jack's little peccadillos in Palm Springs. Sometimes I think Bobby would have killed to protect his brother. Y'know, Hudson lost the lead in *Giant* because of that. They'd already shot two or three weeks of good footage. They junked it all. Nearly shit-canned the whole picture, but Heston jumped in at the last moment and ended up beating out the Dean kid for the Oscar. Like I said, it's a strange business. *Stupid* business.

Sometimes you end up hating the audience for just being the audience. It's not fair, when you think about it. The public wants their heroes to look like they're dashing and romantic and sexy—but they're horrified if they actually behave that way. I mean, could *your* private life stand up to that kind of scrutiny? I'm not sure anybody's could. Hell, the goddamn audience punishes the stars for doing the exact same things they're doing—cheating on their wives, drinking too much, smoking a little weed. If they're going to insist on morality tests for the actors, I think we should start insisting on morality tests for the audience before we let them in the theater. See how they'd like it for a change.

Oh well.

Anyway, the *other* problem was Jack's accent—that goddamn Massachusetts accent. He'd have made a great cowboy. He had the look, he had the build; but he couldn't open his mouth without sounding like a New England lobsterman. I mean, can you imagine Jack Kennedy on a horse or behind a badge—with *that* accent? They brought in the best speech coaches in the world to work with him. A waste of goddamn money. He ended up sounding like Cary Grant with a sinus problem.

You can't believe the parts he didn't get because of his voice. Y'know, at one point Twentieth wanted him for *The Misfits* with Marilyn Monroe—now, that would have been a picture. Can you imagine Kennedy and Monroe? Pure screen magic. But it never happened. His voice again. No, as far as I know, they never even met.

But that was always the problem. Finding the right picture for Jack. George Pal, the Puppetoon guy, gave him his first big break with *War Of The Worlds* over at Paramount, but Jack always hated science fiction. Afraid he'd get typecast. He saw what happened to Karloff and Lugosi. He thought of science fiction as the same kind of stuff.

The funny thing was, the picture was a big hit, but that only made Jack unhappier. He knew the audience had come to see the Martians, not him. That's when he swore, no more science fiction. And yeah, he really did say it, that famous quote: "Never play a scene with animals, children or Martians. They always use the Martian's best take."

Hitchcock had a good sense of how to use Kennedy, but he only worked with him once. *North By Northwest.* Another big hit. Kennedy loved the film—he loved all that spy stuff, he always wanted to play James Bond—but he didn't like the way Hitchcock treated him. And he made the mistake of saying so to an interviewer. Remember? "Hitch doesn't direct. He herds. He treats his actors like cattle." That remark got back to Hitch, and the old man was terribly hurt by it. So, instead of casting Jack in his next film, he went to Jimmy Stewart. Who knows? Maybe that was best for everybody.

Jack spent nine months sitting on his ass, waiting for the right part. Nothing. Finally, he went to Bobby and said, "Help me get some of the good parts." By now, Bobby was running MGM, and this gave him control over one studio and a lot of bargaining power with all the others—he was the biggest deal-maker in town, buying, selling, trading contracts right and left to put together the right package.

Even so, Bobby still had to twist a lot of arms to get Jack into *The Caine Mutiny.* Van Johnson had already been screen-tested. He'd been fitted for his costumes, everything—suddenly, he's out on his ass and here's Jack Kennedy playing opposite Bogart. I can tell you, a lot of feathers were ruffled. Bogey knew how Jack got the part and he never forgave him for it. But, y'know—it helped the picture. Bogey's resentment of Jack shows up on the screen in every scene. Bogey should have had the Oscar for that one, but Bobby bought it for Jack. There was so much studio pressure on the voting—well, never mind. That's a body best left buried.

Anyway, in return, Bobby asked Jack to help him out with one or two of his problems. And Jack had no choice but to say yes. See, when Bobby took over MGM, one of the projects about to shoot was a thing called *Forbidden Planet*. Shakespeare in outer space. Dumb idea, right? That's what everybody thought, at the time. They couldn't cast it.

They were having real trouble finding a male lead, and they were about to go with . . . oh, let me think. Oh, I don't remember his name. He ended up doing a cop show on ABC. Oh, here's a funny. At one point, they were even considering Ronald Reagan for the lead. Very strongly. But they finally passed on him—I guess Bobby remembered the McCarthy business. And that's why Reagan went and did *Queen Of Outer Space*. Never mind, it doesn't matter. Bobby finally asked Jack to play the captain of the spaceship.

And I gotta tell you. Jack didn't want to do it—more of that science fiction crap, right?—but he couldn't very well say no, could he? So he goes ahead and does it. Bobby retitles the picture *The New Frontier*. And guess what? It's the studio's biggest grossing picture for the year. Go figure. But everybody's happy.

After that, Jack had a couple of rough years. One disaster after another. The biggest one was that goddamned musical. That was an embarrassment. The man should never have tried to sing. Even today, nobody can mention *Camelot* without thinking of Jack Kennedy, right? And those stupid tights.

You want my opinion, stay out of tights. Your career will never recover. It was all downhill for Errol Flynn after *Robin Hood*, and the goddamned tights killed poor George Reeves. *Superman*'s another one of those unproduceable properties. Nobody's ever going to make that one work. Or *Batman*. Tights. That's why.

Anyway, back to Kennedy—his career was in the dumper. So, when he was offered the chance to do a TV series, it didn't look so bad any more. Most of the real action in town was moving to TV anyway. So Jack went over to Desilu and played Eliot Ness in *The Untouchables*. Y'know, that was one of J. Edgar Hoover's favorite shows. Hoover even wrote to Kennedy and asked him for his autograph. He visited the set once just so he could get his picture taken with Jack. Hoover had to stand on a box. They shot him from the waist up, so's you'd never know, but the photographer managed to get one good long shot.

Meanwhile, back over at MGM, Bobby's looking at all the money that Warner Brothers and Desilu are making off TV and he's thinking—there's gotta be a way that he can cut himself a slice of that market, right? Right. So he starts looking around the lot to see what he's got that can be exploited.

Well, *Father Knows Best* is a big hit, so Bobby thinks, "Let's try turning *Andy Hardy* into a TV series. And how about *Dr. Kildare* too? The Hardy thing flopped. Bad casting. And it was opposite Disney on Sundays. It didn't have a chance. But the Kildare property caught well enough to encourage him to try again.

So, Bobby Kennedy's looking around, right? And here's where all the pieces come together all at once. NBC says to him, "How about a science fiction series? You did that *New Frontier* thing. Why don't you turn that into a TV series for us?"

There's this other series that's just winding down—a war series called *The Lieutenant*—Bobby calls in the producer, a guy named Roddenberry and tells him that NBC wants a sci-fi show based on *The New Frontier*. Can he make it work? They've still got all the costumes, the sets, the miniatures, everything. Roddenberry says he doesn't know anything about science fiction, but he'll give it a try. He tells his secretary to rush out and buy up every science fiction anthology she can find and do summaries of all the stories that have spaceships in them.

What with one thing and another, it's 1964 before they ever start filming the first pilot. But all the MGM magic is applied, and they end up with one of the most beautiful—and most *expensive*—TV pilots ever made. Of course, Roddenberry put in all his own ideas, and by the time he was through, the only thing left from the movie was in the opening lines of the title sequence: "Space, the new frontier. These are the voyages...et cetera, et cetera."

NBC hated the pilot—they said it was "too cerebral"—but they liked the look of the show, so they say to Bobby, let's try again, give us another pilot. Bobby says no. Take it or leave it. MGM bails out, so Roddenberry goes over to Desilu, where they make a second pilot. He changes the name to *Star Track*, and the show goes on the air in 1966. You know the rest.

Two years later, MGM buys Desilu. Bobby Kennedy strong-arms NBC to move the show to an eight o'clock time slot, and it's a big hit. But then, to settle some old grudge—Bobby hated being wrong—he fires Roddenberry. The rumor mill said it was women—maybe. I don't know and I'm not going to speculate. Dorothy Fontana takes over as producer, and surprise, the show just gets better. Meanwhile, *The Untouchables* gets cancelled and Jack Kennedy is out of work again.

The timing was everything here. See, Shatner and Nimoy were feuding. Not only feuding, they were counting each other's lines. Nimoy threatens to quit. Shatner does too. They're both demanding the same thing: "Whatever he gets, I get."

Bobby agrees and fires both of them. He starts looking around for a new Captain.

He doesn't have to look very far.

In hindsight, yes. It was the perfect decision. John F. Kennedy as Captain Jack Logan of the starship *Enterprise*. The man was perfect. Who wouldn't want to serve under him? But—at the time, who knew? It sounded crazy. Here's this old fart who's career is clearly fading fast— why cast him in *Star Track*?

And Jack didn't want to do it. By now, he hated science fiction so much, he once took a poke at Harlan Ellison at the Emmy Awards. He didn't understand it. He had to have it explained to him. Once, he even called down to the research department and asked, "Just where is this planet Vulcan, anyway?"

And that was the other thing—Jack had already seen how Shatner got upstaged by the Vulcan. To him, it was the goddamn Martians all over again. The man was almost fifty—he looked great, but he was terrified of becoming a has-been, of ending up like Ronald Reagan.

But Bobby had a vision. He was good at that stuff. He promised to restructure the show in Jack's favor. Jack agreed—very reluctantly—to listen. That's enough for Bobby. He calls in the staff of the show and says my brother wants to be captain. "Make it so."

I gotta tell you. That was not a happy meeting. I'd just come aboard as story editor, so I just sat there and kept my mouth shut. Harlan argued a little, but his heart wasn't in it. Maybe he was afraid he'd get punched again. He didn't like the Kennedys very much. Dorothy did most of the talking for us—but Bobby didn't want to hear. He listened, maybe he just pretended to listen, but when everything had been said, he just answered, "Do it my way." We were not happy when we left.

For about three days, we were pissed as hell, because we'd finally gotten the show settled into a good solid working formula, and then suddenly—*poof!*—Roddenberry, Nimoy and Shatner are gone, and Bobby Kennedy is giving orders. But then it sort of hit us all at the same time. Hey, this is an opportunity to reinvent *Star Track*. So we made a list of all the shit that bothered us—like the captain always having to get the girl, the captain always beaming down to the planet, that kind of stuff, and we started thinking about ways to fix it.

We knew Jack couldn't do the action stuff believably. He was already gray at the temples, and his back problems were legendary on the set of *The Untouchables,* so we knew we were going to have to introduce a younger second lead to pick up the action. That's where the Mission Team came from. So Jack wouldn't have to do it.

We really had no choice. Jack had to be an older, more thoughtful captain who stayed on the ship and monitored the missions by remote control. The Mission Team would be headed by the first officer. But this was perfect because it kept the captain in command at all times, and it also made it impossible for the first officer to become a sidekick, or a partner. Jack would be the undeniable star.

We also figured we'd just about milked the Vulcan idea to death, so we eighty-sixed the whole Vulcan species and brought in an android to take Spock's place as science officer. The android would be curious about humanity—kind of like an updated Pinocchio. The opposite of Spock; he *wants* to be human.

Just as we were starting to get excited about the possibilities of the new format, Jack suggested adding families to the crew of the starship to attract a family audience. Maybe the android's best friend could be a teenage computer genius... the kids would *love* that. We ended up calling the android REM—it means Rapid-Eye-Movement—and casting Donald Pleasance. Billy Mumy came aboard as Dr. McCoy's grandson, Wesley.

To be fair, Pleasance made the whole android thing work, but none of us ever really *liked* the idea very much. We tried arguing against it, but who ever listens to the writer's opinion? Whatever Jack wanted, Jack got. Bobby made sure of that. So, there we were—lost in space with Jack Kennedy.

And then...to make it even worse, Jack started reviewing outlines, sending us memoes about what Jack Logan would or wouldn't do. Clearly, he was having trouble telling the difference between the character and the actor who played him. Jack killed a lot of good ideas. I had one where these little furballs started breeding like crazy—kind of like the rabbits in Australia? Dorothy thought it had a lot of whimsy. Everybody liked it. But Jack killed it. He said it made Logan look foolish. He didn't want to look foolish, said it wasn't right for his image.

His *image?* Give me a break. It doesn't matter much now, though, does it? He's got the best image of all. He's an *icon.*

Harlan quit the show first—which surprised all of us, because he was always the most patient and even-tempered of human beings. Y'know, he did that *est* thing and just mellowed out like a big pink pussycat. Ted Sturgeon used to come to him for advice.

Dorothy quit three months after Harlan. I tried to stick it out, but it wasn't any fun without them. I didn't get along with the new producer, and I finally tossed in the towel too.

The worst part of it, I guess, was that after we left, the ratings went up. It was pretty disheartening. I mean, talk about a pie in the face.

What happened to the original crew? I thought you'd never ask.

Roddenberry went over to Warners and worked for a while on *Wagon Train: The Next Generation.* Shatner showed up in a couple of guest spots, then landed the lead in a cop show; when he lost his hair, he took up directing—I hear he's pretty good at it. Nimoy, of course, gave up show business and ran for office. He's been a good governor; I guess he'll run for the Presidency. Walter Cronkite called him one of the ten most trusted men in America.

Dorothy was head of new projects at Twentieth for a while, then she started up her own production company. Harlan moved to Scotland. And me—well, my troubles were in all the newspapers, so I don't have to rehash them here, do I? But I'm doing a lot better these days, and I might even take up writing again. If I can figure out how to use a computer. Those things confuse me.

You don't need me to tell you anything else about *Star Track,* do you? You can get the rest of it from the newspapers.

Yeah, I was there when it happened. We all were. I was as close to Jack as I am to you.

I dunno, I guess none of us realized what a zoo a *Star Track* convention could be. Not then, anyway. It was still early in the phenomenon.

I mean, we had no idea what kind of impact the show had made on the fans. We thought there might be a couple hundred people there. You know how big the crowd was? Nobody does. The news said there were fifteen thousand inside the hotel. We had no idea now many more were waiting outside.

We just didn't know how seriously the fans took the show. Of course, the Ambassador Hotel was never the same afterwards.

Anyway, Harlan was there, so was Dorothy. Gene came by, but he didn't stay very long. I think he felt disgraced. And of course, all the actors. De, Jimmy, Grace, Nichelle, Walter, George, Majel, Bruce, Mark, Leonard, Bill—all the also-rans, as they were calling themselves by then. I guess Bobby had put the screws on. Attend or else. There wasn't a lot of good feeling—at least, not at first.

But then the fans started applauding. One after the other, we all went out and chatted and answered questions, and the excitement just grew and grew and grew.

Of course, when Jack came out, the place went wild. It was like election night. There were people there wearing KENNEDY FOR PRESIDENT buttons. Like he was really the character he played. They loved him. And he loved being loved. Whatever else you might say about Jack Kennedy, he knew how to make love to an audience. Style and grace. That was Jack all over.

Y'know, I saw the Beatles at the Hollywood Bowl. All three concerts. And I never saw that kind of hysteria, not even when Ringo threw jellybeans at the audience. But the Trackers—I thought they were going to scream the walls down.

Jack was glowing. His wife had just turned to him and whispered, "Well, you can't say they don't love you now—" when it happened.

At first, I thought it was a car backfiring. It didn't sound like a gunshot at all. In fact, most people were puzzled at the sound. It all happened so fast. Then Jack grabbed his throat, and I guess for a second, we all thought he was joking. Y'know how you do: "Augh, they got me—" But he had this real stupid look on his face—confused, like. Then the second and third shots went off—and it was the third shot that killed him. And that's when the screaming started. And the panic. All those people injured and killed, suffocated in the crush. It was terrible. Everybody running. I can still see it. I still get nightmares.

I've always been amazed they caught the little bastard who did it. Sirhan Sirhan. I'll never forget his name. Another one of those nerdy little geeks who never had a life of his own. He lived inside the TV. He thought it was real. Half a dozen of those really big women we see at all the conventions just jumped the poor son of a bitch and flattened him. They were outraged that someone would dare to attack *their* captain. Sirhan was lucky to escape with his balls still attached.

Y'know, later some of the witnesses said that Sirhan kept yelling, "Wait, wait—I can explain!" Like you can explain a thing like that? It didn't make any sense then. It doesn't make any sense now, no matter how many articles William F. Buckley and Norman Mailer and Tom Wolfe write about it.

You know what it was? Sirhan never forgave us for replacing Kirk and Spock with Logan and REM. He said we'd ruined the whole show.

But that's not even the half of it. You want to know the rest of the cosmic joke? Bugliosi, the district attorney, told me later on. Sirhan was aiming at Bobby and missed. Three times! Bobby was standing just behind Jack, but that kid couldn't shoot worth shit. I think if he'd have hit Bobby, the industry would have given him a medal. Instead, he got the gas chamber and a movie of the week.

But now—y'know, I think back on it, and I see how stupid we all were. We didn't know the power of television. None of us did. We didn't even suspect.

Jack knew, I think. Bobby knew for sure. He knew that you could change the way people think and feel and vote just by what you put on the screen. Bobby knew that. He had the vision. But he was never the same after that. How could you be? The whole thing scared the hell out of all of us—the whole industry. NBC cancelled the show, but they couldn't cancel the nightmares.

Y'ask me, I think that was the turning point in the sixties—the killing of Kennedy. That's when it all started going bad. That's when we all went crazy and started tearing things down. But, oh, hell—that's old news. Everybody knows it.

Now, we've got the Kennedy mystique and *Star Track: The New Voyages*. And…it's all shit. It's just…so much merchandise. Whatever might have been true or meaningful or wonderful about *Star Track* is gone. It's all been eaten up by the lawyers and the fans and the publicity department.

Don't take this personally, but I don't trust anybody under thirty. I don't think any of you understand what happened then. It was special. We didn't understand it ourselves, but we knew it was special.

See...it's like this. Space isn't the new frontier. It never was.

What is the new frontier? You have to ask—? That proves my point. You're looking in the wrong place. The new frontier isn't out there. It's in here. In the heart. It's in us. Dorothy said it. If it's not in here, it's not anywhere.

Ahh—you know what, you're going to go out of here, you're going to write another one of those goddamn golden geezer articles. You'll miss the whole point, just like all the others. Shut that damn thing off and get the hell out of here before I whack you with my cane. Nurse! Nurse—!

If real life was as heroic as the movies, we wouldn't need the movies.

The Firebringers

THE GUNNERS, TAYLOR AND JOHNSON, stood apart by themselves, whispering about something. I wondered if they were going to take their traditional good-luck piss under the tail of the plane before take-off. Would they even dare with all the guards looking on and all the brass who were supposed to be here? The rest of us stood around under the plane like we always did, smoking, worrying and pretending not to care.

There were twenty armed marines spaced in a circle around the plane, so most of us in the crew stayed close to the boarding hatch and kept our eyes averted from their weapons. We weren't sure we appreciated the honor. Were the guards there to keep everyone else out—or us in?

We looked from one to the other and traded lights off each other's cigarettes. We talked about whisky, poker, women we had known, chocolate, beer, cigarettes, everything but what really counted. Our terror.

Meanwhile, the fog kept rolling in. It was so thick that even the specially outfitted B-32 above us was only a darker shape in the gloom. The ground crew would be putting out flares all the length of the runway. If we went. I was beginning to wonder. The case under my arm, with all my weather charts and maps was getting heavy. I didn't know if I wanted to go or not. I didn't want my work to be wasted. On the other hand . . . .

The sound of an engine was followed by the ruddy glare of head-lights, and then three trucks came rolling up to the belly of the ship. The middle one had a flat bed, with a tarp-covered shape clamped securely into place. The other two trucks were hooded and carried more armed marines. They spilled out of their vehicles in silence and quickly formed a secure circle around the loading operation.

Ollie, one of the two ordinance officers, climbed out of the shot-gun side of the second truck and began gently cooing instructions to the bomb crew; he was so polite it was eerie. The scuttlebutt was such that you could roll a Jeep over his foot and he wouldn't even say ouch. He was a corpulent man, but he moved like a dancer—and he was scrupulous about the loading, watching over every move like a mother hen with a single egg. He demanded precision and delicacy. Before the war, he and his partner Stan had been piano movers. Stanley was the quiet one. Once we were in the air, they'd actually arm the device.

Bogey, the bombardier, chewed an unlit stogie and looked skeptical. He'd had that stogie since the war started and he wasn't going to light it until he was sure he could get another one to replace it. He held a couple of steel ball-bearings in his right hand, which he rotated nervously while he waited. Despite our incessant drilling and practicing and studying, Bogey remained outspokenly skeptical. He was only going along for the ride, he said. After the war, he was going to reopen his gambling salon in Morocco. Uh-huh. Most of us didn't believe he'd ever been farther east than the Brooklyn Bridge. But it was his finger on the button. He'd look through the Norden bombsight, he'd press the release when the moment came. Maybe his tough-guy attitude was his way of not letting himself think about it too much.

While we watched, the bomb crew lowered specially designed clamps from the plane and attached them to matching hooks on the bomb, then they locked each one carefully into place, with two men checking each clamp. The clamps wouldn't be unlocked until just before release. They handed one set of keys to Lt. Bogart. The other set of keys would be given to Colonel Peck.

As soon as the last clamp was secured, they began the arduous and delicate process of hoisting the bomb up into the belly of the ship. The chains began to clank. The slack was taken up, there was a hesitation and then the vehicle eased itself and sighed as the weight was lifted away. Simultaneously, the plane *groaned*. We could hear its back straining. That baby was *heavy*.

Slowly, slowly the bomb rose up, hanging precariously in the space between us. We watched its studied ascent with a mixture of curiosity and fear. We had all seen the test in Nevada. We were still dazed by the memory of that white-flashing roar of heat and wind. We were terrified of what it would do to a city. White-faced, Jaeckel had screamed to Bogey, "Holy smokes! What is that?" Bogey had answered grimly, "It's the stuff that screams are made of."

Even now, it was still difficult to believe that so much destructive power could be contained in this solid black cylinder. Someone had written in bold white chalk on the side, "Heil *this*!" But as it rose, I saw that someone else had carefully inscribed in bright yellow paint: "*Sh'ma Yisrael, Adonai Elohainu Adonai Ehod.*" Beside it was a list of names—the men who had actually designed and built the bomb. I'd heard there had been quite a fight about the prayer and the names; but apparently Dr. Karloff and Dr. Lorre had told General Tracy, "No prayer, no names—no bomb." I couldn't imagine "Spence the Fence" saying no to either one of those two grand old gentlemen, and I was glad he hadn't.

But there were a lot of rumors floating around. We weren't supposed to repeat them, but we did anyway. We'd heard that Dr. Lugosi was already designing a more powerful bomb. We'd heard that Dr. Karloff was having second thoughts, that he'd written to the president and asked him to demonstrate the bomb on an uninhabited island so the Axis nations could see its power before we actually used it on a city. Rumor had it that Secretary of War Capra had advised against that as "too humanitarian." We needed to hurt the enemy *hard*—so hard that the war would come to a screeching halt.

President Cooper never said what he was thinking throughout the entire debate, but when the question was finally asked, he simply issued his characteristic "Yup" and that was the end of that. The prayer on the side of the bomb probably represented a compromise.

It bothered me. I understood—at least I thought I did—the urge behind it; but at the same time, I didn't think a bomb, and certainly not *this* bomb, was the right place to paint a prayer of any kind. But then again, I wasn't Jewish. I wondered how I'd feel about it if I were.

All of us were volunteers. At the beginning, we hadn't known what we were volunteering for, only that it was dangerous and important.

Then they'd taken us out to Nevada and shown us. We were going to end the war. We were going to obliterate a city. We were going to kill a hundred thousand people in a brilliant bright flash of light.

We had dark goggles to protect our eyes. And radiation meters. Jaeckel, the new kid, would have the best view of all. He was the belly-gunner. He'd been issued a 16mm Bolex loaded with special Eastman-color film. He was supposed to photograph everything we saw. He was excited about the opportunity, even though it meant he had to wear lead-foil underwear.

And then, the bomb was secured and the trucks were rolling away. We still hadn't seen Colonel Peck. Or Colonel Reagan, our co-pilot, either. And the fog wasn't clearing up. Worse, it was getting thicker. My shirt collar was sticking damply to my neck. I checked my watch. So far, we were still on schedule, but time was tight. If we were going to get in the air at all this morning, it would have to be soon.

I was pretty sure that Colonel Peck was uneasy about the mission. I knew him too well, all his mannerisms. He'd been brooding about this ever since Nevada. And the closer we got to take-off, the more irritable he became. He kept ordering me to check the maps, over and over, plotting alternate courses, fuel consumption figures, alternate targets, everything. His tension was infectious. None of us were happy.

And now this. A morning so gloomy it felt like twilight. Could we even get off the ground?

We stood around underneath the plane, an uncomfortable clump of men in baggy flight-suits, and listened to the awful stillness of the fog. Far away sounds were simply swallowed up. Nearby sounds were amplified. Lieutenant Hope—I was suddenly struck by the irony of his name—wouldn't shut up. Even when I moved away to the other side of the bird, I could still hear his inane little jokes. "This is Bob 'fogged-in' Hope calling anybody. Is anybody out there? Say, did you guys hear the one about the leprechaun and the penguin?" There were groans and a *thump* as somebody hit him with a parachute. "Don't worry about me, fellas," he said, climbing back to his feet. "I'm goin' home after this. I'm not spending *my* Christmas with the army."

A chorus of hoots and catcalls greeted this response. I turned away in annoyance and saw the headlights coming out of the fog. I stubbed out my cigarette and called out, "Ten-*hut!*" The crew snapped to attention where they stood.

Generals Gable and Donleavy climbed out of the Jeep. Colonel Peck and Colonel Reagan climbed out after them, followed by the new sky-pilot. "At ease," said General Donleavy; he looked unhappy. General Gable stepped forward and spoke gruffly. "I just wanted to come out here myself and...wish you godspeed. I know some of you have been having second thoughts about this. I don't blame you. I would too. I've been having second thoughts about this since the day I was first briefed.

"But I want you to know that despite all my fears and concerns, that I fully support this operation. In fact, *I envy you.* You men are going to save a lot of lives today. If this device works as well as we hope, then millions of young men—on both sides of this terrible war—will not have to meet on the battlefield. You have it in your power today to save millions of lives, both civilian and military, and spare the world years of suffering and destruction. Just keep that thought in mind and you'll do fine." He glanced over at Captain Fonda. "If any of you want to see the chaplain before you take off...."

At first, most of us were too embarrassed, but then Stan and Ollie stepped over to Captain Fonda and bowed their heads. And then Bogey. And Colonel Peck. I followed. And the others came behind me. All except Taylor and Johnson, the skeptics. They strode down to the tail end of the plane and...upheld their military traditions. General Gable glanced over, decided not to say anything, and deliberately turned his back.

Captain Fonda was slim and gentle, almost too gentle for a war. He had a long, lanky way of speaking; the words came softly out of him like honey poured from a jar. He was a different kind of sky-pilot. He didn't talk about God so much as he talked about the spirit of God inside each and every one of us. "You know what's right in the world," he said. "Stand for it. And others will stand with you." It made me feel good to listen to him.

Afterward, I noticed, Jaeckel, the new kid, hung behind and knelt to confess. Captain Fonda made the sign of the cross over him, then helped him back to his feet with a friendly clap on the shoulder. That was what I liked about him; he knew how to be just an ordinary guy.

Colonel Peck collected his keys from Ollie, then the two of them, the pilot and the copilot, walked slowly around the plane, shining flash-lights up into the wheel housings and looking for oil leaks under the engines. When they finished, they came back, saluted the generals and shook their hands; then they ordered the rest of us up into the bomber. From here on out, the responsibility for delivering the device was all ours, nobody else's.

The solemnity of the moment left us all subdued. That plus the unusual circumstances of two generals and a chaplain coming all the way out to the end of the field for our departure. There was none of the usual wiseass chatter as we climbed into our seats, hooked up our oxygen and buckled our harnesses. We went through our checklists without the usual banter. Even Hope kept his mouth shut for a change. Finally, Colonel Peck started the engines and they clattered explosively to life. They sputtered and smoked and then abruptly caught with a bang. The bird began to vibrate like a 1932 Ford on a rutted road. Colonel Reagan fussed with the fuel mixture to compensate for all the water vapor in the air.

We rolled out onto the end of the runway and turned into the wind. Colonel Peck closed his eyes for a moment—a silent prayer?—then picked up his microphone and asked the tower for permission to take off. The tower's reply was crisp. "Go with God." It would be our last communication. From here on out, strict radio silence would be observed.

Colonel Peck ran the engines up, louder and louder until the plane was howling like a banshee. He turned in his seat to look at the left wing; Reagan turned to look at the right. Satisfied, they both turned back. Colonel Peck put his hands firmly on the wheel, bit his lip and let the plane leap forward. I glanced out the front windshield, but all I saw was a gray wall of haze. He had to be steering by the line of flares along the sides of the runway. I glanced out the side window and tried to gauge our speed by the passing red pinpoints. Faster and faster—they leapt out of the gloom ahead of us and vanished into the gloom behind. Colonel Reagan began calling out airspeed numbers.

At first I didn't think we were going to make it into the air. The bird was heavy and the air was thick and wet. The engines weren't happy. The bird was bouncing and buffeting. Colonel Peck must have been having a hell of a time keeping us on the concrete. And the end of the runway had to be getting awfully close...but at the last moment, the colonel gunned it, grabbed hold of the sky and pulled us up over the trees—so close, I could feel the branches scraping our belly.

We bounced up through the damn fog, shaking and buffeting and cursing all the way. But the bird held together, and at last we climbed up into the clear blue sky above the gray blanket. Suddenly, the warm June sun poured down on us like a welcome smile, filling the plane with lemon-yellow light. The air smoothed out and the bird stopped complaining. Colonel Peck glanced back to me with a smile. I gave him a big thumbs-up.

We were on our way to Germany. And Berlin. And history.

Crossing the channel, we saw some fishing boats. Even in the midst of war, men still cast their nets into the sea to feed their families. I wondered if they looked up and wondered about us in turn. Did they ever think about the planes that crossed back and forth across the channel, and if so, did they wish us well—or did they just resent the burden of the war.

I scribbled notes in the log. Time, position, heading. At the opposite end of the plane, Van Johnson was probably writing another love letter to his fiancée, June. He wrote one every mission and mailed it as soon as we landed. She wrote back every time she got a letter from him. We teased him about it, but we envied him the letters and the connection to someone back home.

"Okay, Jimmy," Colonel Peck turned around to me. "What's it going to be? Paris or Amsterdam?"

I pulled out my lucky silver dollar, flipped it, and caught it on the back of my wrist. I lifted my hand away to show him. "Uh—ah—it looks like Paris," I said. I glanced at the compass. "Uh, you wanna come right about—ah, forty degrees, skipper."

This was part of the security around this operation. Once we were in the air, not even the ground stations were supposed to know where we were. We had been instructed to plot three separate courses to the target; we were forbidden to choose our final heading until we were out over the channel, away from all possible ground observers. Of course, all the flight crews knew that there were U-boats in the channel, tracking the comings and goings of all flights, but we didn't worry about it. Much. Colonel Peck and I favored two different courses, Amsterdam and Paris, each named for the city we'd head toward before turning toward Berlin.

Our group had been sending single flights out over the continent for months, spotting troop movements, checking weather conditions, drop-

ping leaflets, taking photos, surveying bomb damage, all that stuff—a
lot more flights than we needed to. They were decoys to get the jerries
used to the sight of a single Allied plane crossing their skies. Some of
the fellows resented the duty. They'd rather have been dropping bombs,
and nobody would tell them why their flights were so important, but
they were.

We'd flown a a lot of the flights too, mostly the missions over Berlin
and our secondary targets. In the past week, we'd even made two leaflet
drops, dropping the package and then pulling up and away sharply to
the right exactly as we would do later today. The leaflets had warned the
Berliners to leave the city, because we were going to destroy it. We implied that we'd be sending a thousand planes across the channel, dark-
ening their skies with the roar of engines and the thunder of bombs.
We'd heard they were installing ack-ack guns from here to the Rhine
and we wondered if they'd test them on us today.

Once, we'd also dropped an agent into Germany. A fellow named
Flynn. His job was to contact members of the underground and warn
them to get out of Berlin before the sixth. I wondered where he was now.
I hoped he had gotten out. A nice fellow, I guess, but I wouldn't have his
job. He'd seemed foolhardy to me.

Colonel Peck glanced at the altimeter, tapped it to make sure it wasn't
stuck, and then spoke into his microphone. "All right, Stan, Ollie. We're
at cruising altitude. You can start arming the device." He waited for
their confirmations, then switched off again.

We'd heard that the Nazis had forbidden the civilian population to
flee Berlin, but our intelligence sources were telling us that at least a
third of the civilians had evacuated anyway and more were streaming
out every day. Even if the bomb failed, we would still have seriously
disrupted the economy of the Reich's capital. Most of the overlords of
the Reich had already moved themselves away from the city—except
for that pompous turnip, Goering. He had publicly boasted that not a
single allied bomb would fall on Berlin. I wondered if he would be in
Berlin today. I wondered about all the others too. Goebbels, Heydrich,
Eichmann, Hess, Himmler, and the loudmouthed little paper-hanger.
Would they be close enough to see the blast? What would they think?
What would they do?

Some of the psych boys said that they believed that Corporal Shickel-
gruber would sooner die in the holy flames of martyrdom than ever let

himself be captured and put on trial for war crimes. Worse, he would take the nation down with him.

If the bomb worked—

Of course it worked. We'd seen it work in Nevada. I couldn't get it out of my head—that terrible mushroom cloud climbing into the morning sky, churning and rising and burning within. It was a preview of Hell. Afterward, we were given the chance to withdraw from the mission. None of us did. Perhaps if we hadn't already been a crew, some of us would have. I'd have considered it, but I couldn't let the other fellows down. Later, we spent long hours talking among ourselves. If we ended the war, we'd be heroes. But...just as likely, we might be war criminals. Nobody had ever used a bomb like this before.

But never mind that—if the bomb worked the way we wanted it to, we'd paralyze the Third Reich. The armies would stop fighting. The generals would surrender rather than let their troops be incinerated. Perhaps even they'd overthrow the murderous bastards at the top and save the rest of the world the trouble of hanging them. Perhaps.

And perhaps they'd do something else. Perhaps they'd launch a ferocious counter-attack beyond our abilities to comprehend. Perhaps they'd unleash all the poison gases and deadly germs they were rumored to have stockpiled. Who knew what they'd do if they were scared enough?

But that wasn't our worry. All we had to do was deliver the device. Behind us, taking off at fifteen-minute intervals, thirty other planes would be following; each one equipped with cameras and radiation-detectors. The visible aftermath of this weapon would be on movie screens all over the world within the week.

I tried to imagine what else might be happening today. Probably the French resistance was being signaled to do whatever they could to scramble communications and transportation among the Nazis. Our ambassadors were probably preparing to deliver informative messages to other governments. We'd entered the war in 1939. Everybody expected us to invade Europe before the end of the summer. I wondered if our troops were massing even now to follow us into Germany.

Lieutenant Bogart came forward then with a thermos of coffee. It was his habit to come up to the cockpit for a while before we reached enemy territory. Today, he had more reason than ever. Despite his frequent protestations otherwise, the thought of the bomb in our belly clearly disturbed him as much as the rest of us. Perhaps him more than any-body. He looked burnt and bitter. "Which way are we headed, skipper? We going over Paris?"

Colonel Peck nodded. "It's the long way around, but I want to give Stan and Ollie plenty of time to arm the device."

I looked at Bogey suddenly. There was something odd in his eyes, but I couldn't identify the look. Anger perhaps? Some long-remembered hurt?

"Uh, ahh-h—you've been to Paris?" I asked.

He nodded. "I was there. For a while. Just before the jerries moved in."

"I never made it myself. I always wanted to go, but something always came up. I had to stay home and help Pop with the business."

"After the war is over," Colonel Peck said, "We'll all meet for cham-pagne on the Champs Elysees." He got a wistful look on his face then. "It's one of the most beautiful streets in the world. Lined with cafes and shops and beautiful women. You could spend your days just sitting and sipping coffee. Or you could stuff yourself with mushrooms and fish poached in butter. You could follow it with little thin pancakes filled with thick rich cream. And the wine—we had champagne and caviar on toast so crisp it snapped. I never had a bad meal anywhere in France. They could make even a potato a work of art."

He looked to Bogey for agreement, but the bombardier just shrugged. "I spent most of my time on the left bank, drinking the cheap wine. I didn't get to the same joints you did, Colonel."

"You saw a lot of Europe before the war, skipper?" Reagan asked.

Peck shook his head. "Not as much as I wanted to. But I have good memories." He stared off into the distance as if he were seeing them all again. "I remember the tulip gardens in Copenhagen—so bright they dazzle the eyes. And the dark canals of Amsterdam, circling around the center of the city. All the buildings are so narrow that the staircases are almost like ladders." He shook his head sadly. "I can still taste the thick layered pastries of Vienna. And I remember wandering through the sprawling parks of Rome—do you know there are wild cats living all over the ruins of the Colosseum? They've probably been there since Caesar's time. And the rumpled hills of Athens, the Parthenon look-ing down over the city, and ouzo in your belly like licorice fire. Berlin. The beerhalls and the nightclubs. The screech of the trains. The smell of coal. The old opera house. On Sundays, you could go to the afternoon concerts; if you were a student, you paid half price. That's where I first heard Beethoven and Wagner. What a marvelous dichotomy the Germans represent, that they could produce such sublime music—and such incredible horrors too."

"Uh, ah—you've seen Berlin?" I asked. This was the first time he'd ever admitted it.

Colonel Peck nodded. "A long time ago." His eyes were shaded grimly. "It's a funny old town. When I was there it was full of students and workmen, shopkeepers and grandmothers in babushkas. No one was angry then. The streets were clean and the people were stolid and happy. It was spring, and the world was green and fresh and full of butterflies and hope. It was a long time ago, and I was very...young."

Bogey and Reagan exchanged a look then. Worried. Was the colonel having second thoughts?

Almost as if in answer to their question, Colonel Peck added, "It was the music. I was sure that Berlin had to be the most marvelous city in the world for such incredible music to live there." And then, as if realizing again where he was and what he'd just said, he shook his head grimly. "I've never liked this idea. Bombing a city. Civilians. It's—" He didn't finish the sentence. Instead he reached over and flipped the fuel tank switches. It was time to lighten the left side of the plane for a while.

After a moment, he turned around again and looked at the three of us. First Reagan, then me, then finally Bogey. "All right," he said. "What is it?"

"Ah, uh—are you feeling all right, skipper?"

Colonel Peck nodded with his chin, in that grim way of his. "If you're worrying if I can do the job, stop worrying. This is what we've trained for."

"Right," said Bogey, clapping one hand on the Colonel's shoulder. "We don't need Berlin. We'll always have Paris." I couldn't tell if he was joking or not.

Bogey was the weirdest one in the crew, always saying things that were either bitter jokes or just plain bitter. Colonel Peck wasn't sure what Bogey meant either. He just looked at him sideways for a long moment. The two of them studied each other the way two men do when they first meet, sizing each other up, getting a sense of whether they're going to be friends or enemies.

These two jokers had known each other for a long time, but right now, at this moment, it was as if they'd never really seen each other before. Bogey shifted the cigar from one side of his mouth to the other and grinned fiercely at Peck. Peck's expression relaxed, widened into a matching grin. And then suddenly, we were all grinning and laughing nervously.

"We're starting to take ourselves a little too seriously," said Peck. "Take over, Ronnie, I'm going back to check on the boys." He levered himself out of his seat and climbed past Bogey into the rear of the plane.

We waited until we were sure he was gone. None of us dared speak. Finally, I had to ask it. "Ah, ah—do you fellas think he's gonna be all right?"

Bogey shifted his cigar from one side of his mouth to the other, then back again. "I dunno. I've seen a lot of men do a lot of strange things. When the crunch comes, that's when you find out what a man's made of." He added. "He's got a look in his eye all right."

Reagan didn't say anything for a moment. He looked like he was rehearsing his next words. At last, he said, "I had a private briefing with General Donleavy last night." We waited for him to continue. "He said...he said that if for any reason Colonel Peck was unable to carry out the mission...I was to take over and make sure the device was delivered. I asked him if he thought that was likely. He said no, but...well, the top brass just wanted to cover every possibility, that's all."

"Ah, uh, you can't be serious," I stammered.

"Well, General Donleavy suggested that if I thought I had to do such a thing, I should talk it over with the bombardier and the navigator and maybe the flight engineer. I wouldn't have said anything, but—" He glanced backward.

"Uh—you *can't* do it," I said. "You just can't. The colonel didn't mean anything by what he said. You saw him. He's just—I mean, anybody'd feel bad having to do this. You would, wouldn't you?" I looked to Bogey, alarmed at the way the conversation was going.

Bogey's expression was dark. "I'm not going to have any trouble dropping this bomb. I've seen the Nazis face-to-face." He looked to Reagan.

"Well," said Reagan. "I guess...a man's gotta do what a man's gotta do."

"Ah, uh, you can't do this, Colonel. You gotta give him a chance. You do this, you'll wreck his career—"

Bogey poked me hard in the shoulder then, and I shut up just as Colonel Peck climbed back into the cockpit. If he'd heard anything, he didn't show any sign. He glanced around at us with gentle eyes, and I *knew* he knew.

"All right, men," he said. "Let's talk about it."

"Eh?" said Bogey, blandly. "We don't know what you're talking about."

Peck let out his breath in a sigh, glancing downward while he collected his thoughts. When he met our eyes again, his face was grim. "I wanted to have this talk with you before," he said. "But I realized that there was no safe way to have this talk until we were safely in the air. From here on in, this *thing* is our responsibility. It's up to us. We've been entrusted by our government with the single most important mission of the war. But I want you to think about something for a moment. There is a law that transcends the laws that mere men can make."

I glanced to Bogey, then to Reagan. Bogey's grim smile revealed nothing of what he was thinking. But everything Reagan was feeling was written on his face so clearly, he could have been a neon sign.

Peck saw it. He put his hand across the intervening space and laid it on Reagan's shoulder. "Ronnie, I want you to think about the precedent we're about to set. We'll be validating that it's all right to bomb civilians, to wipe out whole cities. This is the first atomic war. If we do this, it won't be the last. Yes, I've been thinking; maybe the most courageous thing we can do today is *not* drop this bomb. Maybe we should jettison it into the ocean. It'll be three months before the next one is ready. But we could take a stand today, that soldiers of the United States will not kill innocent civilians. And if we did that, our government leaders would have three months to change their minds about using the next one. Perhaps they'd think differently if we gave them a reason to reconsider—"

"And perhaps they'll just put us in Leavenworth and throw away the key," said Bogey. "Count me out. I've seen enough prisons, thank you."

"You're talking treason, sir," said Reagan.

"Yes, in one sense, I guess I am. But is it treasonous to place one's loyalty to God and all humanity above everything else? If our government is about to do something terribly terribly wrong, shouldn't we oppose it—just like all those brave men and women who have been trying to oppose the evils of the Third Reich for so many years? Do two wrongs make a right?"

"Ahh-h-h," I stammered. They all looked at me. "I hear the sense of your words, Colonel, but this is the wrong time to have second thoughts. The time to bail out of this mission was before we took off."

Peck looked to Bogey. He raised an eyebrow questioningly; what do you think?

Bogey chewed on the soggy end of his cigar for a moment before answering. "Colonel, you're one of the most decent men in the world. Perhaps too decent. You're certainly too decent for this job. And I wish I had your courage, because you're speaking what a lot of us have been thinking. But...I'm also a realist. And there comes a time when even decent men have to do indecent things. That's the obscenity of war. Especially this one. Lives are cheap. We drop this thing, they're going to get cheaper still. But if we don't—well, I don't see there's much decency in the alternative."

Colonel Peck nodded thoughtfully while he considered Bogey's words. He nodded and kept nodding. I could see that he was thinking through the logic step by step. That was Colonel Peck. Careful.

But he never got the chance to finish his thinking. Colonel Reagan unbuttoned his jacket pocket and pulled out a set of orders. He unfolded them and handed them to Colonel Peck. "Colonel, you are hereby relieved of command of this mission. I'm sorry, Greg. I was given those orders last night by General Donleavy. If you showed any signs of not being able to carry out this mission, he told me to place you under arrest and take over." And then he added, "I hope you won't make this difficult. Sir."

Colonel Peck read the orders without comment. "These appear to be in order," he said. He passed them to Bogey, who glanced at them, and handed them to me. I pulled my logbook around and wrote in the change of command. My hand shook as I did so.

"Colonel Reagan, your orders appear to be valid. The mission is yours." He folded his arms. "You've helped me make up my mind, and I thank you for that. The fact that General Donleavy felt that such an order might be necessary confirms the ugliness of this mission." He glanced at his watch. "We still have two hours before we're over Berlin. You might spend it thinking about what kind of a world we'll be living in after you drop that bomb. You too, Bogey, Jimmy." He looked to Reagan. "Do you want me to ride in the back?"

"If you promise not to interfere with the operation of this mission, I'd rather you stay up here, sir."

"Thank you. I'd like that."

Ronnie picked up his microphone then. "Attention, all hands. This is Colonel Reagan. Colonel Peck has been taken ill. I'm taking command. We will proceed with the mission as directed." He put the microphone down.

Colonel Peck nodded. "Thank you, Colonel Reagan."

"Thank you for your cooperation, Colonel Peck."

We flew in silence for a while. The plane droned across the bright green fields of France, heading toward the distant blue mountains and then the long run north toward Berlin.

"Colonel?" Lt. Laurel's softly accented tenor came through our headphones.

"Yes, Lieutenant?"

"Ollie and I would like to report that the device is armed."

"Thank you, Lieutenant." Reagan glanced at his watch. "You're ahead of schedule. Good job."

Reagan looked around at me, at Bogey. "Either of you fellows having second thoughts?"

I shook my head. "I'm fine." Bogey held up his thumb. *The* thumb. The one he'd use to press the button. I glanced at my watch, then wrote the time in the log. *Device armed.* The words looked strange on the page.

I wondered what the people of Berlin were doing now? Were they going about their daily lives without concern, or were they studying the skies and worrying? Did the husbands go to work this morning? Were they busy at their offices? Were the children reciting lessons in their classrooms? Were the wives and housekeepers out shopping for sausage and cheese? Were the students sitting in cafes, sipping coffee and arguing philosophy? Did the orchestras still rehearse their concerts of Beethoven and Wagner? Or was the music cancelled for the duration?

We flew on in silence. The engines roared and vibrated. The big machine talked to itself in a thousand different noises. We had our own symphony, here in the sky.

Colonel Peck looked curiously relaxed, as if he were finally at peace with himself. The bomb might fall, but it would not be his doing. Reagan, on the other hand, could not have looked unhappier. He must have felt betrayed by the colonel. Worse, he must now be feeling the same burden that Colonel Peck had been carrying around for the last few months.

Reagan exhaled, loudly. I could tell he was trying to figure it out. "I don't get you, skipper. You're one of the smartest guys I know. How can you betray your country like this?" He had an angry edge to his voice.

"I'm not betraying my country. I'm holding her true to her principles. We're not killers."

"The Germans started this war," Reagan said. "The Nazis are an evil empire. This bomb will destroy them. We have to follow our orders."

Colonel Peck nodded. "Ron, it's an officer's duty to refuse to obey any order that he knows is wrong. We're about to drop the equivalent of fifteen kilotons of TNT on an unarmed civilian population. Do you think that's correct?"

Reagan didn't answer. Even from the back, I could see the expression on his face; he was so angry his hair was clenched.

"Maybe the whole idea of war has gone too far," Peck said. "Maybe it's time for someone to just say no."

"That's got to be the stupidest thing I've ever heard anyone say," Reagan replied, shaking his head. I could tell he wasn't thinking straight anymore. I'd seen him get like this before. He'd get so angry that he'd refuse to listen to anyone, even when he knew they were right.

"Maybe. Maybe it is—and maybe someday, someone else will have an atomic bomb—maybe the Russians or the Chinese or even some crazy little Arab hothead—and maybe they'll be thinking about dropping their bomb on an American city, maybe New York or Chicago or Los Angeles. I don't know. But whoever it is, they'll have the precedent of our actions today, Ron. They'll know *exactly* what the horror will look like. The whole world is watching. If we turn back today, we'll be saying that this bomb is too *terrible* for anyone to use.

"But—if we use it, then every nation will want to have one—will *need* to have one—if only to defend themselves against the United States, because we'll have demonstrated ourselves as willing to inflict such horror on our enemies. Oh, if it were only the war, Ron, I'd drop the bomb. What's the difference between a bellyload of little blockbusters or one big city-killer? Only the size of the boom. But it's not just this war, Ron. It's everything. It's all the consequences. It's tomorrow and tomorrow and all the tomorrows that come after."

"We'll be over Germany soon," Reagan said to Bogey. He hadn't heard a thing that Colonel Peck had said.

Bogey grunted a noncommittal response.

Reagan looked to Peck. "It's time. Give him your keys."

Peck nodded. He unclipped the keys from his belt and handed them to Bogey. Bogey clapped the colonel on the shoulder, a gesture of respect and affection, then ducked out of the cockpit.

We flew on. The engines droned and roared. I bent back to my table, my charts, my numbers, my logbook, my frustration. They were both right, each in their own way.

"How long to Berlin, Jimmy?"

"Uh, ah—ah-h, twenty minutes."

"Thank you." Reagan spoke into his mike. "Bombardier?"

Bogey's voice came through the headphones. "I've got a problem— I'm coming back up."

Reagan and Peck looked at each other in puzzlement. Peck glanced back to me. I shrugged.

Bogey pulled himself back into the cockpit, scratching the stubble on his chin. "I dunno how to tell you this, Colonel—" he said to Reagan. "—but I dropped the other set of keys. I can't unlock the bomb."

"Well, find 'em, dammit!" Reagan was getting red in the face.

"Uh, that'll be a little hard, Colonel. I dropped 'em out the window."

For a moment Reagan didn't get it. Peck realized it first, and a big grin started spreading across his face.

Reagan started to unfasten his seat-harness. "All right, I'll cut the damn chains if I have to—"

"That won't work either, sir. Stan and Ollie are already disarming the bomb." Bogey looked to Peck. "We're going to have to turn back."

"You'll be court martialed for this! Both of you!" Reagan snapped.

"Oh, hell," said Bogey. "Let 'em. If they want to put me in jail for standing for what's right, then our country's got a lot bigger problem than this little war. You and I, Colonel—our problems don't amount to a hill of beans in this crazy world. But if I let you take this plane to Berlin, I'll regret it for the rest of my life...."

Colonel Peck put his hands back on the controls of the aircraft. He looked over to Ron—

"Dammit! We have our orders—" Reagan protested.

"I know, Ron, I know." Colonel Peck said softly, regretfully. He picked up his microphone. "Lt. Hope. This is the Captain speaking. Break radio silence. Send the mission aborted signal. We're coming home." And then he began banking the plane around to the left.

Bogey took the cigar out of his mouth and grinned at me. "Hey, Jimmy, you got a light?"

Being a superhero is hard, thankless work. If you're good at it, you don't get rewards—you just get bigger problems. That's why superheroes go psychotic.

Franz Kafka, Superhero!

THE RATTLE OF THE RED ROACH PHONE—a noise like an angry cicada—brought him to instant wakefulness. He rolled out of bed in a single movement, scooped up the handset and held it to his ear. He didn't speak.

The familiar voice. The words crisp and mellifluous. "One-thirty-three. How soon can you leave?"

He bent to the nightstand and switched on the lamp with a loud click. He opened the World Atlas that lay directly under the glow to page 133. A map of Vienna. He glanced at the clock. The minute hand had long since fallen off, but he'd become fairly proficient at telling the time by the position of the hour hand alone. "I'll be on the ten-thirty train."

"Good," said the voice. The line clicked and went silent.

He undid the laces tying up the throat of his nightshirt, letting the wide neck of the garment fall open and away. He began shrugging it down off his shoulders, pulling it down to his waist, shedding it like an insect pushing its way out of its cocoon, all the while darting his eyes about the room in quick, nervous little glances. It fell forgotten to the floor. He stepped out of it, pink, naked and alert. A whole new being. His eyes glistened with anticipation and excitement.

He dressed quickly, efficiently. He put on a shiny black suit. He se-

50

lected a matching black tie. He buttoned his dark red vest meticulously. He wound his watch and tucked it into his vest. He opened the top drawer and selected his two best handkerchiefs; then, after a moment's consideration, he selected a third one as well—his *silk* handkerchief, the one he only used for special occasions.

He pulled on his heavy wool overcoat. He grabbed his carpet bag from the closet, already packed. He was ready to go.

As he walked, he considered. Fifteen minutes to the train station. Five minutes to buy a ticket. Twenty minutes to spare before the train arrived. Yes. He could purchase a newspaper and have a coffee and a croissant in the cafe while he waited. Good.

He could feel the power in his step. He was ready for battle. His mind was clear. This time, he would confront the arch-fiend PsycheMan in his lair. Yes! The enemy would know the taste of ashes and despair before *this* day was through.

In his ordinary life, he pretended to be just another faceless dark slug—sweaty, confused, trapped by circumstance. He moved through the maze of twisty gray streets, almost unnoticed. If by chance he did attract the attention of another being, they would see him only as a squat dark shape, brooding, uncommunicative.

In his ordinary life, he pretended to be a writer of grotesque fantasies, a mordant storyteller of obscure, deranged, and unpublishable dreads. His visions were tumbled and stifling—almost repulsive in their queerness. People avoided the possibility of close contact, which was exactly what he wanted and needed—

—Because in his *extra*ordinary life, he was Bug-Man! *The human insect!*

Transformed by a bizarre experiment in Marie Curie's laboratory—accidentally exposed to the life-altering rays of the mysterious element *radium*—he had become a *whole new kind of being*. A strange burst of power had expanded throughout his entire body, shredding the very cells of his flesh.

For a single bright instant, he comprised the entire universe, he knew *everything,* understood *everything*. His skin glowed white as the very essence of life itself infused his whole being. For just that single instant, he became a creature of *pure energy!* And then the transforming bath of radioactive power ebbed and the entire cosmos collapsed again, down into a single dark node at the bottom of his soul. When his vision cleared, he realized that the insect specimen he had been holding had vanished completely, its essence subsumed throughout his flesh.

That night, under the intoxicating rays of the full moon, he discovered a new plasticity to his flesh. His bones had become malleable. His muscles could be used to pull his body into a shape that was at first painful and frightening, then curious, and finally invigorating and powerful. His skin toughened like armor. He turned and saw himself in the mirror as something strange and beautiful. A shining black carapace. Glistening faceted eyes. Trembling antennae. He could taste symphonies in the air that he had never known before. He could hear colors previously undreamt. The strength in his limbs was alarming! Thrilling! He had become a master of *metamorphosis*. Franz Kafka, superhero!

In the days that followed, he learned to control his new powers, leaping from buildings, tunneling, biting, scrabbling through the earth in the dead of night. The cost of his ability to metamorphosize was a ferocious hunger. He satisfied it by preying on the predators of society. He became a force to be reckoned with, seeking out those who preyed on the weak, snapping them in two and feeding on their flesh. Soon, the dark underworld elements of Austria learned the fury of his appetites. The word spread. *The night belonged to Bug-Man.*

Soon he became an ally to the great governments of Europe, battling arch-fiends all over the continent. His exploits became world-famous. His twilight battles were the stuff of legend. Where evil spread its nefarious claws, the cry would soon go up: "This is a job for Bug-Man!"

Now, he hurried to Vienna, eager for the final confrontation with the greatest monster of them all: the terrible master of confusion, Sigmund Freud—more commonly known to the League Of United Superheroes Everywhere as *PsycheMan!*

The evil doctor Freud terrorized his victims by summoning up the monsters of the id. He used their own fears against them, plundering their treasures and leaving them feeble and empty. Freud's victims babbled in languages of their own, meaningless chatter. They capered like monkeys, simpered like idiots, grinning and drooling; he filled the asylums with his victims. Franz Kafka could not wait to catch this monster on his own overstuffed couch. He dabbed at his chin with his handkerchief, lest someone observe him drooling in anticipation.

The train lurched and rattled and crawled across the Austrian countryside. By the time it finally clattered into the Vienna station, it was nearly four in the afternoon. Dusk would be falling soon, and with it would come his terrible hunger. No matter, tonight he intended to feed well. He would soon suck the marrow from the bones of Dr. Freud. He could hardly wait to sink his gleaming pincers into the soft white flesh of the little Viennese Jew, injecting him with his venom, then tasting the liquefied flesh, inhaling its aroma, taking it hungrily into his meta-morphosed self, refreshing himself, invigorating his energies. He would turn the monster's very flesh into fuel for his own divine crusade against evil!

Wiping his mouth again, covering his excitement with his now-sod-den handkerchief, Kafka hurried to the post office window and asked if a letter had been left for him. The squint-eyed clerk handed it across without comment. Kafka shoved it into his coat pocket without look-ing at it and scuttled away out of the glare of the bright lights overhead. At last he flattened himself into a dark comer and opened the envelope quickly. Inside was a small square of paper with an address neatly typed on it. Kafka repeated the address to himself three times, memorizing it, then wadded up the paper and shoved it into his mouth, chewing fran-tically. It was several moments before he was able to swallow the wad, and during the entire time his little dark eyes flicked back and forth, watching for suspicious strangers. But no, nobody had noticed the dark little creature in the corner.

Kafka swallowed the last of the paper and left the station, relieved to be away from the screech of the trains and the crush of so many people. He headed north, walking briskly, but not so fast as to call attention to himself. He headed directly for the address on the paper. He had to see the house before the sun set. The narrow cobbled streets of Vienna echoed with his footsteps.

All the buildings were clustered like newborn wedding cakes, close and ornate. The streets and alleys between them were already sunk in romantic gloom, and the first smells of the evening meal were already filling the streets. He passed open shop doors and restaurants. His heightened senses told him of the spices in the sausages, the honey in the pastries, the butterfat in the cream. A horse-drawn wagon clattered by, dragging with it the animal scent of manure and sweat. Smoke from the chimneys climbed up into the oppressive sky. The heavy flavor of coal pervaded everything.

Kafka found the street he was looking for and turned left into it as if he was a long-familiar resident. He slowed his pace and studied the houses on the opposite side of the avenue, one at a time, examining each as if none of them held any specific interest for him. They were tall, narrow structures, each hiding behind a wrought-iron fence. The high peaked roofs offered multiple opportunities to hide and possible easy access through the gabled windows; but Kafka ignored them. He let his attention wander to the cobbled street itself, the sewers and the drains. If he was satisfied with what he saw, he gave no sign. He continued on down the street toward the end.

At the end of the block, he turned right, crossed the street and headed up toward the next block. He turned right and headed up the row of houses looking thoughtfully at each one. As luck would have it, the building directly behind Dr. Freud's suspected lair was a small hotel for retired gentlemen.

He climbed up the front steps, entered and rang the bell at the registration desk. Shortly, a wizened old clerk appeared and Kafka inquired politely if there were a quiet room available in the back of the inn. There was, and he immediately secured it for two days. He would need a private place in which to accomplish his metamorphosis, and time to recover afterward. He considered himself extremely fortunate to be so close to his quarry.

Wiping his chin, he let himself into the room, put down his carpet bag just inside the door, turned and locked the door behind him. At last! He was so close to his arch-enemy he could almost taste his blood! He crossed to the window and parted the curtains. Across a narrow garden, he could see the shuttered rear windows of Dr. Freud's house. He wondered what nefarious deeds were going on behind those walls.

He'd know soon enough; the moon was already visible above the rooftops. He pulled the curtains aside and opened the window, the better to admit the healing rays of moonlight. He began pulling off his clothes, almost clawing his way out of them, exposing his pallid flesh to the intoxicating luminance.

He opened the carpet bag and began laying out the equipment that he would need. A large rubber sheet—he spread it across the floor. A large block of wood—battered, chipped and scarred; he placed that carefully on the sheet.

The transformation began slowly. He felt the first twinges in his shoulders and in his knees. He began to twitch. The long hours cooped

up in the train had left him stiff and uncomfortable; this metamorphosis would be a painful one. Good! A flurry of little shudders shook his
body; he grabbed hold of a chair for support until the seizure eased. He
knew he had to be careful, he knew he didn't dare risk losing consciousness; he had to stay awake and deliberately shape himself for the battle
ahead.

His head. Most important. His mandibles—

His teeth began to lengthen in his mouth, pushing his jaw painfully
out of its sockets. He shoved his fingers into his mouth and started
pulling his teeth painfully forward, shaping them into the digging and
grinding tools that he would shortly need.

Next, his skull. He put his right hand under his chin and his left hand
on top of his head and pressed them toward each other as hard as he
could. The bones of his skull creaked and gave. His head began to flat-
ten. His chin spread, his eyes bulged sideways, his jaw widened out, his
teeth splayed forward, his eyebrows sprang out like antennae—blood
began to pour from his nose. He pressed harder and harder, until the
pain became unbearable, but still he pressed until he no longer had the
strength in his arms or the leverage with which to press.

Already his spine was softening, could no longer support his weight.
He dropped to the floor, grunting as the air was forced from his lungs.
His arms flopped wildly. He pulled his knees up and grabbed hold of
his feet as hard as he could. As he straightened his legs again, his arms
began to lengthen. His elbows popped, the bones pulling out of their
sockets—he screamed with pain, rolled over and grabbed the block of
wood in his mouth, bit it as hard as he could. He did this again and
again, stretching his arms into long, black, hairy appendages.

Yes, the hair! It was sprouting all over his arms and legs. His legs were
softening now. He pulled his knees up to his chest, and now, grabbing
them again with his hardening arms, he pulled at his knees until the
sockets popped and now his legs could lengthen naturally. He clutched
his feet, working them into clawlike shapes, stretching his toes, pulling
at them mercilessly, grunting with the pain, and still continuing to pull.
And yes, now the side appendages were large enough to grab, to pull,
to stretch. He worked his muscles savagely, massaging them into shape,
strengthening them. Yes, this was going to be one of the best! The more
pain he experienced, the better the transformation!

He rolled around on the floor, rubbing his back and sides against the rubber sheet, hardening his carapace. He wiped at his multifaceted eyes with his front legs, cleaning them of bloody residue. His antennae twitched. He was almost done. Almost there—and yes, in a final spasm of completion, he *ejaculated!* Spurt after spurt after spurt of sickly yellow-looking ichor. The shaft of his metallic-looking penis retreated again inside his chitiny shell, and Bug-Man raised himself aloft on his six exquisite legs, chittering with satisfaction and joy!

Bug-Man was a simple being. He had no knowledge of anything but the blood of his enemy. He cared nothing for Franz Kafka or the League Of United Superheroes Everywhere. He knew little of trains and croissants and newspapers. Bug-Man was a creature of hunger and rage. He knew only the ferocious desire for vengeance. He lived for the hot red fulfillment of delicious gluttony. His mandibles clattered in soft anticipation. He drooled with excitement. He wanted one thing only—the flesh of PsycheMan! He could not rest until he'd crunched the skull of Sigmund Freud between his diamond-hard teeth!

He leapt to the window, flinging it open, pulling himself out onto the balustrade, poising himself, stretching himself up into the darkness and the holy glow of the full moon above. Across the way, he heard a gasp, and then the sound of a window slamming. A light vanished. He heard the sounds of running footsteps. He ignored them all. He leapt.

He landed lightly on the soft black earth of the garden below. Instantly, he began digging, down and down into the deep delicious soil, his six legs working frantically, flinging the dirt backward and upward, scattering it in every direction. His mandibles chewed and cut. In moments, he was gone, sliding into the cool dark space beneath the lawn, tunneling his way toward the house of Sigmund Freud, the monster.

The night fell silent. The moon rose higher and higher until it was directly overhead, casting its lambent radiance down across the gabled old houses of sleeping Vienna. And then a noise ...

The sound of something creaking, cracking, crackling as it broke—

The ancient floorboards came away in ragged chunks. The hole widened. Something was chewing up through the ground, widening the hole in quick, malicious bites. And then it was climbing up and into the cellar of the house. Bug-Man was here! Inside the house of his arch-enemy! He scrabbled purposefully across the floor, sniffing the air with his antennae. He slid up the stairs, not bothering to open the door at the top, breaking through it instead like a flimsy construction of cardboard.

He was in the pantry! The overwhelming pantry, reeking with conflict-ing flavors and aromas—all the spices and ingredients of a thousand differ-ent meals, coffee-chocolate-butter-garlic-sausage-cheese-pepper-bread—they all repulsed him now. He moved swiftly to the kitchen, to the din-ing room, to the stairway in the hall, and up the stairs, breaking away the banister as he climbed to give himself room.

There was no dark at the top of the stairs. The light came on abruptly. Someone was moving up there. Bug-Man's glistening multifaceted eyes caught the image in a shattered reality. There—silhouetted against the glare of the electric lamp beyond—stood the terrible demonic form of Sigmund Freud, the *PsycheMan!*

He stood alone, wearing only a nightshirt, a robe, and fuzzy blue slip-pers. He rested one hand on the top of the broken banister to support him-self. He looked incredibly frail, but his eyes gleamed with turquoise pow-er! His high forehead bulged abnormally, the fringe of white hair around it was not enough to conceal its freakish expanded shape. His predatory chin was concealed by the long white beard. His bony knees stuck out from beneath the hem of his garment like awkward chicken legs.

The transformed Kafka lifted himself up, as if about to leap. He ut-tered a low sound, a moan of anticipatory lust, a growl of warning, a challenge, a chittering of danger.

"Ach!" said Freud. "It's only you. Well, come in, come in. I've been expecting you. You're late again." He waggled his finger warningly. "You superheroes, you think you can come calling any time, day or night, without an appointment—"

He started to turn away, then suddenly, turned back toward Bug-Man, his eyes blazing with red fire! *"Well, I won't have it!"* He knocked the ash off his cigar into his hand and carefully pocketed the residue. Then he lifted the cigar like a baton, holding it outstretched toward the man-bug. With his other hand he stroked the cigar, once, twice, a third time—suddenly the cigar emitted a crackling bolt of blue-white lightning down the staircase. BugMan ducked his head just in time. The blast of fire splattered off his back singing the walls, scorching the wall-paper, striking little fires among the chips and sawdust of the broken banister all the way down and leaving the air stinking of ozone.

Kafka was stunned. For a moment, he almost forgot that he was Bug-Man. Freud was much stronger than he had thought. He must have been gaining converts faster than they had realized, far more than they had estimated. He must have been draining the life force of hundreds, perhaps thousands of hapless souls, distilling their very being down into his own evil essence.

Bug-Man recovered himself then. He stopped thinking, stopped considering, stopped caring—he remembered his purpose. To *feed on the flesh of Sigmund Freud!* He charged up the stairs after the monstrous little man. But Freud's frail demeanor was only another deceit. The old man scampered away like an animated elf, disappearing into the darkness at the far end of the hall.

Bug-Man followed relentlessly, his six long hairy legs scrabbling loudly on the hardwood floor. His claws left nasty scratches in the polished surface. He plunged into the darkness—

And found himself in a maze of twisty little passages, all alike. A maze. The maze. Twisty little passages. A twisty little maze. All alike.

His eyes swiveled backward and forward—and he hesitated. For a moment, he had to be Kafka again. Had to rely on his innate human intelligence instead of his insect instinct. Reminded himself. *Freud has no power of his own. He borrows the power of others. He summons monsters from the id and lets them fight his battles for him. But it's all illusion.. You will destroy yourself fighting empty manifestations of your own fears. Ignore the illusions. Concentrate on what's real!*

Bug-Man's hesitation stretched out forever. His chitiny shell began to soften. His mandibles clattered in confusion. *But—but how do I know what's real?* he wondered. *Everything that a being can know is ultimately experiential. I have no way to stand apart from the experiential nature of existence! So how can I access what is real and distinguish it from illusion?*

It seemed as if all time was standing still. Kafka's mind raced, his thought processes accelerated. *Be who you are!* he shouted to the Bug-Man! *Don't let him define you! He is a walrus. You are the Bug-Man! You are the greatest superhero ever! Ignore the lies! Anything that contradicts the Bug-Man is a lie! Remember that!*

The Bug-Man snarled. Unconfused. He knew himself again, submerged himself once more in crimson fury and fire; the hunger and rage suffused his body like a bath of acid. He clicked his mandibles, reached out with his pincers and started pulling down the ugly twisty little walls and their dripping veins and wires, started pulling down the twisty little maze of darkness and fury, sending creatures of indeterminate shape scuttling out into the fringes, started pulling down the twisty little passages all alike, pulling and chewing and breaking through—

He was in a tunnel. Blackness behind him. Blackness ahead.

The tunnel slanted downward into the bottomless dark. The walls were straight; they were set wide apart, but the ceiling was low. Everything was cut from dark wet stone. The water dripped from the walls and slid downward into the gloom ahead. His eyes refocused. What little light there was seeped into the air from no apparent source.

Far in the distance below, something moved. He could smell it. His antennae quivered in anticipation. He lifted his pincers. He readied his stinger, arching his tail high over his head. His venom dripped.

The thing ahead was coming closer. In the blackness below, a formless form was growing. It opened its eyes. Two bright red embers, glowing ferociously! The eyes were screaming toward him now!

Stinger?!

Bug-Man remembered just in time. *Ignore the lies!*

The red eyes went hurling past him, vanishing into darkness. The screams of rage faded into distant echoes that hung in the air like dreadful memories—

I could have stung myself, right behind the brain case—he realized. And then, realizing again how narrowly he had escaped the trap of the Freudian paradigm, he warned himself again. *You are the Bug-Man! Don't let him define you or your reality! Monsters from the id aren't real!*

The Bug-Man headed down the tunnel. Its angle of descent increased abruptly, getting steeper and steeper, until he was slipping, sliding, skidding, tumbling—

—onto the hard-baked surface of a place with no sun, no moon, no sky and no horizon. Tall black cylinders surrounded them, leaping up into the gloom and disappearing overhead. They looked like the bars of a cage.

Freud stood beside one of the bars, surveying him thoughtfully. "You are resisting the treatment," he said. "I can't help you if you do not want to be helped." He waggled his finger meaningfully. *"You must really want to change!"*

Bug-Man roared in fury. It consumed him like volcanic fire. He became a core of molten energy. The blast of emotion overwhelmed him. Enraged, he charged.

Bug-Man galloped across the space between them, tearing up the floor with his six mighty claws. He thundered like a bull, hot smoke streaming from the vents of his nostrils. The black leviathan leapt—

—and abruptly, Freud was gone!

Bug-Man smashed against the bars of the cage like a locomotive hitting a wall, his legs flailing, his body deforming, the air screaming out from his lungs like a steam whistle. He shrieked in rage and frustration and pain. He fell back, legs working wildly, righted himself, whirled around, eyes flicking this way and that, focusing on Freud again. The *PsycheMan* waited for him on the opposite side of the cage. The Bug-Man didn't hesitate! He charged again—

—and again, he came slamming up against the bars. Helpless for an instant, he lay there gasping and wondering what he was doing wrong. Transformed Kafka shuddered in his shell. But he pushed the thought aside, levered himself back to his feet, focused again on his target, readied his charge, sighted his prey—

This time, he would watch to see which way the *PsycheMan* leapt. He would snatch him from the air. He held his pincers high and wide. Instead of charging, he advanced steadily, inexorably, closing on his elusive prey like some ghastly mechanical device of the industrial revolution gone mad. His mandibles clicked and clashed. His eyes shone with unholy fury. A terrible guttural sound came moaning up out of his throat—

—came slamming hard against the bars of the cage as if he'd been fired into them by a cannon. The discontinuity left him rolling across the floor in pain, clutching at his aching genitals and crying in little soft gasps. He pulled himself back to his knees, his feet, trying to solidify his form again. He stood there, wavering, almost whimpering.

"What's wrong?" he asked himself. "What am I doing wrong?"

Kafka looked across the cage. Freud stood there grinning nastily. The old man laughed. "You battle yourself!" he said thickly. "The rigidity of your constructed identity cannot deal with events occurring outside of its world view. You become confused and you attack shadows and phantoms!"

Kafka took a deep breath. Then another, and another. "I am Franz Kafka, superhero!" he said to himself "I am here to destroy the evil paradigm of Dr. Freud! I will not be defeated."

No!—he realized abruptly. *That way doesn't work! I am the master of metamorphosis. I must metamorphose into something that the doctor cannot defeat!* At first he thought of giant squids and vampire bats, cobras

and bengal tigers, raging elephants, bears, dragons, manticores, gob-
lins, trolls—Jungian archetypes! *But, no*—he realized. *That would be just
more of the same! Just another monster! To fight a monster I must change
into something ELSE—*

He stood there motionless, staring across the cage at his fiendish
opponent, considering. His mind worked like a precision machine, a
clockwork device ticking away at superfast speed. His thoughts raced,
exploring strange new possibilities he had never conceived before.

Ego cogito sum—he considered. *I have been reacting to his manipula-
tions. Reactive behavior allows him to control the circumstance. Proactive
behavior puts me in control. I should attack him, but attacking him is still
reaction. Yet, if I don't attack him, I cannot defeat him. How can I be proactive without being reactive?*

Bug-Man wavered. His confusion manifested itself as a softening of
his shell, a spreading pale discoloration of his metallic carapace. His
mandibles began to shrink. His arms and legs began to plump out,
seeking their previous shape. *No!* he shrieked to himself. *No! Not yet! I
haven't killed him yet*

Bug-Man felt himself weakening, growing ever more helpless in the
face of his enemy. He felt shamed and embarrassed. He wanted to scuttle
off and hide in the woodwork. His bowels let loose, his bladder emptied.
His skin became soft and pallid again. He stood naked before Freud.
Franz Kafka, superhero. But the Bug-Man was defeated, discredited—

No! said Kafka. *No! I won't have it. I am Franz Kafka, superhero! I don't
need to be a giant cockroach to destroy the malevolence of Freud! I can stop
him with my bare hands.*

—And then he knew!

"Your paradigm is invalid," Kafka said. "It's powerful, yes, but ultimately, it has no power over those who refuse to give it power; therefore,
it is not an accurate map of the objective reality, only another word-game
played out in language." Freud's eyes widened in surprise. Kafka took two
steps toward him. "You're just a middle-aged Viennese Jew who smokes
too much, talks too much and suffers from—your word—*agoraphobia*.
You can't even cross the street without help!" Freud held up a hand in protest, but Kafka kept advancing, continuing his unflinching verbal assault.
"You're a dirty old man. You can't stop talking about sex, you want to kill
your father and copulate with your mother—and you believe that everybody else feels the same thing, too! You're despicable, Sigmund Freud!"

Freud's chin trembled. "You—you don't understand. You're functioning as a paranoid schizophrenic with psychotic delusions. You've constructed a world view in which explanations are impossible—"

"That won't work, Siggie. It's just so much language. It's just a load of psyche-babble. The distinctions you've drawn are arbitrary constructions that only have the meaning that we as humans invest them with. Well, I withdraw my investment. Your words are meaningless. I will not be *psychologized*. You are just a disgusting little man who likes to talk about penises!"

The old man made one last attempt to withstand the withering assault of Kafka's logic. "But if you withdraw all meaning from the paradigm—" he protested, "—what meaning can you replace it with?"

"That's just it!" exulted Kafka, delivering the death blow. *"Life is empty and meaningless!"*

Horrified, Freud collapsed to the floor of his parlor, clutching at his chest.

Kafka stood over him, triumphant. *"It's meaningless, you old fart!"*

Freud moaned—

"It doesn't mean anything! And it doesn't even mean anything that it doesn't mean anything! So we're free to make it up any way we choose!"

"Please, no. Please, stop—"

But Kafka wasn't finished. "Your way is just a possible way of being, Sigmund—but it isn't the only way! The difference between you and me is that because I know the bindings of my language, I also know my freedom within those bindings! You have been focusing on the bindings, you old asshole, *not the freedom."*

Freud was shuddering now, impaled on Kafka's impeccable truths. He trembled uncontrollably on the patterned rug, sick and despairing at the chaotic darkness gathering around him. The broken shards of his shattered paradigm had sliced his soul mercilessly, leaving the poor defeated man twitching in the growing puddles of his own terminal *Weltschmerz.* "Forgive me, please. I didn't know what I was doing."

Kafka knelt to the floor, gathered Freud up in his arms, held him gently, cradling him like a child. He placed one soft hand on the old man's forehead. "It's all right now, Siggie," he soothed. "It's all over. You can stop. You can rest."

Freud looked up into Kafka's calm expression, questioning, hoping. He saw only kindness in the superhero's eyes. Reassured, he let himself relax; he allowed peace to flood throughout his body. All stiffness fled. Sigmund Freud rested securely in Franz Kafka's arms. "Thank you," he whispered. "Thank you."

"No," said Kafka. "On the contrary. It is *I* who should thank *you*." And with that he plunged his needle-sharp teeth into Sigmund Freud's pale exposed neck, ripping it open. He bent his head and fed ferociously. The hot rush of blood slaked his incredible thirst, and he moaned in delirious ecstasy.

Triumph was delicious.

Wouldn't you love a pet dinosaur? I would. A dinosaur would make a great pet. Soft, cuddly, useful….

Rex

"DADDY! THE TYRANNOSAUR is loose again! He jumped the fence."

Jonathan Filltree replied with a single word, one which he didn't want his eight-year-old daughter to hear. He punched the *save* key on his keyboard, kicked back his chair and headed toward the basement stairs with obvious annoyance. He resented these constant interruptions in the flow of his work.

"Hurry, Daddy!" Jill shouted again from the basement door. "He's chasing the stegosaurs! He's gonna get Steggy!"

"I warned you this was going to happen—" Filltree said angrily, grabbing the long-handled net off the wall. "No! Wait here," he snapped.

"That's not fair!" cried Jill, following him down the bare wooden stairs. "I didn't know he was going to get this big!"

"He's a meat-eater. The stegosaurs and the apatosaurs and all the others look like lunch to him. Get back upstairs, Jill!"

Filltree stopped at the bottom and looked slowly around the basement that his wife had demanded he convert into a miniature dinosaur kingdom for their spoiled daughter. Hot yellow lights bathed the cellar in a prehistoric ambience. A carboniferous smell permeated everything. He wrinkled his nose in distaste. For some reason, it was worse than usual.

The immediate problem was obvious. Most of the six-inch stegosaurs had retreated to the high slopes that butted up against the north wall, where they milled about nervously. Their bright yellow and orange colors made them easy to see. Quickly, he counted. All three of the calves and their mother were okay; so were the other two females; but they were all cheeping in distress. He spotted Fred and Cyril, but Steggy was not with the others. The two remaining males were emitting rasping peeps of agitation; and they kept making angry charging motions downslope.

Filltree followed the direction of their agitation. "Damn!" he said, spotting the two-foot-high tyrannosaur. Rex was ripping long strips of flesh off the side of the fallen Steggy and gulping them hungrily down. Already he was streaked with blood. His long tail lashed furiously in the air, acting as a counterweight as he bent to his kill. He ripped and tore, then rose up on his haunches, glancing around quickly and checking for danger with sharp bird-like motions. He jerked his head upward to gulp the latest bloody gobbet deeper into his mouth, then gulped a second time to swallow it. He grunted and roared, then lowered his whole body forward to again bury his muzzle deep in gore.

"Oh, Daddy! He's killed Steggy!"

"I told you to wait upstairs! A tyrannosaur can be dangerous when he's feeding!"

"But he's killed Steggy—!"

"Well, I'm sorry. There's nothing to do now but wait until he finishes and goes torpid." Filltree put the net down, leaning it against the edge of the table. The entire room was filled with an elaborate waist-high miniature landscape, through which an improbable mix of Cretaceous and Jurassic creatures prowled. The glass fences at the edges of the tables were all at least thirty-six inches high and mildly electrified to keep the various creatures safely enclosed. Until they'd added Rex to the huge terrarium, they'd had one of the finest collections in Westchester, with over a hundred dinos prowling through the miniature forests. And every spring, the new births among the various herbivores usually added five to ten adorable little calves to their herds.

Now, the ranks of their menagerie had been reduced to only a few light-footed stegosaurs, some lumbering apatosaurs, two armored anklosaurs, the belligerent triceratops herd and the chirruping hadrosaurs. Most of those had survived only because their favorite grazing grounds were at one end of the huge U-shaped environment, and Rex's corral was all the way around at the opposite end. Rex wandered around the herbivore grounds only until he found something to attack. Like most of the mini-dinos, Rex didn't have a lot of gray matter to work with; he almost always attacked the first moving object he saw. In the six months since his installation in what Filltree had once believed was a secure corral, Rex had more than decimated the population of the Pleasant Avenue Dinosaur Zoo. He was now escaping regularly once or twice a week.

Slowly, Filltree worked his way around the table to the corral, examining all the fences carefully to see where and how the tyrannosaur might have broken through the barriers. He had thought for sure that the thirty-inch high rock-surfaced polyfoam bricks he had installed last week would finally keep the carnivore from escaping again to terrorize the more placid herbivores. Obviously, he had been wrong.

Filltree frowned as he studied the thick blockade. It had not been broken through in any place, nor had the tyrant-lizard dug a hole underneath it. The rocks were not chewed, but they were badly scratched in several places. Filltree leaned across the table for a closer look. "Mm," he said.

"What is it, Daddy? Tell me!" Jill demanded impatiently.

He pointed. The sides and tops of the bricks were sharply gouged. Rex had leapt up onto the top of the wall, surveyed the opposite side, and leapt down to feed. Judging from the numerous marks carved into the surface, today's outing was clearly not the first. "See. Rex can leap the fence. And that probably explains the mysterious disappearance of the last coelophysis too. This is getting ridiculous Jill. I can't afford this anymore. We going to have to find a new home for Rex."

"Daddy, no!" Jill became immediately belligerent. "Rexie is part of our family!"

"Rexie is eating up all the other dinosaurs, Jill. That's not very family-like."

"We can buy new ones."

"No, we can't. Dinosaurs cost money, and I'm not buying any new animals until we get rid of him. I'm sorry, kiddo; but I told you this wasn't going to work."

"Daddy, pleeeaase—! Rexie is my favorite!"

Jonathan Filltree took his daughter by the hand and led her back around to where Rexie was still gorging himself on the now unrecognizable remains of the much smaller stegosaur. "Look, Jill. This is going to keep happening, sweetheart. Rexie is getting too big for us to keep. It's all that fresh beef that you and Mommy keep feeding him. Remember what the dinosaur-doctor said? It accelerates his growth. But you didn't listen. Now, none of the other dinosaurs can escape him or even fight back. It isn't fair to them. And it isn't fair to Rexie either to keep him in a place where he won't be happy."

That last part was a complete fabrication on his part, and Filltree knew it even as he spoke it. If Rexie was capable of happiness, then he was probably very happy to be living in a place where he was the only carnivore and all of the prey animals were too small to resist his attacks. According to the genetic specifications, however, Rexie and the other mini-dinosaurs would have had to borrow the synapses necessary to complete a thought. Calling them stupid would have been a compliment.

"But—but, you can't! He'll miss me!"

Filltree sighed with exhaustion. He already knew how this argument was going to end. Jill would go to Mommy, and Mommy would promise to talk to Daddy. And then Mommy would sulk for two weeks because Daddy wanted her to break a promise to their darling little girl. And finally, he'd give in just to get a little peace and quiet again so he could get some work done. But he had to try anyway. He dropped to one knee in front of his daughter and put his hands on her shoulders. "We'll find a good place for him, Jilly, I promise." And even as he said it, he knew it was a promise he'd never be able to keep.

He knew he wouldn't be able to sell Rex. He'd seen the ads in the Recycler. There was no market for tyrant-lizards anymore—of any size. And Rexie was more than two feet high, and rapidly approaching the legal maximum of thirty-six inches. Rexie required ten pounds of fresh meat a week; he'd only eat dry kibble when the alternative was starvation. They still had half a bag of Purina Dinosaur Chow left from when they'd first bought him. The dinosaur would go for almost a week without eating before he'd touch the stuff, and even then he'd only pick at it.

Nor did Filltree think he'd even be able to give the creature away. The zoo didn't want any more tyrannosaurs, of *any* size. They were expensive to feed and they already had over a hundred of the little monsters, spitting and hissing and roaring—and occasionally devouring the smaller of their brethren.

At one time it had been fashionable to own your own miniature T. Rex; but the fad had passed, the tyrant-lizards had literally outgrown their welcome, the price of meat had risen again (due to the Brazilian droughts), and a lot of people—wearying of the smells and the bother—had finally dropped their pets off at the zoo or turned them over to the animal shelters. Because they were protected under the Artificial Species Act, the cost of putting a mini-dino down was almost prohibitive. Some thoughtless individuals had tried abandoning their hungry dinosaurs in the wild, not realizing that the animals were genetically traceable. The fines, according to the newspaper reports, had been astonishing.

"I promise you, Jilly, we'll find a place for Rexie where he'll be happy and we can visit him every week, okay?"

Jill shook his hands off, folded her arms in front of her, and turned away. "No!" she decided. "You're not giving Rexie away! He's my dinosaur. I picked him out and you said I could have him."

Filltree gave up. He turned back to the diorama. Rexie had stopped gorging himself and was now standing torpidly near his kill. Filltree grabbed the metal-mesh net and quickly brought it down over the dinosaur. Rexie struggled in the mesh, but not wildly. Filltree had learned a long time ago to wait until the tyrant-king had finished eating before trying to return him to his corral. He swung the net across the table, taking care to hold the dinosaur well away from him and as high as he could. Jill tried to reach up to grab the handle of the net, and instinctively he yanked it up out of her reach—but for just a moment, the temptation flickered across his mind to let her actually grab Rexie. Then he'd see how much she loved the little monster.

But...if he did, he'd never hear the end of it, he knew that—and besides, there was the danger that the mini-dino might actually do some serious damage. So he ignored Jill's yelps of protest and returned Rexie to his own kingdom. Temporarily at least. Then he went back and scooped up the bloody remains of poor Steggy and wordlessly tossed that into Rexie's domain as well.

"Aren't we going to have a funeral for Steggy?"

"No, we're not. We've had enough funerals. All it does is annoy the tyrannosaur. Let Rexie have his meal. It'll keep him from jumping the fence for another week or two. Maybe. I hope. Come on. I told you to stay upstairs. And you didn't listen. Just for that, no dessert—"

"I'm gonna tell Mommy!"

"You do that," he sighed tiredly, following her up the stairs—realizing that of all the animals in the house, the one he resented most was the one who was supposed to know better. She was eight and a half years old—at that age, they were supposed to be almost human, weren't they? He felt exhausted. He knew he wasn't going to get any more work done today. Not after Jilly finished crying to Mommy about Daddy threatening to get rid of poor little Rexie. "Rexie didn't mean to do anything wrong," he mimed to himself. "He was hungry because Daddy forgot to feed him last night."

Filltree both hated and envied Rexie. Jill gave all her attention and affection to the dinosaur, speaking to Daddy only when demanding something else for her collection of creatures. And Mommy was another one—she paid more attention to preparing the little tyrant's meals than to his. The dinosaur got fresh beef or lamb three times a week. He got soy-burgers.

For a long while, he'd been considering the idea of a separation—maybe even a divorce. He'd even gone so far as to log onto the Legal-Net website and crunch the numbers on their divorce-judgment simulator. Although Legal-Net refused to guarantee the accuracy of its legal software, lest they expose themselves to numerous lawsuits, the divorce-judgment simulator used the same Judicial Engine as the Federal Divorce Court and was unofficially rated at ninety percent accuracy in its extrapolations.

All he wanted was a tiny little condo somewhere up in the hills, a place where he could sit and work and stare out the window in peace without having to think about tyrants, either the two-foot kind or the three-foot kind. Tyrant lizards, tyrant children—the only difference he could see was that the tyrant lizard only ate your heart out once and then it was done.

According to CompuServe, he could afford the condo; that wasn't the problem. *Unfortunately*, also according to Legal-Net's Judicial Engine he could not afford the simultaneous maintenance of Joyce and Jill. The simulator gave him several options, none of them workable from his point of view. A divorce would give him freedom, but it would be prohibitively expensive. A separation would give him peace and quiet, but it wouldn't give him freedom—and he'd still have to keep up the payments on Joyce and Jill's various expensive habits.

Grunting in annoyance, he pulled the heavy carry cage out of the garage and lugged it awkwardly back down the basement stairs. Jilly followed him the whole way, whining and crying. He slipped easily into his robot-daddy mode, disconnecting his emotions and refusing to respond to even her most provocative assaults. "I don't love you any more. You promised me. I'm not your daughter any more. I'm gonna tell Mommy. I don't like you. You can go to hell."

"Don't tempt me. I might enjoy the change," he muttered in reply to the last remark.

Back downstairs, Filltree discovered that Rexie had not only finished his meal; he was already standing on top of the rock barrier again, lashing his tail furiously and studying the realm beyond. He looked like he was preparing to return to his hunting. At the opposite end of the room, the remaining stegosaurs were mooing agitatedly.

Rexie spotted them then. He turned sharply to glare across the intervening distance, cocking his head with birdlike motions to study them first with one baleful black eye, then the other. Perhaps it was just the shape of his head, but his expression seemed ominous and calculating. The creature's eyes were filled with hatred for the soft pink mammals who restricted him, as well as insatiable hunger for the taste of human flesh. Filltree wondered why he'd ever wanted a tyrannosaur in the first place. Rexie hissed in defiance, arching his neck forward and opening his mouth wide to reveal ranks of knife-sharp little teeth.

Filltree frowned. Was it his imagination or had the little tyrannosaur grown another six inches in the last six minutes? The creature seemed a lot bigger than he remembered him being. Of course, he'd been so angry at the little monster that he hadn't really looked at him closely for a while.

"He's awfully big. Have you been feeding him again?" he demanded of his daughter.

"No!" Jill said, indignantly. "We've only been giving him leftovers. Mommy said it's silly to waste food."

"In addition to his regular meals?"

"But, Daddy, we can't let him to *starve*—"

"He's in no danger of starving. No wonder he's gotten so voracious. You've accelerated his appetite as well as his growth. I told you not to do that. Well...it's over now. We should have done this a long time ago." Filltree picked up the net and brought it around slowly, approaching Rexie from his blind side, taking great care not to alarm the two-foot tyrant king. The thing was getting large enough to be dangerous.

Rexie hissed and bit at the net, but did not try to run. Tyrannosaurs did not have it in their behavior to run. They attacked. They ate. If they couldn't do one, they did the other. If they couldn't do either, they waited until they could do one or the other. The creatures had the single-mindedness of lawyers.

Working quickly, Filltree caught Rexie in the net and swung him up and over the glass fence of the terrarium. He lowered the dinosaur into the open carry cage, turned the net over in one swift movement to tumble the creature out, lifted it away and kicked the lid shut. He latched it rapidly before Rexie could begin bumping and thumping at it with his head. Jill watched, wide-eyed and resentful. She had stopped crying, but she still wore her cranky-face.

"What are you going to do with him?" she demanded.

"Well, he's going to spend tonight in the service porch where it's warm. Tomorrow, I'm going to take him to...the dinosaur farm, where he'll be a lot happier." *To the animal shelter, where they'll put him down...for a hefty fee.*

"What dinosaur farm? I never heard of any dinosaur farm."

"Oh, it's brand new. It's in...Florida. It's for dinosaurs like Rexie who've gotten too big to live in Connecticut. I'll put him on an airplane and send him straight to Florida. And we can visit him next year when we go to Disney World, okay?"

"You're lying—" Jill accused, but there was an edge of uncertainty in her tone. "When are we going to Disney World?"

"When you learn to stop whining. Probably when you're forty or fifty." Filltree grunted as he lifted the carry cage from behind. He could feel its center of gravity shifting in his arms as Rexie paced unhappily within, hissing and spitting and complaining loudly about being confined. The little tyrant was not happy. Jill complained in unison. *Neither* of the little tyrants were happy.

Somehow Filltree got the heavy box up the stairs and into the service porch. "He'll be fine there till tomorrow, Jill." In an uncharacteristic act of concession, he said, "You can feed him all the leftovers you want tonight. The harm has already been done. And you can say goodbye to him tomorrow before you go to school, okay?"

Jill grumped. "You're not fair!" she accused. She stomped loudly out of the service porch and upstairs to her bedroom for a four-hour sulk, during which time she would gather her strength for the daughter of all tantrums. Filltree waited until after he heard the slam of her door, then exhaled loudly, making a horsey sound with his lips. Considering the amount of agida produced, he wondered if he'd locked up the right animal.

Dinner was the usual resentful tableau. The servitors wheeled in, laid food on the table, waited respectfully, wheeled back, then removed the plates again. His wife glared across the soup at him. His daughter pouted over the salad. Not a word was said during the fish course. Instead of meat, there was soy-burger in silence again. Filltree had decided not to speak at all if he could possibly avoid it. Joyce couldn't start chewing at him if he didn't give her an opportunity.

Idly, he wondered how much meat it would take to accelerate Rexie's growth to six feet tall. The idea of Rexie stripping the flesh from Joyce's bones and gulping it hungrily down gave him an odd thrill of pleasure.

"What are you smiling about?" Joyce demanded abruptly.

"I wasn't smiling—" he said, startled at having been caught daydreaming.

"Don't lie to me. I *saw* you!"

"I'm sorry, dear. It must have been a gas pain. You know how soy-burger disagrees with me."

He realized too late his mistake. Now that the conversational gauntlet had been flung, picked up and flung back, Joyce was free to expand the realm of the discussion into any area she chose.

She chose. "You're being very cruel and unfair, you know that," she accused. "Your daughter loves that animal. It's her *favorite*."

Filltree considered the obvious response: "That animal gets more hamburger than I do. I'm the breadwinner in this family. I'd like to be treated as well as Rexie." He decided against it; down that way lay domestic violence and an expensive reconciliation trip to Jamaica. At the very least. Instead, he nodded and agreed with her. "You're right. It is cruel and unfair. And yes, I know how much Jill loves Rexie." He tasted the green beans. They were underdone. Joyce had readjusted the servitors again.

"Well, I don't see why we can't rebuild the terrarium."

"It isn't the terrarium," Filltree pointed out quietly. "It's Rexie. He's been accelerated. Nothing we do is going to contain him anymore." He resisted the temptation to remind her that he had warned her about this very possibility. "If he gets any bigger, he's going to start being a hazard.

I don't want think we should take the risk, do you?" He inclined his head meaningfully in Jill's direction.

Joyce looked thwarted. Jonathan had hit her with an argument she couldn't refute. She pretended to concede the point while she considered her next move. Perhaps it was just the shape of her new coiffure, but her expression seemed ominous and calculating. Filltree wondered why he'd ever wanted to marry her in the first place.

His wife patted the tinted hairs at the back of her neck and smiled gently. "Well, I don't know how you intend to make it up to your daughter...but I hope you have something appropriate figured out." Both she and Jill looked to him expectantly.

Filltree met their gaze directly. He returned her plastic smile with one of equal authenticity. "Gee, I can't think of anything to take Rexie's place."

Joyce tightened her lips ever so delicately. "Well, I can. And I'm sure Jill can too, can't you sweetheart...?" Joyce looked to Jill. Jill smiled. They both looked to Daddy again.

So. That was it. Filltree recognized the ploy. Retreat on one battlefield, only to gain on another. Jamaica appeared inescapable. He considered his options. Option. Dead end. "You've already made the booking, haven't you?" His artificial smile widened even more artificially.

"I see," his wife said curtly. "Is that what you think of me...?" He recognized the tone immediately. If he said anything at all—*anything*—she would escalate to tactical nukes within three sentences. The *worst* thing he could say would be, "Now, sweetheart—"

Instead, he opened his mouth and said, "We can't go, in any case. I have research to do in Denver." This time, he amazed even himself. Denver? Where had *that* idea come from? "I'll be gone for a month. Maybe two. At least. I'm sorry if this ruins your plans, dear. I would have told you sooner, but I was hoping I wouldn't have to go. Unfortunately...I just heard this afternoon that no one else is available for this job." He spread his hands wide in a gesture of helplessness.

Joyce's mouth tightened almost to invisibility—then reformed itself in a deliberate smile. "I see," she said, in a voice like sugared acid. She refused to lose her temper in front of Jill. It was a bad role model, she insisted. She had declared that eight years ago, and in the past five, Jonathan Filltree had amused himself endlessly by seeing how close to the edge he could push her before she toppled over into incoherence. Tonight—with Denver—he had scored a grand slam home run, knocking it all the way out of the park and bringing in all three runners on base. "We'll talk about this later," she said with finality, her way of admitting that she was outflanked and that she had no choice but to retreat and regroup her energies while she reconnoitered the terrain. She would be back. But for the moment, the conversation was temporarily suspended.

"I'll be up late," Filltree said genially. "I have a report to finish. And I have to pack tonight too." He took a healthy bite of soy-burger. It was suddenly delicious.

Joyce excused herself to escort Jill upstairs to get her ready for bed. "But, Mommy, don't I get dessert..." the child wailed.

"Not while your Daddy is acting like this—"

Jonathan Filltree spent the rest of the evening working quietly, almost enjoying himself, anticipating what it would be like to have a little quiet in the house without the regular interruption of Rexie's intolerable predations. If only he could get rid of Jill and Joyce as easily.

Filltree wondered if he should sleep on the couch in his office tonight, but then decided that would be the same as admitting a) that there had been a battle, and b) he had lost. He would not concede Joyce one inch of territory. Before heading upstairs, he took a look in at Rexie.

The tyrannosaur was working at the left side wall of the carry cage, scratching at it with first one foot, then the other, trying to carve an opening for itself. It bumped its head ferociously against the side; already the thick polymoid surface was deformed and even a little cracked. Filltree squatted down to get a closer look at the box, running his hands over the strained material. He decided that the damage inflicted was not sufficient to be worrisome; the carry cage would hold together for one more day. And one more day was all he needed.

He headed upstairs to bed, smiling to himself. It was a small victory, but a victory nonetheless. The knowledge that he'd be paying for it for months to come didn't detract from the satisfaction he took in knowing that he'd finally held the line on something. Today, Rexie; tomorrow, the soy-burger.

He was awakened by screaming—unfamiliar and agonized. Something was crashing through the kitchen. He heard the clattering of utensils. Joyce was sitting up in bed beside him, screaming herself, and clawing at his arm. "Do something!" she cried.

"Stay here!" he demanded. "See to Jill!" Wearing only his silk boxers, and carrying a cracked hockey stick as his weapon, he went charging down the stairs. The screaming was getting worse.

A male voice was raging, "Goddammit! Get it off of me! Help! Help! Anyone!" This was followed by the sound of someone battering at something with something. High-pitched shrieks of reptilian rage punctuated the blows.

Filltree burst through the kitchen door to see a man rolling back and forth across the floor—a youngish-looking man, skinny and dirty, in bloody t-shirt and blue jeans. Rexie had his mouth firmly attached to the burglar's right arm. He hung on with ferocious determination, even as the intruder swung and battered the creature at the floor, the walls, the stove. Again and again. The screaming went on and on. Filltree didn't know whether to strike at the burglar or at the dinosaur. The man had been bitten severely on both legs, and across his stomach as well. A ragged strip of flesh hung open. His shirt was soaked with blood. Gobbets of red were flying everywhere; the kitchen was spattered like an explosion.

The man saw Filltree then. "Get your goddamn dinosaur off of me!" he demanded angrily, as if it were Filltree's fault that he had been attacked.

That decided Filltree. He began striking the man with the hockey stick, battering him ineffectively about the head and shoulders. That didn't work—he couldn't get in close enough. He grabbed a frying pan and whanged the hapless robber sideways across the forehead. The man grunted in surprise, then slumped to the floor with a groan, no longer able to defend himself against Rexie's predacious assault. The tyrant-lizard began feeding. He ripped off a long strip of flesh from the fallen robber's arm. The man tried to resist, he flailed weakly, but he had neither strength nor consciousness. The dinosaur was undeterred. Rexie fed unchecked.

Behind him, Joyce was screaming. Jill was shrieking, "Do something! Daddy, he's hurting Rexie!"

Filltree's humanity reasserted itself then. He had to stop the beast before it killed the hapless man; but he couldn't get to the net. It was still in the service porch—and he couldn't get past Rex. The creature hissed and spit at him. It lashed its tail angrily, as if daring Filltree to make the attempt. As if saying, "This kill is mine!"

Filltree held out the frying pan in front of him, swinging it back and forth like a shield. The small tyrant-king followed it with its baleful black eyes. Still roaring its defiance, it snapped and bit at the frying pan. Its teeth slid helplessly off the shining metal surface. Filltree whacked the creature hard. It blinked, stunned. He swung the frying pan again, and, reflexively, the dinosaur stepped back; but as the utensil swept past, it stepped right back in, biting and snapping. Filltree recognized the behavior. The beast was acting as if it were in a fight with another predator over its kill.

Filltree swung harder and more directly, this time not to drive the creature back, but to actually hit it and hurt it badly. Rexie leapt backward, shrieking in fury. Filltree stepped in quickly, brandishing the frying pan, triumphantly driving the two-foot dinosaur back and back toward the service porch. As soon as Rexie was safely in the confines of the service porch, screaming in the middle of the broken remains of the carry cage, Filltree slammed the door shut and latched it—something went thump from the other side. The noise was punctuated with a series of angry cries. The door thumped a second time and then a third. Filltree waited, frying pan at the ready. . . .

At last, Rexie's frantic screeching ebbed. Instead, there began a slow steady scratching at the bottom of the door.

When Filltree turned around again, two uniformed police officers were relievedly reholstering their pistols. He hadn't even heard them come in. "Is that your dinosaur, sir?"

Shaken, Filltree managed to nod.

"Y'know, there are laws against letting carnivores that size run free," said the older one.

"We'd have shot him if you hadn't been in the way," said the younger officer.

For a moment, Filltree felt a pang of regret. He looked at the fallen burglar. There was blood flowing freely all over the floor. The man had rolled over on his side, clutching his stomach, but he was motionless now, and very very pale. "Is he going to make it—?"

The older officer was bending to examine the robber. "It depends on the speed of the ambulance."

The younger cop took Filltree aside; she lowered her voice to a whisper. "You want to hope he doesn't make it. If he lives, he could file a very nasty lawsuit against you. We'll tell the driver to take his time getting to the E.R. . . ."

He looked at the woman in surprise. She nodded knowingly. "You don't need any more trouble. I think we can wrap this one up tonight." She glanced around the room. "It looks to me like the burglar tried to steal your dinosaur. But the cage didn't hold and the creature attacked him. Is that what happened?"

Filltree realized the woman was trying to do him a favor. He nodded in hasty agreement. "Yes, exactly."

"That's a mini-rex, right?" she asked, glancing meaningfully at the door.

"Uh-huh."

"Lousy pets. Great guard-animals. Do yourself a favor. If you're going to leave him running loose at night, get yourself a permit. It won't cost you too much, and it'll protect you against a lawsuit if anyone else tries something stupid."

"Oh, yes—I'll take care of that first thing in the morning, thank you."

"Good. Your wife and kid know to be careful? Those rexies can't tell the difference between friend and foe, you know—"

"Oh, yes. They know to be *very* careful."

Later, after the police had left, after he had calmed down Joyce and Jill, after he had cleaned up the kitchen, after he had had a chance to think, Jonathan Filltree thoughtfully climbed the stairs again.

"I've made a decision," he said to his shaken wife and tearful daughter. They were huddled together in the master bedroom. "We're going to keep Rexie. If I'm going to be in Denver for two months, then you're going to need every protection possible."

"Do you really mean that, Daddy?"

Filltree nodded. "It just isn't fair for me to go away and leave you and Mommy undefended. I'm going to convert the service porch into a big dinosaur kennel, just for Rexie. Good and strong. And you can feed him all the leftovers you want."

"Really?"

"It's a reward," Filltree explained, "because Rexie did such a good job of protecting us tonight. We should give him lots and lots of hamburger too, because that's his favorite. But you have to promise me something, Jill—"

"I will."

"You must *never* open the kennel door without Mommy's permission, do you understand?"

"I won't," Jill promised insincerely.

Turning back to Joyce, Filltree added, "I promise, I'll finish up my work in Denver as quickly as possible. But if they need me to stay longer, will that be okay with you?"

Joyce shook her head. "I want you to get that thing out of the house tonight."

"No, dear—" Filltree insisted. "Rexie's a member of our family now. He's earned his place at the table." He climbed into bed next to his wife and patted her gently on the arm, all the time thinking about the high price of meat and what a bargain it represented.

If it is true that you are what you read, then it is even more true that you are what you write.

. . . And Eight Rabid Pigs

WHEN I FIRST BECAME AWARE of Steven Dhor, he was talking about Christmas. Again.

He hated Christmas—in particular, the enforcement of bliss. "Don't be a scrooge, don't be a grinch, don't be a Satan Claus taking away other people's happiness." That's what his mother used to say to him, and twenty years later, he was still angry.

There were a bunch of them sitting around the bar, writers mostly, but a few hangers-on and fringies, sucking up space and savoring the wittiness of the conversation. Bread Bryan loomed all tall and spindly like a frontier town undertaker. Railroad Martin perched like a disgruntled Buddha—he wore the official Railroad Martin uniform: t-shirt, jeans and pot belly. George Finger was between wives and illnesses; he was enjoying just being alive. Goodman Hallmouth pushed by, snapping at bystanders and demanding to know where Harold Parnell had gone; he was going to punch him in the kneecap.

"Have a nice day, Goodman," someone called.

"Don't tell me to have a nice day," he snarled back. "I'll have any damn kind of a day I want."

"See—" said Dhor, nodding at Hallmouth as he savaged his way out again. "That's honest, at least. Goodman might not fit our pictures of the polite way to behave, but at least he doesn't bury us in another layer of dishonest treacle."

"Yep, Goodman only sells honest treacle," said Railroad Martin.

"Where do you get lie-detector tests for treacle?" Bread Bryan asked, absolutely deadpan.

"There's gotta be a story in that—" mused George Finger.

"—but I just can't put my *finger* on it," said one of the nameless fringies. This was followed by a nanosecond of annoyed silence. Somebody else would have to explain to the fringie that a) that joke was older than God, b) it hadn't been that funny the first time it had been told, and c) he didn't have the right to tell it. Without looking up, Bread Bryan simply said, "That's one."

Steven Dhor said, "You want to know about treacle? Christmas is treacle. It starts the day after Halloween. You get two months of it. It's an avalanche of sugar and bullshit. I suppose they figure that if they put enough sugar into the recipe, you won't notice the taste of the bullshit."

"Don't mince words, Stevie. Tell us what you really think."

"Okay, I will." Dhor had abruptly caught fire. His eyes were blazing. "Christmas—at least the way we celebrate it—is a perversion. It's not a holiday; it's a brainwashing." That's when I started paying *real* attention.

"Every time you see a picture of Santa Claus," Dhor said, "you're being indoctrinated into the Christian ethic. If you're good, you get a reward, a present; if you're bad, you get a lump of coal. One day, you figure it out; you say, hey—Santa Claus is really Mommy and Daddy. And when you tell them you figured it out, what do they do? They tell you about God. If you're good, you get to go to heaven; if you're bad, you go to hell. Dying isn't anything to be afraid of, it's just another form of Christmas. And Santa Claus is God—the only difference is that at least Santa gives you something tangible. But if there ain't no Santa, then why should we believe in God either?"

Bread Bryan considered Dhor's words dispassionately. Bread Bryan considered everything dispassionately. Despite his nickname, even yeast couldn't make him rise. Railroad Martin swirled his beer around in his glass; he didn't like being upstaged by someone else's anger—even when it was anger as good as this. George Finger, on the other hand, was delighted with the effrontery of the idea.

"But wait—this is the nasty part. We've taken God out of Christmas. You can't put up angels anymore, nor a cross, nor even a crèche. No religious symbols of any kind, because even though everything closes down on Christmas day, we still have to pretend it's a secular celebration. So, the only decorations you can put up are Santa Claus, reindeer, snowmen and elves. We've replaced the actual holiday with a third-generation derivation, including its own pantheon of saints and demons: Rudolph, Frosty, George Bailey, Scrooge and the Grinch—Santa Claus is not only most people's first experience of God," Dhor continued, "it's now their *only* experience of God."

Dhor was warming to his subject. Clearly this was not a casual thought for him. He'd been stewing this over for some time. He began describing how the country had become economically addicted to Christmas. "We've turned it into a capitalist feeding frenzy—so much so that some retailers depend on Christmas for fifty percent of their annual business. I think we should all 'Just Say No to Christmas.' Or at least—for God's sake—remember whose birthday it is and celebrate it appropriately, by doing things to feed the poor and heal the sick."

A couple of the fringies began applauding then, but Dhor just looked across at them with a sour expression on his face. "Don't applaud," he said. "Just do it."

"Do you?" someone challenged him. "How do you celebrate Christmas?"

"I don't give presents," Dhor finally admitted. "I take the money I would normally spend on presents and give it to the Necessities of Life Program of the AIDS Project of Los Angeles. It's more in keeping with the spirit." That brought another uncomfortable silence. It's one thing to do the performance of saint—most writers are pretty good at it—but when you catch one actually *doing* something unselfish and noteworthy, well...it's pretty damned embarrassing for everyone involved.

Fortunately, Dhor was too much in command of the situation to let the awkward moment lie there unmolested. He trampled it quickly. "The thing is, I don't see any way to stop the avalanche of bullshit. The best we can do is ride it."

"How?" George Finger asked.

"Simple. By adding a new piece to the mythology—a new saint in the pantheon. *Satan Claus.*" There was that name again. Dhor lowered his voice. "See, if Santa Claus is really another expression of God, then there has to be an equally powerful expression of the Devil too. There has to be a balance."

"Satan Claus...." Bread Bryan considered the thought. "Mm. He must be the fellow who visited my house last year. He didn't give me anything I wanted. And I could have used the coal too. It gets *cold* in Wyoming."

"No. Satan Claus doesn't work that way," said Dhor. "He doesn't give things. He takes them away. The suicide rate goes up around Christmastime. That's no accident. That's Satan Claus. He comes and takes your soul straight to hell."

Then Railroad Martin added a wry thought—"He drives a black sleigh and he lands in your basement."—and then they were all doing it.

"The sleigh is drawn by eight rabid pigs—big ugly razorbacks," said Dhor. "They have iridescent red eyes, which burn like smoldering embers—they *are* embers, carved right out of the floor of hell. Late at night, as you're lying all alone in your cold, cold bed, you can hear them snuffling and snorting in the ground beneath your house. Their hooves are polished black ebony, and they carve up the ground like knives."

Dhor was creating a legend while his audience sat and listened enraptured. He held up his hands as if outlining the screen on which he was about to paint the rest of his picture. The group fell silent. I had to admire him, in spite of myself. He lowered his voice to a melodramatic stage-whisper: "Satan Claus travels underground through dark rumbling passages filled with rats and ghouls. He carries a long black whip, and he stands in the front of the sleigh, whipping the pigs until the blood streams from their backs. Their screams are the despairing sounds of the eternally tormented."

"And he's dressed all in black," suggested Bread Bryan. "Black leather. With silver buckles and studs and rivets."

"Oh, hell," said George Finger. "*Everybody* dresses like that in my neighborhood."

"Yes, black leather," agreed Martin, ignoring the aside. "But it's made from the skins of reindeer."

"Whales," said Bryan. "Baby whales."

Dhor shook his head. "The leather is made from the skins of those whose souls he's taken. He strips it off their bodies before he lets them die. The skins are dyed black with the sins of the owners and trimmed with red-dyed rat fur. Satan Claus has long gray hair, all shaggy and dirty and matted; and he has a long gray beard, equally dirty. There are crawly things living in his hair and beard. And his skin is leprous and covered with pustules and running sores. His features are deformed and misshapen. His nose is a bulbous monstrosity, swollen and purple. His lips are blue and his breath smells like the grave. His fingernails are black with filth, but they're as sharp as diamonds. He can claw up through the floor to yank you down into his demonic realm."

"Wow," said Bread Bryan. "I'm moving up to the second floor."

The cluster of listeners shuddered at Dhor's vivid description. It was suddenly a little too heavy for the spirit of the conversation. A couple of them tried to make jokes, but they fell embarrassingly flat.

Finally, George Finger laughed gently and said, "I think you've made him out to be too threatening, Steve. For most of us, Satan Claus just takes our presents away and leaves changeling presents instead."

"Ahh," said Railroad. "That explains why I never get anything I want."

"How can you say that? You get t-shirts every year," said Bread.

"Yes, but I always want a tuxedo."

After the laughter died down, George said, "The changeling presents are made by the satanic elves, of course."

"Right," said Dhor. He picked up on it immediately. "All year long, the satanic elves work in their secret laboratories underneath the South Pole, creating the most horrendous ungifts they can think of. Satan Claus whips them unmercifully with cat o'nine tails; he screams at them and beats them and torments them endlessly. The ones who don't work hard enough, he tosses into the pit of eternal fire. The rest of them work like little demons—of course they do; that's what they are—to manufacture all manner of curses and spells and hexes. All the bad luck that you get every year—it comes straight from hell, a gift from Satan Claus himself." Dhor cackled wickedly, an impish burst of glee, and everybody laughed with him.

But he was on a roll. He'd caught fire with this idea and was beginning to build on it now. "The terrible black sleigh isn't a sleigh as much as it's a hearse. And it's filled with bulging sacks filled with bad luck of all kinds. Illnesses, miscarriages, strokes, cancers, viruses, flu germs, birth defects, curses of all kinds. Little things like broken bones and upset stomachs. Big things like impotence, frigidity, sterility. Parkinson's disease, cerebral palsy, multiple sclerosis, encephalitis—everything that stops you from enjoying life."

"I think you're onto something," said Railroad. "I catch the flu right after Christmas, every year. I haven't been to a New Year's party in four years. At least now I have someone to blame."

Dhor nodded and explained, "Satan Claus knows if you've been bad or good—if you've been bad in any way, he comes and takes a little more joy out of your life, makes it harder for you to want to be good. Just as Santa is your first contact with God, Satan Claus is your first experience of evil. Satan Claus is the devil's revenge on Christmas. He's the turd in the punch bowl. He's the tantrum at the party. He's the birthday-spoiler. I think we're telling our children only half the story. It's not enough to tell them that Santa will be good to them. We have to let them know who's planning to be bad to them."

For a while, there was silence as we all sat around and let the disturbing quality of Dhor's vision sink into our souls. Every so often someone would shudder as he thought of some new twist, some piece of embroidery.

But it was George Finger's speculation that ended the conversation: "Actually, this might be a dangerous line of thought, Steve. Remember the theory that the more believers a god has, the more powerful he becomes? I mean, it's a joke right now, but aren't you summoning a new god into existence this way?"

"Yes, Virginia," Dhor replied, grinning impishly, "There *is* a Satan Clause in the holy contract. But I don't think you need to worry. Our belief in him is insufficient. And unnecessary. We can't create Satan Claus—because he already exists. He came into being when Santa Claus was created. A thing automatically creates its opposite, just by its very existence. You know that. The stronger Santa Claus gets, the stronger Satan Claus must become in opposition."

Steven had been raised in a very religious household. His grandmother had taught him that for every act of good, there has to be a corresponding evil. Therefore, if you have heaven, you have to have hell. If you have a God, you have to have a devil. If there are angels, then there have to be demons. Cherubs and imps. Saints and damned. Nine circles of hell—nine circles of heaven. "Better be careful, George! Satan Claus is watching." And then he laughed fiendishly. I guess he thought he was being funny.

I forgot about Steven Dhor for a few weeks. I was involved in another one of those abortive television projects—it's like doing drugs; you think you can walk away from them, but you can't. Someone offers you a needle and you run to stick it in your arm. And then they jerk you around for another six weeks or six months, and then cut it off anyway—and one morning you wake up and find you're unemployed again. The money's spent, and you've wasted another big chunk of your time and your energy and your enthusiasm on something that will never be broadcast or ever see print. And your credential has gotten that much poorer because you have nothing to show for your effort except another dead baby. You get too many of those dead babies on your resume and the phone stops ringing altogether. But I love the excitement, that's why I stay so close to Hollywood—

Then one Saturday afternoon, Steven Dhor read a new story at Kicking The Hobbit—the all science-fiction bookstore that used to be in Santa Monica. I'm sure he saw me come in, but he was so engrossed in the story he was reading to the crowd that he didn't recognize me. "*...the children believed that they could hear the hooves of the huge black pigs scraping through the darkness. They could hear the snuffling and snorting of their hot breaths. The pigs were foaming at the mouth, grunting and bumping up against each other as they pulled the heavy sled through the black tunnels under the earth. The steel runners of the huge carriage sliced across the stones, striking sparks and ringing with a knife-edged note that shrieked like a metal banshee.*

"*And the driver—his breath steaming in the terrible cold—shouted their names as he whipped them, 'On, damn you, on! You children of war! On Pustule and Canker and Sickness and Gore! On Monster and Seizure and Bastard and Whore. Drive on through the darkness! Break through and roar!*" Dhor's voice rose softly as he read these harrowing passages to his enraptured audience.

I hung back away from the group, listening in appreciation and wonder. Dhor had truly caught the spirit of the Christmas obscenity. By the very act of saying the name aloud in public, Dhor was not only giving his power to Satan Claus, he was daring the beast to visit him on Christmas Eve.

"*...And in the morning,*" Dhor concluded, "*there were many deep, knife-like scars in the soft dark earth beneath their bedroom windows. The ground was churned and broken and there were black sooty smudges on the glass....But of their father, there was not a sign. And by this, the children knew that Satan Claus was indeed real. And they never ever laughed again, as long as they lived.*"

The small crowd applauded enthusiastically and then crowded in close for autographs. Dhor's grin spread across his cherubic face like a pink glow. He basked in all the attention and the approval of the fans; it warmed him like a deep red bath. He'd found something that touched a nerve in the audience—now he responded to them. Something had taken root in his soul.

I saw Dhor several more times that year. And everywhere, he was reading that festering story aloud again: "*Christmas lay across the land like a blight, and once again the children huddled in their beds and feared the tread of heavy bootsteps in the dark....*" He'd look up from the pages, look across the room at his audience with that terrible impish twinkle and then turn back to his reading with renewed vigor. "*...Millie and little Bob shivered in their nightshirts as Daddy pulled them onto his lap. He smelled of smoke and coal and too much whiskey. His face was blue and scratchy with the stubble of his beard and his heavy flannel shirt scratched their cheeks uncomfortably. 'Why are you trembling?' he asked. 'There's nothing to be afraid of. I'm just going to tell you about the Christmas spirit. His name is Satan Claus, and he drives a big black sled shaped like a hearse. It's pulled by eight big black pigs with smoldering red eyes. Satan Claus stands in the front of the carriage and rides like the whirlwind, lashing at the boars with a stinging whip. He beats them until the blood pours from their backs and they scream like the souls of the damned—*'"

In the weeks that followed, he read it at the fund-raiser/taping for Mike Hodel's literacy project. He read it at the Pasadena Library's Horror/Fantasy Festival. He read it at the Thanksgiving weekend Lost-Con. He read it on Hour 25, and he had tapes made for sale to anyone who wanted one. Steven was riding the tiger. Exploiting it. Whipping it with his need for notoriety.

"'*Satan Claus comes in the middle of the night—he scratches at your window, and leaves sooty marks on the glass. Wherever there's fear, wherever there's madness—there you'll find Satan Claus as well. He comes through* the wall like smoke and stands at the foot of your bed with eyes like hot coals. He stands there and watches you. His hair is long and gray and scraggly. His beard has terrible little creepy things living in it. You can see them crawling around. Sometimes, he catches one of the bugs that lives in his beard, and he eats it alive. If you wake up on Christmas Eve, he'll be standing there waiting for you. If you scream, he'll grab you and put you in his hearse. He'll carry you straight away to Hell. If you get taken to Hell before you die, you'll never get out. You'll never be redeemed by baby Jesus....'"

And then the Christmas issue of *Ominous* magazine came out and *everybody* was reading it.

"*Little Bob began to weep and Millie reached out to him, trying to comfort his tears; but Daddy gripped her arm firmly and held her at arm's length. 'Now, Millie—don't you help him. Bobby has to learn how to be a man. Big boys don't cry. If you cry, then for sure Satan Claus will come and get you. He won't even put you in his hearse. He'll just eat you alive. He'll pluck you out of your bed and crunch your bones in his teeth. He has teeth as sharp as razors and jaws as powerful as an axe. First he'll bite your arms off and then he'll bite off your legs—and then he'll even bite off your little pink pee-pee. And you better believe that'll hurt. And then, finally, when he's bitten off every other part of you, finally he'll bite your head off! So you mustn't cry. Do you understand me!' Daddy shook Bobby as hard as he could, so hard that Bobby's head bounced back and forth on his shoulders and Bobby couldn't help himself; he bawled as loud as he could.*"

People were calling each other on the phone and asking if they'd seen the story and wasn't it the most frightening story they'd ever heard? It was as if they were enrolling converts into a new religion. They were all having much too much fun playing with the legend of Satan Claus, adding to it, building it—giving their power of belief to Father Darkness, the Christmas evil...as if by naming the horror, they might somehow remain immune to it.

"*'Listen! Maybe you can hear him even now? Feel the ground rumble? No, that's not a train. That's Father Darkness—Satan Claus. Yes, he's always there. Do you hear his horn? Do you hear the ugly snuffling of the eight rabid pigs? He's coming closer. Maybe this year he's coming for you. This year, you'd better stay asleep all night long. Maybe this year, I won't be able to stop him from getting you!'*"

Then some right-wing religious zealot down in Orange County saw the story; his teenage son had borrowed a copy of the magazine from a friend; so of course the censorship issue came bubbling right up to the surface like a three-day corpse in a swamp.

Dhor took full advantage of the situation. He ended up doing a public reading on the front steps of the Los Angeles Central Library. The *L.A. Times* printed his picture and a long article about this controversial new young fantasy writer who was challenging the outmoded literary conventions of our times. Goodman Hallmouth showed up of course—he'd get up off his death bed for a media event—and made his usual impassioned statement on how Dhor was exposing the hypocrisy of Christmas in America.

"The children trembled in their cold, cold beds, afraid to close their eyes, afraid to fall asleep. They knew that Father Darkness would soon be there, standing at the foot of their beds and watching them fiercely to see if they were truly sleeping or just pretending."

Of course, it all came to a head at Art and Lydia's Christmas Eve party. They always invited the whole community, whoever was in town. You not only got to see all your friends, but all your enemies as well. You had to be there, to find out what people were saying about you behind your back.

Lydia must have spent a week cooking. She had huge platters piled with steaming turkey, ham, roast beef, lasagna, mashed potatoes, sweet potatoes, tomatoes in basil and dill, corn on the cob, pickled cabbage, four kinds of salad, vegetable casseroles, quiche and deviled eggs. She had plates of cookies and chocolates everywhere; the bathtub was filled with ice and bottles of imported beer and cans of Coca-Cola. Art brought in champagne and wine and imported mineral water for Goodman Hallmouth.

And then they invited the seven-year locusts.

All the writers, both serious and not-so, showed up; some of them wearing buttons that said, "Turn down a free meal, get thrown out of the Guild." Artists too, but they generally had better table manners. One year, two of them got trampled in the rush to the buffet. After that, Lydia started weeding out the guest list.

This year, the unofficial theme of the party was "Satan Claus is coming to town." The tree was draped in black crepe, and instead of an angel on top, there was a large black bat. Steven Dhor even promised to participate in a "summoning."

"Little Bob still whimpered softly. He wiped his nose on his sleeve. Final-

ly, Millie got out of her bed and crept softly across the floor and slipped into bed next to little Bob. She put her arms around him and held him close and began whispering as quietly as she could. 'He can't hurt us if we're good. So we'll just be as good as we can. Okay. We'll pray to baby Jesus and ask him to watch out for us, okay?' Little Bob nodded and sniffed, and Millie began to pray for the both of them. . . ."

I got there late, I had other errands to run; it's always that way on the holidays.

Steven Dhor was holding court in the living room, sitting on the floor in the middle of a rapt group of wanna-bes and never-wases; he was embellishing the legend of Satan Claus. He'd already announced that he was planning to do a collection of Satan Claus stories, or perhaps even a novel telling the whole story of Satan Claus from beginning to end. Just as St. Nicholas had been born out of good deeds, so had Satan Claus been forged from the evil that stalked the earth on the night before Jesus' birth.

According to legend—legend according to Dhor—the devil was powerless to stop the birth of baby Jesus, but that didn't stop him from raising hell in his own way. On the eve of the very first Christmas, the devil turned loose all his imps upon the world and told them to steal out among the towns and villages of humankind and spread chaos and dismay among all the world's children. Leave no innocent being unharmed. It was out of this beginning that Satan Claus came forth. At first he was small, but he grew. Every year, the belief of the children gave him more and more power.

"The children slept fitfully. They tossed and turned and made terrible little sounds of fear. Their dreams were filled with darkness and threats. They held onto each other all night long. They were awakened by a rumbling deep within the earth, the whole house rolled uneasily—"

Dhor had placed himself so he could see each new arrival come in the front door. He grinned up at each one in a conspiratorial grin of recognition and shared evil, as if to say, "See? It works. Everybody loves it." I had to laugh. He didn't understand. He probably never would. He was so in love with himself and his story and the power of his words, he missed the greater vision. I turned away and went prowling through the party in search of food and drink.

"They came awake together, Millie and little Bob. They came awake with a gasp—they were too frightened to move.

"Something was tapping softly on the bedroom window. It scraped slowly at the glass. But they were both too afraid too look."

Lydia was dressed in a black witch's costume, she even wore a tall pointed hat. She was in the kitchen stirring a huge cauldron of hot mulled wine and cackling like the opening scene in Macbeth, "Double, double toil and trouble, fire burn and cauldron bubble—" and having a wonderful time of it. For once, she was enjoying one of her own parties. She waved her wooden spoon around her head like a mallet, laughing in maniacal glee.

Christmas was a lot more fun without all those sappy little elves and angels, all those damned silver bells and the mandatory choral joy of the endless hallelujahs. Steven Dhor had given voice to the rebellious spirit, had found a way to battle the ennui of a month steeped in Christmas cheer. These people were going to enjoy every nasty moment of it.

"A huge dark shape loomed like a wall at the foot of their bed. It stood there, blocking the dim light of the hallway. They could hear its uneven heavy breath sounding like the inhalations of a terrible beast. They could smell the reek of death and decay. Millie put her hand across little Bob's mouth to keep him from crying.

"'Oh, please don't hurt us,' she cried. She couldn't help herself. 'Please—'"

I circulated once through the party, taking roll—seeing who was being naughty, who was being nice. Goodman Hallmouth was muttering darkly about the necessity for revenge. Writers, he said, are the Research and Development Division for the whole human race; the only *specialists* in revenge in the whole world. Bread Bryan was standing around looking mournful. George Finger wasn't here, he was back in the hospital again. Railroad Martin was showing off a new t-shirt; it said, "Help, I'm trapped inside a t-shirt."

And of course, there was the usual coterie of fans and unknowns—I knew them by their fannish identites: the Elephant, the Undertaker, the Blob, the Duck.

"And then—a horrible thing happened. A second shape appeared behind the first, bigger and darker. Its crimson eyes blazed with unholy rage. A cold wind swept through the room. A low groaning noise, somewhere between a moan and an earthquake, resounded through the house like a scream. Black against a darker black, the first shape turned and saw what stood behind it. It began to shrivel and shrink. The greater darkness enveloped the lesser, pulled it close, and—did something horrible. In the gloom, the children

could not clearly see; but they heard ever terrible crunch and gurgle. They heard the choking gasps and felt the floor shudder with the weight.

"*Millie screamed then; so did little Bob. They closed their eyes and screamed as hard as they could. They screamed for their very lives. They screamed and screamed and kept on screaming—*"

Steven Dhor got very drunk that night—first on his success, then on Art and Lydia's wine. About two in the morning, he became abusive and started telling people what he really thought of them. At first, people thought he was kidding, but then he called Hallmouth a poseur and a phony, and Lydia had to play referee. Finally Bread Bryan and Railroad Martin drove him home and poured him into bed. He passed out in the car, only rousing himself occasionally to vomit out the window.

The next morning, Steven Dhor was gone.

Art stopped by his place on Christmas morning to see if he was all right; but Dhor didn't answer his knock. Art walked around the back and banged on the back door too. Still no answer. He peeked in the bedroom window, and the bed was disheveled and empty, so Art assumed that Steven had gotten up early and left, perhaps to spend Christmas with a friend. But he didn't know him well enough to guess who he might have gone to see. Nobody did.

Later, the word began to spread that he was missing.

His landlady assumed he'd skipped town to avoid paying his rent. Goodman Hallmouth said he thought Steven had gone home to visit his family in Florida, and would probably return shortly. Bread Bryan said that Steve had mentioned taking a sabbatical, a cross-country hitchhiking trip. Railroad Martin filed a missing person report, but after a few routine inquiries, the police gave up the investigation. George Finger suggested that Satan Claus had probably taken him, but under the circumstances, it was considered a rather tasteless joke and wasn't widely repeated.

But ... George was right.

Steven Dhor had come awake at the darkest moment of the night, stumbling out of a fitful and uncomfortable sleep. He rubbed his eyes and sat up in bed—and then he saw me standing there, watching him. Waiting.

I'd been watching him and waiting for him since the day he'd first spoken my name aloud, since the moment he'd first given me shape and form and the power of his belief. I'd been hungry for him ever since.

He was delicious. I crunched his bones like breadsticks. I drank his blood like wine. The young ones are always tasty. I savored the flavor of his soul for a long long time.

And, of course, before I left, I made sure to leave the evidence of my visit. Art saw it, but he never told anyone: sooty smudges on the bedroom window, and the ground beneath it all torn up and churned, as if by the milling of many heavy-footed creatures.

This is another story about Christmas. Consider this a warning. It is not safe to eat the fruitcake just before going to bed.

The Ghost of Christmas Sideways

WHEN THE GHOST APPEARED, Kris Kringle was humping an elf.

The centuries-old oak bed was creaking and groaning like a whale with indigestion, as Kringle pounded furiously away. The headboard banged against the panelled wall with every thrust. Kringle's red pants were down around his ankles, so were his silk boxers. The flabby pink mounds of flesh that were his buttocks shook like two great bags of jelly; they looked like Christmas puddings, all blotchy and purple with veins.

"*Kriiiinnngllllle....*" the sepulchral voice repeated ominously, this time accompanied by the rattle of rusty old chains.

The fat man didn't hear it—or maybe he didn't want to hear it. He kept grunting with lust, again and again, while beneath him, the elf—almost smothered by his weight—shrieked in ecstasy or discomfort. It was impossible to tell.

"*Kringle! Goddammit! Stop that now!*" demanded the voice.

Kris Kringle rolled over abruptly, rising up on one elbow, his tumescence shrinking and disappearing into the folds of flesh at his groin. "Ho ho ho!" he boomed jovially. "Mmmmeeeeerrrrrrryyyyy CCChh-hhrrriiisssstttmmmaaaaassss!! And what would you like Santa to bring you, little boy?" Beside him, the elf lowered its knees from where they had been pressed against his chest. He wore an annoyed expression as he struggled to sit up, straightening his long blonde wig, and at the same time trying to pull down the nearly-transparent nightie to cover his childish modesty. His lipstick was badly smeared.

"*Kringle . . . !*" The apparition's words came from the darkest depths of the grave; they were hollow and raspy and carried the weight of years. "*I have come for you!*" Again, there came the hopeful rattle of moldering chains.

"Wait a minute, goddammit!" squeaked the elf. It reached up onto the headboard behind itself, fumbling for the remote control. At last, it found the clicker and hastily punched the pause button. Santa stopped booming in the middle of a loud enthusiastic "Ho—!" His deep voice trailed off slowly, the bright twinkle faded from his eyes, and some of the redness faded from his bulbous nose. The machinery whirred softly to a halt and Santa sat silently waiting, his naked lap open.

"Odds bodkins!" squeaked the elf. "What is it *this* time?"

In response, the tall gray specter elongated itself, stretching out one bony arm to reach across the intervening distance. It plucked the elf up out of the cushiony feather bed and held it aloft. "Do you recognize me, Brucie Kringle? *Ho ho ho . . . !*" it moaned.

The elf's eyes widened in sudden horror. "Ye gods and little fishes!" He chittered like a cockroach with a thyroid problem. "I thought we *killed* you!"

"*You did!*" rasped the wraith. "*Ho ho ho—!*" It rattled its long popcorn chains and leered malevolently. Its eyes burned like ornaments.

The ghost made a mysterious gesture and—

Suddenly, the two of them were standing out in a frozen cold wilderness, the blue sun was a bitter pill on the horizon. A furious wind whipped at the elf's nightgown. Nearby, a red and white striped pole stood next to a tiny cottage. "*Look!*" pointed the ghost, stabbing with a bony finger at the tiny house. A yellow window glowed with beckoning warmth. Framed by red and white curtains, Santa's body, stuffed to an ample girth with styrofoam peanuts, rocked steadily back and forth in a motorized chair. It puffed merrily at its pipe. Periodically it lifted its hand and waved out the window, while a synchronized recording repeated Santa's infectious laughter against a background of Jingle Bells.

"*A very good job you did, little sprite! You left no detail unattended to.*"

"Thanks," blushed the elf, forgetting for the moment its precarious predicament.

The ghost made another mysterious gesture and—

Suddenly, the two of them were standing in a cold gray field—no horizon, only gray mist and cruel grass. Nearby, stood three men clad in hunters' garb and carrying rifles. Suddenly, one pointed upward. The other two raised their rifles, took careful aim and fired off three quick shots each. The reports of their weapons sounded small and flat against the silent tundra—but far in the distance, a dark object plummeted heavily to the ground, smacking into it with a terrible wet impact.

"*You sold my reindeer to a hunting farm!*" the apparition accused.

The elf squirmed in the bony grip. "Hey! That wasn't my idea. The lawyers ordered it. They said we should downsize the operation. We needed to invest in new transportation. And we got a terrific detail from the Airbus Consortium. The goddamn elk were too old and too slow anyway—and you never paid any attention to how much those hayburners ate, did you? The upkeep was horrendous! If we didn't act when we did, the whole thing would have gone into Chapter 11. Down the tubes without a flush. At least this way, we have a chance to compete against the Japanese—"

"*Always with the excuses, Bruce! Remember, an excuse only satisfies the person who makes it.*"

"Yeah, yeah, yeah—the old-fashioned ways are always the best. The time-honored tradition of the Christmas spirit—and all that jazz. But have you seen how Christmas is celebrated lately?" This time the elf made a mysterious gesture. "Look at this, you fat old fart—"

This time, the haunt and the elf found themselves in a gaily-lit concourse, a suburban mall filled with joyous music, dazzling decorations, towering displays, spotless storefronts and crowds of anxious looking people milling from one ramp to the next with desperate expressions on their faces. Many of them were parents, escorting small children.

The children wore costumes of all kinds. The girls were mostly dressed as glittery princesses, ballerinas, winged fairies with plastic wands, mermaids, cowgirls and witches—a lot of little witches. The costumes of the boys reeked of violence—they were killers of all kinds: gunslingers, terminators, ninjas, turtles, batmen, supermen, vampires and pirates. Many of the costumes seemed to be generic, probably purchased from the Disney outlet in the mall. At each store, tired-looking employees in gay apparel smiled wanly and passed out generic candies.

"This is Christmas now!" declared Bruce Kringle, pointing at a shop window showing Santa waving from a pumpkin patch, another shop window showing Santa riding on the back of a witch's broom, a third display showing the gay old saint passing out candy to costumed children at the front door of his North Pole workshop, and a fourth one showing Santa sitting in the command seat of the starship Enterprise while a dozen little Vulcans in green uniforms smiled and waved.

"But this is not Christmas—" the spook whispered. "It's only Halloween."

"Yeah, that's another thing. We had to merge the holidays. Greater profit potential. Longer selling season. We had to drop the Christ angle, of course. Too tricky. But now, we get into high gear the first weekend before Halloween and we go straight through until the middle of January."

"What have you done?" the ghost demanded cavernously.

"Hey—this was all your idea," the elf replied strongly. "We pick up another five percent just with the post-season white sales. We've got a Japanese conglomerate funding the expansion, and we're looking at an eventual extension of the selling season all the way into Valentine's Day. Of course, the long-term goal is to make Christmas a year-round festival. You always said, you wanted people to have the spirit of Christmas all year round. Well, this is the necessary first step—merchandising."

Brucie Kringle was about to explain about cost-leveraging and swing-markets, when suddenly, from nearby, came a blood-curdling shriek of terror.

"What's that?" asked the ghost.

"Uh—it's just a little extra innovation. Something to shake them up a bit. An idea we got from the amusement parks."

"Tell me!" demanded the wraith.

"Um—better yet, I'll show you." Shaking free from the bony grasp of the specter, the elf jumped down to the tiled floor, grabbed the haunt by its cobwebby robe and dragged it toward a ramshackle-looking structure; it seemed to have been dropped in a heap in front of the entrance to the Broadway. A short line of people waited to enter. Periodically, a hunchback would stagger out of the entrance, grinning and drooling, to wave another small group of people inside. As they watched, another terrifying scream came floating over the top of the walls.

"*What's happening in there?*" said the spook.

"It's called a haunted house. We're scaring the bejesus out of them. It helps to put them in a buying mood—"

The ghost and the elf joined the line—nobody paid them any undue attention. Shortly, the hunchback guided them into the interior of the fabricated structure, where they were treated to a series of tableaus portraying the worst excesses of vampires, chain-saw murderers and back-alley abortionists. The rooms were decorated with coffins, skeletons and big glass jars with strange-looking creatures floating in amber alcohol. They saw corpses, dismembered body-parts and all manner of hairy little bugs and slimy snakes and worms. Deformed mutants leapt out of the walls at them. All around them, the costumed children laughed and shrieked in delight. Flashes of lightning and crashes of thunder punctuated the screams of the banshees and the moans of the zombies.

"See!" said the elf, when they found themselves out in the crush of the mall again. "It's all in fun. Nobody gets hurt. Okay, yeah—so it's not dancing sugarplums. But you were out of touch with all that sugary crap. Don't you know that sugar is bad for kids. This is more realistic—more educational. It's more in tune with the times. I mean, just look at yourself! Do you think you really represent the spirit of Christmas?"

The ghost was sorely offended. It stiffened to its full height. "*I am the spirit of Christmas!*"

"Right, sure," said the elf. "And just how jolly do you think you're going to make people feel, looking like that? At least we've got them laughing at their fears—"

"*Laugh at this!*" said the spook, grabbing the elf by the arm and dragging him into a kitchen appliance store. He seized a cordless electric knife from the wall display—"No More Hassles Carving Your Christmas Turkey!"—and began hacking off the elf's arms and legs. With each cut, the ghost reminded the screaming elf of who it had been when it was still alive. "*I used to bust my ass all year long just for the privilege of working like a frenzied demon racing the dawn on what was supposed to be the holiest night of the year. I had a spastic colon, two crushed vertebrae, a double hernia, hemorrhoids, varicose veins, swollen ankles, colitis, phle-*"

bitis, an ulcerated bowel, psychosomatic impotency and chest pains strong enough to fell a horse. But I did it for the children—and you've turned it into a mockery!"

By this time, the elf had been sliced into seven or eight different-sized pieces, all of them wriggling excitedly on the floor, reforming and growing even as the undead spirit watched. Each piece of the elf was becoming a whole new elf. Almost immediately, they were leaping to their feet, chittering and squeaking in their little high voices. "Now, there are eight of us! Eight little Brucies! H'ray! We can have a daisy-chain!"

The ghost began grabbing them one by one, cackling hideously as it shoved them all into an industrial size food processor. The elves screamed in agony as the ghost punched up the *puree* setting. The many shrieks of "I'm melting—" died away quickly, smothered by the sounds of tiny bones crunching into soup.

Before the fragments could reform into a Brucie-blob, the ghost slid the whole pitcher into a brand-new Radar-Range Microwave oven (with carousel and browning circuits) and programmed it for popcorn. Almost instantly, myriads of little gremlin-like creatures began spurting out of the pitcher, yelping and sparking as the microwaves sleeted angrily through their bodies. They cursed and swore, but their voices were way too thin to be audible. Instead, they sounded like the angry buzz of summer cicadas. Soon, they began smoking and popping, vaporizing painfully into nothingness—

Brucie Kringle, the elf, woke up in a cold sweat. "Oh, my goodness—what a nightmare," he piped. Beside him, the naked Santa-droid rested heavily in the feathery mattress. Bruce leaned over and mopped the cold sweat from his face with Santa's beard. "Whoa," he said to himself. "That was scary. I just gotta watch what I eat before going to bed. I think there was more gravy than grave in that one." And then his words stuck in his mouth. Fear grabbed his throat with icy claws.

Standing at the foot of the bed was a tall dark wraith; its ample girth and jolly posture revealed its nature even before it spoke. *"He he he!"* it cackled. *"Thank you, Bruce, thank you! You have taught me a very valuable lesson. The time is right for a whole new spirit of Christmas—you will get the Christmas that you deserve. And this time, my little sugar-plum, no one will never be able to kill the Christmas spirit! Ho ho ho!"*

Yes, Virginia, there really was a Lennie Smish, a walking elbow-wrinkle of a man who could curdle milk just by walking through the room. His sole delight in life was hurting other people and the damage he did was infamous. I'm sorry I didn't push him out the fourth-story window when I had the chance, but the universe achieved its own revenge, a much more appropriate termination—his proctologist discovered he had a malignant brain-tumor. I sent a get-well card to the tumor.

This story is nowhere near the tribute that Lennie Smish has fairly earned, but it will have to do for now.

A Wish For Smish

DO YOU KNOW WHY they call it slime?

Because the name Smish was already taken.

Lennie Smish was a lawyer. A Hollywood lawyer.

Let me explain that.

Hollywood is heaven for lawyers. There's always somebody with a deal, a contract, a claim or a grudge. The movie isn't over until the last lawsuit is settled; a legal case in Hollywood isn't merely a legal matter, it's a whole career. You have to do it for your children, because you won't live long enough to win.

In Hollywood, Lennie was a legend. He handled one case where settlement was delayed until not only all of the original combatants had died, but most of their heirs as well. By that time, legal fees had eaten up ninety percent of the award. When lawyers spoke of their idols, Lennie's name was always on the list.

No one knew how old Lennie was. It was said of him that even a stake through his heart wouldn't slow him down. It was said that he was already dead, but the devil had refused to take him; so Lennie was left to wander the earth and trouble the sleep of the living. This was what Lennie's *colleagues* said about him.

To say that Lennie was a vampire was more than an understatement, it was like saying the *Titanic* had a rough crossing. Lennie was a super-star of greed.

Lennie Smish had an amazing demeanor. He looked unwashed and disreputable. He was flabby, misshapen, swollen, mottled, discolored, uneven, lumpy, pickled and pocked. He had the large hairy pores of a walrus, the wattles of a turkey and the gravelly skin of an armadillo. He had the charm of a three-day-old Texas roadkill. His clothes were shabby and dirty; his shirts were rumpled and spotted. His tie—he only had one—was a wrinkled collection of soup stains. His hair was stringy and colorless, not quite gray, not quite anything else. Some of it lay flat, not quite covering his bald spot; the rest of it stuck out at odd angles. When he spoke, his voice rasped and scraped as if the words were being pulled one at a time out of a dry scabby throat. Lennie Smish was the only man in the world who could say, "Have a nice day," and make it sound like a threat.

In short, Lennie Smish was so unappetizing, so unpleasant to look upon, so disheartening to deal with, that nobody ever scheduled a meeting with him before lunch.

How the lamp got to Hollywood is obvious. In 1946, in his quest for Arabic authenticity, Louis B. Mayer ordered the purchase of as many Moroccan oil lamps as it took to find the right lamp for the new Douglas Fairbanks, Jr., Maureen O'Hara picture. Fifteen hundred lamps later, somebody finally worked up the courage to tell him that the lamp was actually in the story of Aladdin, not Sinbad. For years thereafter, the MGM prop department was the place to go if you needed an authentic Arabian lamp.

How *the* lamp fell into the hands of Lennie Smish is another story— the usual combination of greed, deceit and underhanded dealings. The short version: Lennie was cataloguing the property he'd seized from the estate of a client who shortsightedly had not provided for Lennie's fees in his will, and had attached the lamp as part of his booty. In keeping with tradition, Lennie was cleaning the lamp when it went off.

The *djinn* came pouring out of the lamp, hacking and wheezing with a dreadful cough—Lennie had been using a chemical cleaner. It expanded itself to a comfortable size, twelve feet, then, seeing the low ceilings in Lennie's apartment, retracted again down to seven feet, ten inches. The *djinn* was a traditional *efrit*. It was as big as it could be in such cramped qaurters; it was bronze of skin and muscled like a bull elephant who worked out at Gold's Gym. It wore a red fez, a black vest, a green sash, a curved bronze scimatar, yellow flowing pantaloons and black pointy-toed shoes. There was no doubt that this was a major genie. It had no hair, no eyebrows, but long black mustaches. It had sharp-pointed ears. It grinned down at Lennie with a mouth full of golden teeth.

Lennie Smish blinked.

To his credit, he did not for an instant doubt the authenticity of the experience. He'd seen stranger sights on Santa Monica Boulevard and hadn't doubted the reality of those apparitions either. His first words were, "Right. How many wishes and how long do I have to make up my mind?"

The genie settled itself comfortably on the floor. It sat down crosslegged on the rug and swelled again to its full size. "In your case," the genie said, "you get one wish only. But you may take as long as you need to decide."

"Hm," said Lennie, thoughtfully. The last time Lennie had said "Hm" so thoughtfully, a major studio head had abruptly announced his retirement. But then, suddenly, Lennie realized what the genie had said. "What do you mean—in *my* case?"

The *djinn* shrugged. "Policy," it said. "That's just the way these things work." But, seeing the look on Lennie's face, it pulled a document out of thin air. "See here? This is the 1990 rider attached to the 1988 contract extension. Section 12, Article II, Paragraph 6, Item A, Schedule 2. Lawyers and other primordial scum. That's you."

Lennie leaned forward to examine the document, but abruptly the genie snatched it back and stashed it away again in thin air. "Sorry, that's a confidential Guild document. I can't let you see it."

"Guild?" Lennie asked.

"WGAW," the *efrit* explained.

"Wizards, Genies, Angels, Warlocks?" Lennie asked. "I dealt with them once. A fellow named Faust, I think—"

"Writers Guild of America, West," the genie corrected. *"Our* executive director is a pit bull."

At last, Lennie's incredulity surfaced. "The *Writers Guild?* But you can't be—"

"Yes, I can," the *djinn* replied huffily. "I've been a member since 1949. Well, only an associate member, but when I finish my screenplay, I'm sure it'll sell. I have a cousin who knows Spielberg and—"

"Never mind," said Lennie, waving his hand in annoyance. "Let's talk about the bottom line here, my wish."

"As you command, my master." The *djinn* spread its hands in a florid arm gesture and inclined its muscular upper body in a semblance of a bow. "How much wealth, love, honor, fame, glory, beauty and power do you want? I am required by law to caution you, however, that while I must honor your wish to the letter, I must take advantage of every loophole in your wording to thwart the spirit of it."

"Hm," said Lennie again. And this time he meant it.

The *djinn* flinched. He knew who Lennie Smish was.

"I'll tell you," said Lennie. "If there's one thing I've always wanted, it's respect."

"Is that your wish?"

"No," said Lennie. "Not yet. What I want is the respect that comes with success at one's craft. I have always wanted to be a $10,000 an hour lawyer."

"Ahh," said the *djinn*. "That's your wish."

"No," said Lennie. "I am not yet ready to wish. Not until I find a way to phrase this so that there are no loopholes—so you can't thwart it."

"Ahhhhh," said the *efrit,* approvingly. "A challenge." It licked its chops; its tongue was long and pink and forked. "Those are the *tastiest* kind."

Lennie reached over to the table beside his chair and picked up his yellow legal pad and a pencil. At the top of it, he wrote: *Ten thousand dollars an hour.* After a moment, he added, *As many clients as it takes to make me happy.* After a moment's more thought, he scratched that out and wrote, *More than enough work to keep me busy.*

Underneath that, he began making notes:
Clients who can afford to pay.
Clients with winnable cases.
Clients with cases that cannot be settled too quickly.
Resolutions that my clients will be satisfied with.

Lennie Smish thought for a while. He stared across the room at the *djinn* and pursed his prune-like lips. He gnawed on the end of his pencil while he considered all the ways he might phrase his wish and all the ways that the *efrit* might thwart the results.

The *djinn* grinned at him.

Lennie Smish said, "I think I'm beginning to understand the depth of this problem."

The *djinn*'s grin widened. Its golden teeth flashed like sunset. Sunset Boulevard.

"I believe," said Lennie, "that I am going to have to spend some time researching this. Will you negotiate with me? Will you sign a fair contract?"

The *djinn* laughed. Its voice boomed like a kettle drum. "I will sign any contract you care to draft. Even you, the great Lennie Smish, cannot write a contract that cannot be thwarted."

"Hmm," said Lennie. A new thought occurred to him and he began scribbling more notes onto his yellow pad. His handwriting was crabbed and tiny; his words looked like spider-tracks. "This is going to take some time," said Lennie.

"No problem," said the *djinn*. "I can work on my screenplay." The creature materialized a laptop computer and began carefully typing. Occasionally, it chuckled. Once, it materialized a dictionary in mid-air, paged through it to check the meaning of the word *scrofulous*, then dematerialized the volume and returned to its labors.

Across the room, Lennie scribbled furious notes. More and more ideas kept occurring to him. But one thought overrode every other consideration—this had to be the *greatest* contract of his career, perhaps even the greatest contract that anyone had ever negotiated anywhere. This document would be a model of airtight, watertight, *unbreakable*, krell metal-clad intention.

At one point, the *djinn* looked up and said, "Oh, by the way—don't forget to add a clause that I can't alter you, your behavior, your motivations, your desires or your conception of your results. I wouldn't do it anyway, that would be cheating, but you need to be aware that some *efrits* consider that a fair trick."

Lennie stared at the *djinn*, astonished. It was *helping* him? But, he dutifully noted the clause. Then he made a note to himself to examine the *efrit*'s suggested phrasing. Was the genie giving him that clause specifically to set up a loophole big enough to drive a producer's ego through?

At last, Lennie put the yellow pad aside and said, "All right, I've outlined the areas I'll need to research. It's going to take longer than I thought, several months at least. But I think I can do it. I can't rely on boilerplate. I'm going to have to do the whole thing by hand. I'll probably have to release most of my other clients just to put this thing together—"

The *djinn* didn't even look up. "Of course," it acknowledged. "That's the way these things work. You're not the first, you know. I doubt you'll be the last."

"We'll see," said Lennie. "We'll see."

For the next nine months, Lennie devoted himself solely—eighty hours a week—to his contract. He researched contract law all the way back to Noah. He studied every precedent from Faust to Daniel Webster. He consulted with demonologists, mediums, exorcists and karmic gurus. He met with scholars of the supernatural from seven different cultures. He interviewed three supreme court justices. He studied linguistics and communication to make sure he understood the precise semantic definition of the words he was using and the distinctions he was drawing. He studied torts, retorts and curses. He even met with an emissary from the Pope to ensure that his immortal soul would not be endangered by the contract. He cashed in his savings bonds, withdrew his life savings, sold his Paramount stock and hired a staff of twelve research assistants; he broke them into three teams—each one would write a clause and the other two teams would try to find a loophole.

After nine exhausting months, Lennie was finished. It took another two weeks to get the contract printed, proof read, corrected, reprinted, proof read again, corrected again, reprinted again, etc. Lennie could not allow even a typographical error to mar the perfection of this document. A forgotten comma had once cost a shipping company forty million dollars. By now, of course, the *djinn* had finished its screenplay and had begun sending it out to agents. While it waited, the *djinn* worked patiently on the novelization.

At last, Lennie presented his contract to the *djinn*. The creature took the document, paged through it slowly, nodding and grunting in reaction to various clauses, sub-clauses, articles, sections, paragraphs, schedules, tables and footnotes. It read the contract all the way through to the last page and looked up at Lennie with a happy grin. "This is really a very nice piece of work," it said. "My compliments. This work is definitely worth $10,000 an hour."

"So you'll sign it?"

"Of course," said the *djinn*. "Hand me that pen, will you?"

"You have to sign this with your legal name!" Lennie Smish insisted.

The *djinn* looked up annoyed. "Give me a break," it said. "A contract this elegant requires a loophole every bit as elegant—and every bit as carefully worked out." It scrawled its signature in elegant Arabic script.

"Aha!" said Lennie Smish, grabbing the contract and waving it in the *djinn*'s face. "I got you now!"

The *djinn* looked at Lennie without emotion. "You do?" it asked.

"I won't agree to any contract you sign. Because you won't sign it unless you find a loophole. The deal's off."

"I'm afraid it's not that easy," the *djinn* said. "You have to avail yourself of my services."

"No, I don't. I haven't signed. And I have the right to back out of the deal any time before the contract is finalized." Lennie Smish produced his bill. "But whether the contract is executed or not, you still have to pay for the services of the lawyer. Here's my bill for three thousand hours of labor, plus the labors of my staff and associated expenses. It comes to thirty-six million dollars, payable in legal tender only, cash, check or money order—no coins or bills under a hundred, please."

The *djinn* began laughing heartily. "I do believe you have caught me," it said. "I really do believe that you have found a way to get your wish without getting tricked. I'm mightily impressed." It began plucking suitcases out of the air, thirty-six of them in all. Lennie grabbed at the cases and began opening them suspiciously.

The *djinn* shook its head. "The money is legal," it said in annoyance. "United States of America, *e pluribus unum*. All that stuff. I don't cheat. I trick. There's a difference."

Lennie stacked the suitcases in the hall closet, the spare bedroom, the service porch and the kitchen. He hadn't realized that thirty-six million dollars would take up so much space. When he finished, the *djinn* asked him to sign a receipt. He did so suspiciously; but he had no choice.

"All right," said the *djinn*. "Our business is concluded. You got your wish. I get my freedom."

"Begone," said Lennie, glad to have the creature finally out of his apartment.

The *djinn*—and the lamp—vanished.

Two days later, there was a knock on the door. Lennie Smish answered it and a process server handed him a subpoena. He was being sued. By the *djinn*. For failure to negotiate in good faith.

That was only the first subpoena.

In the next three months, forty-six more lawsuits were filed against Lennie Smish. Everything from sexual harrassment in the workplace to violations of the RICO statutes. And that was only the beginning. It seemed as if every court case, every settlement, every contract he'd ever worked on, was bubbling back up to the surface of the legal quagmire.

It took a while, but Lennie finally figured it out. *He'd gotten his wish.*

He was a $10,000 an hour lawyer, and he had more work than he could handle.

It's not about getting even. It's about getting better. Most people never figure that out.

What Goes Around

THE FIRE BLOSSOMS OUTWARD, rosy-petals of orange and black. The bullet spits. The sound pops softly in the sweating August night. Again and again.

It begins.

The door explodes. Horror invades, laughing wildly, screaming with invented rage at invisible monsters, nobody home here, just bodies, it doesn't matter—rage assaults the nearest target.

The screams become a nightmare chorus. On and on. Outrage and shock. The knives begin to work, plunging, tearing—rending first the clothes, then the flesh, and deeper still, into the heart of the beast, and from there into the fibrillating heart of the species. The wounds go deep.

Bitterly the blades keep biting. Slender arms pump up and down, struggling with the dreadful work. Steaming blood pours forth, the muscles pull and strain. The bodies resist; it isn't easy—tendons, cartilage, muscles, bone and spurting hot wet blood; a fountain of gore—it isn't neat, it isn't pretty. Life fights back, it resists the assault; it struggles, fights, bites, kicks, screams, claws, shrieks, begs, wonders, pleads, gasps and refuses to give up, even as it shreds away with dreadful ripping noises.

The gleeful cries go on and on. The harridans, the witches cackle and

107

laugh at the audacity of this vicious celebration. "Die, piggie, die!" The walls are splattered with scarlet slashes. Steel skitters along bone. Cartilage resists, then breaks. Bodies jerk, and still the blood pours forth; the baby slides wetly into dreadfulness.

Saturday morning.

The maid discovered the bodies. She ran screaming down the driveway to a neighbors. The police arrived in a squadron of gleaming vehicles, black-and-whites, and plainclothes—all with their lights blazing, some with sirens screaming.

The young detectives stood at the door of the sprawling house and stared in at the carnage within—stunned beyond words—reluctant to enter, not knowing where to start. It was like a scene out of Hell. That was the metaphor, but it was insufficient.

"Who lives here?" one of them asked.

Another one turned away, gagging.

A third wrote down license numbers and began calling them in.

Few of them had ever seen anything like this in their careers. They'd heard about crimes of horrific violence; they'd seen the casebooks of a few. They'd never really expected to have to investigate one like this. Their training failed them, overpowered by their instinctive human revulsion.

But then the chief of detectives arrived and started barking orders. He barely glanced inside the house. He knew better. He didn't want to know. He didn't want the memories. He didn't want the dead things clogging up his vision, troubling his sleep.

The young officer came back from his black-and-white, holding his notebook open. "The pickup truck is registered to Charles Manson, white, male, age forty-two."

"Manson?" said one of the detectives, frowning. "Why does that name sound familiar?"

The chief of detectives grunted. "There used to be a rock star by that name." He turned to the officer. "Is this the same guy?"

"I don't know."

"Find out," he said—and groaned. Looking past the officer, he saw the arrival of the first carload of vultures. He recognized the reporters from the *Times*. Overhead, a newschopper began clattering through the smoggy air, circling the site around and around. Up the hill, the neighbors were already out on their porches, shading their eyes against the morning sun and staring down at the tableau below.

The newspapers had a feeding frenzy. Banner headlines advertised the gory event as if it were important: **ROCK BAND MURDERED IN ORGY OF VIOLENCE**. Beneath, in smaller type, the article identified the victims: **Charles Manson and 'The Family' Found Stabbed to Death in Manson's Bel-Air Home**.

The articles described the horror without being explicit:

"Even veterans of the LAPD Violent Crimes Division were stunned by the carnage.

"Although officials at the scene refused to go on record about the apparent murder spree, it is believed that the Manson home was invaded by three or more knife-wielding individuals who stabbed all six of the occupants to death. A seventh victim was found shot to death in his car.

"At present, the police have not indicated whether or not they have any leads in the case."

The text went on to explain:

"Although generally unknown to the record-buying public, Charles Manson and 'The Family' were fairly well known in the Los Angeles underground club scene.

"One club-owner who refused to be identified, said, 'Yeah, we knew them. They were bad. Loud and bad. That was why we booked them— as a kind of gag. We'd put them in as a spacer between two good sets. The kids hooted and jeered.

"'Manson ate it up. He loved that shit. He'd get out there and scream at the crowds and they'd scream right back. He was a great warm-up. But, no—he never figured it out that no one took him seriously. You want the truth? Manson was an asshole. And the girls were pigs, pardon my language, but it's true. They were over-the-hill, overweight, out-of-tune and ugly. If Manson liked you, he'd tell his girls to go to bed with you. I hate to think what he'd tell them to do if he didn't like you.'"

LA TIMES: SUCCESS ELUDED ECCENTRIC GROUP

…The Manson Family made only three albums in their short-lived recording career. Their first, *We Are The Nightmare*, released in August 1969, attracted far more attention for the offensiveness of its language than for the quality of the music, most of which was shrieked rather than sung. *Rolling Stone* magazine gave it the lowest rating in its history, a 1/4 star rating, and said the album was at best only good for breaking your lease. Nevertheless, the furor over the album's language guaranteed it enough sales to make it a cult item among radical punk rockers.

Regarding *We Are The Nightmare*, band-member, Charles "Tex" Watson freely admitted, "Hey, man. We didn't intend this as music. It ain't supposed to be listened to. It's supposed to be an initiation into the tribe. You have to inhale this deep into your mind, that's all. It's like, you know, a scream of consciousness. We don't want people sitting around and *listening* to this shit. We want them jumping up and down and shrieking with us. Like the hash-smoking assassins would pump themselves up into a killing frenzy before going out into the world to commit mayhem. Well, that's us. We're freaking fucking out." (Watson was found shot to death in his car in the driveway.)

Manson's second album, *Die, Piggies, Die!*, received an even worse critical drubbing. Cordwainer Bird, writing for the *Rolling Stone*, opined that he hoped that the title of the LP indicated that this disk was a suicide note. "Anyone stupid enough to buy this whiny piece of enervated bat-guano ought to have their ears ripped off their heads and stapled to the walls where they can at least be useful as ashtrays. This record isn't even good enough be called crap. It's an insipid, puerile waste of vinyl, not even of interest to those morbid curiosity seekers who like to stand around and gawk at the scene of a fatal accident."

Manson was so enraged by that review that when he was questioned about it on KPFK's late-night *Under The Rock* program, he erupted into a furious tirade. He threatened to cut out Cordwainer Bird's heart and eat it raw. It is widely believed that "Blind As A Bird," the first of Manson's three singles, was written with Cordwainer Bird in mind. The lyrics, screamed in a near-incoherent rage, included these lines:

You don't know me! You don't know!
You stupid motherfucking little dwarf, you don't know shit!

If I can't make you love me, then I'll make you hate me!
But I won't let you ignore me!

The resultant flurry of threats, lawsuits and injunctions, kept the album in the news long enough for it to sell a modest number of copies. Sludge Records (now defunct) even sold t-shirts labeled 'ONE OF THE MORBIDLY CURIOUS' to those who sent in ten dollars and a proof-of-purchase certificate.

Curiously, it was Manson's third and last album that received the best reviews. *The Cage of Life* was released in 1972 and attracted almost no attention at all. Recorded entirely in Manson's garage, the LP has minimal production values, but the stark simplicity of the arrangements created a sense of the darkness of the LA club-scene. The album's set piece, a brooding seven-minute dirge called "Life Sentence," tells the story of a man who has emptied his life of all value and now waits only for death. But by then, even curiosity-seekers had lost all interest in Manson, and only a few copies of the LP found their way into record stores.

The commentators *tsked*. They couldn't quite bring themselves to mourn Manson; there was nothing to mourn. He'd been a failure in life. He was, at best, a footnote; at worst, an embarrassing asterisk, a nothing.

What made him noteworthy now was not his life, but only his manner of leaving it. So they dwelt on that. They alluded to the rumors of mystic symbols written in blood on the walls of his home—his blood, his walls—and wondered who had been responsible and why.

They licked their lips and spent lugubrious tears on the unborn baby of Patricia Krenwinkle. They worried about Susan Atkin's last terrifying moments. They burrowed through the sordid details of the lives of Squeaky Lynnette Fromme and Leslie Van Houtin.

Perhaps the strange X's cut into their foreheads had something to do with the albums they recorded. The police spent hours playing and replaying the LP's. They paid particular attention to Dyslexic Sadie and Smelter Skelter. They studied an underground video of The Family, trying to understand who these people were and why someone would want to murder them.

Cordwainer Bird opined that the list of suspects should start with anyone who loved music.

Charlie was the lead singer, with a voice as thin and unpleasant as February ice. Tex was the axe-man, posturing and posing—he would have upstaged Charlie were it not for Charlie's riveting, Rasputin-like gaze. The girls danced behind them, backing Manson's incoherent lyrics and Watson's pretentious gruntings with a ragged embroidery of artificial doo-wop noises.

In the meantime . . . the sales of guard dogs, security devices, alarms, fences, cellular phones—and guns, weapons of all kinds—jumped and kept on jumping. August turned into September and the terror hardened into distrust and bitterness. Whatever was out there remained unknown, unidentified, uncontrolled. Would there be more killings?

Brooding late one night in an hour-long soliloquy, Cordwainer Bird devoted one entire show to what he called "the Manson phenomenon."

"It's not Manson," Bird began. "He was a nothing—a gnat's fart, not worth the energy to talk about. He was one of those little scuttlefish that come out of the woodwork, attracted by the light, but totally lacking any understanding of how to create the light in the first place.

"Yeah, right—" Bird said, jabbing his finger at the audience. "I'm an asshole for speaking ill of the dead, is that your point? What do you think, bunky? The act of dying automatically elevates a human being to sainthood? I got news for you—Manson's music sucked. It sucked when he was alive, it ain't gonna get any better now that he's dead.

"And his personal habits—? I'll tell you. He smelled. Yeah, I met him. Three times. And you know what? He was afraid of me. All those threats? He just did a little shuffle and jive and dropped his head and wouldn't look me in the eye. A fucking coward. A yutz.

"You know who he was? He was that skinny kid in the ninth grade, the one who never got any hair on his chest or under his arms or on his balls; the one who picked his nose and ate the boogers when he thought no one was looking; the one who had to be reminded to take a shower once in a while because nobody ever explained to him about deodorants.

"You know all those pictures of him making him look like some kind of scary vampire bat? That was bullshit. He was a scrawny little guy. Shorter than me! Shorter than the average fire hydrant—a shrunken chest, he looked like he was suffering from terminal malnutrition. Yeah, he had a great stare and he was incoherent, whacked out on drugs and booze half the time, and you think that's the sign of a serious craftsman? The fact that he looked weird and you can't understand him.

"Okay—" Bird interrupted himself. "You want me to be compassionate. I'll be compassionate for two seconds. He had a lousy childhood. He can be excused for being an asshole; he had a lousy childhood. Okay, I'm through being compassionate. That's so much crap, it makes my gorge buoyant. I had a lousy childhood! Half the people in this room had a lousy childhood. So fucking what! We got over it. We didn't use it as an excuse to assault the people around us. We got over it. He didn't.

"So what's his claim to fame? No talent and he got himself murdered. And you people are gathering around, sniffing like jackals at a rotting corpse, pissing and moaning about how awful it was that these lives were snuffed out! What the hell—if it weren't for the fact that there's someone out there who is provably crazier than Charlie and his stupid Family, I'd probably want to shake his hand and thank him for improving the average IQ of the human race and removing some seriously sociopathic phenotypes from the gene pool.

"Y'know," Bird said, trotting up into the audience and sitting on the lap of a fat woman. She giggled in delight. "Y'know, if this universe worked the way it was supposed to—like if God had stuck around instead of taking off early for the weekend—Manson's name would be unknown to each and every one of us in this theater. He would have never made a ripple. He would have died forgotten. Instead, what do we get?" He leapt back to his feet. "The bloody awfulness of his death has turned him into a ninety-day wonder, a cultural icon. It's the goddamn Lindbergh baby all over again—only this time we've got CNN giving us hourly updates on how incompetent the Los Angeles Police Department really is. Like that's news to the rest of us? Get real! It's a bloody Frankenstein movie that they keep running because you keep tuning in. It sells toothpaste and tampons, that's all it means.

"And what do you get out of it? You get to play Halloween. How many of you are going to feel safe in your beds tonight? Yeah, none of you, that's right! That's why you do it. You love being scared. You love wallowing in other people's dreadful deaths, without ever stopping to think of the horror of it! Do you assholes know how much horror there is in the world? There's already more than enough for all of us! Why do you want to create more? What do you get from it?

"I'll tell you what you get—you get the feeling of power, the vicarious thrill of going along for the ride during a criminal act of mindless, stupid, thoughtless violence. You're not identifying with the ones who died screaming in the night—you're each of you recreating the act of murder, with yourself playing the lead role as a modern day Jack-the-fucking-Ripper. And by that singular deed, you align yourself with the disease, not the cure!

"Don't you give me that look, lady, that self-righteous, 'It's not my fault' look. I've seen you standing in the supermarket line, all of you, checking out the headlines in the *National Enquirer*. Oh, you don't read the *Enquirer*, right? So this speech is for everybody else. What do you read? *People* magazine? I thought so. Really socially uplifting material, lady. I'm not impressed. And who's that turnip sitting next to you, your husband? You, sir? When was the last time you read something that didn't have the dialog in balloons?

"The horror isn't the murders, you idiots. The horror is that we've made such horrors commonplace in our society. These murders will be forgotten in two years, because somebody else will be murdered in some other place, some other way, and next time we'll have color video of it, and CNN will make some poor sucker rich because he was standing in the right place at the right time with his fucking camcorder turned on. Who really gives a shit about Charles Manson? None of you do. You just wish there was a video of him begging and screaming with his killers for his life so you could ride the adrenalin roller-coaster one more time.

"He was a weasel and he's dead, but the real assassins are the ones who keep him writhing on the knife!"

Around town, those who could reliably claim to have known him—*them*—now had stories they could dine out on:

"Oh, yeah, I knew him…." "What was he like?" Shrug. "Actually, I never saw him get mad. Sometimes, he could be a real charmer. He asked me to engineer an album for him; but nothing ever came of it—"

"The girls? They had a sleazy reputation. Yeah, it was true. If Charlie liked you, yeah, you could end up the meat in a pussy sandwich. But…it wasn't something you wanted to do twice. The girls were—it's hard to describe—I think the best word to use is *traif*. It's a yiddish word, yeah. It means unclean. I got a weird feeling off them, I can't explain it, but they looked at you like you were dead, or like they were waiting for you to be dead, like they were necrophiliacs...."

"I got a friend whose cousin works in the coroner's office, and she said that the bodies were dismembered. The heart was removed from Manson's body and they still haven't found it. The baby was cut out of the mother—I mean, the things she said—it was sick. But they won't put it in the paper, because they're hoping to keep it secret to help catch the killers."

"Okay, I'll tell you what I heard. I got this from the head of legal. He knows one of the detectives on the case. Anyway, the theory is that Charlie and his girls were having a wild party with some drug dealers, gang-members, crack-heads, slam-bangers, whatever they're called, and it got out of control. Charlie tried to stiff them, offered them sex with the girls instead of cash, or maybe he tried to rob them, and the bangers took them down instead. It wasn't supposed to get that violent, but they were all strung out on drugs and you know—"

"No, I swear, this is God's honest truth. The caretaker was having a homosexual affair with Charleton Heston. Heston was there! While it was happening. But when they heard the screams, they climbed out a window and hid naked in the bushes. Then they snuck away. My step-brother is a public defender. He heard it from a secretary in the DA's office. The caretaker's lie detector test was really dirty. They think the caretaker knows more than he's saying."

"Did you see this in the *San Francisco Chronicle*? Manson was a big L. Ron Hubbard fan. Now they think the Scientologists might be involved somehow—"

"You won't believe this, but I was invited up there a few times. Yeah, I could have been up there that night. Yeah, the rumor was that Charlie always had plenty of dope, that he grew it in the basement, that they were always stoned. But that's not true. They were beer-drunks. They sat around drunk all day watching TV. They watched reruns. They watched *Happy Days* and *The Brady Bunch* and *The Partridge Family*, all of those. Charlie loved them. They were supposed to be the nasty boys of rock, and the truth is, they were just a bunch of couch potatoes vegging out on phosphors. It was boring, man. Stupid. Killing them was redundant. They were already dead from the neck up."

The investigative task force spread out across the city. Charlie's connections to the music community, the drug community, the gay community, the prison community, the science fiction community, the Scientologists and the underground club scene were all investigated. Nothing substantial developed, but everything was pursued. Something had to fit somewhere; the crime couldn't have been simply a random happenstance. If a band of drug-crazed hippies could burst into anyone's home on a murderous killing spree, then what purpose was there to civilization?

Days stretched into months. No new leads developed. Old trails dried up. Publicly, the police said they were still investigating every possibility. Privately, they acknowledged that they were getting nowhere fast.

A panel of criminal psychologists and detectives appeared on the Cordwainer Bird talk show to discuss the apparent failure of the LAPD to produce substantial results. Bird had intended to focus on the issue of public safety, but instead allowed himself to be distracted into more speculation on the unsolved murders.

"What puzzles me the most," said one of headshrinkers, "is the silence. There had to be at least three killers—probably more. The violence in the Manson house was…well, it wasn't describable. I was in Vietnam, and I never saw anything like this. But even assuming there were only three killers, that's three people who would know. More, if you include other gang members, family members—or anyone else who knew them who would have a reason to be suspicious. Whoever did it would have come home drenched with the blood of their victims. That couldn't have gone unnoticed. So, why haven't we gotten a call from someone's girl friend or neighbor or cleaning lady? A secret this big—it's got to break sooner or later."

Bird seized on this thought as the channel for the discussion that followed. "All right," he demanded. "What are the possibilities then?"

A forensic pathologist suggested, "The violence of the crime scene seems to rule out that it was an execution; but maybe it was an execution gone bad. In any case, if it was an execution, the killers were professional. They're probably out of the country by now. I'd look in the Bahamas, somewhere around there."

The first detective shook his head. "No, I think the killers are dead, at least one or two of them anyway. Maybe the victims fought back and the murderers died of their wounds later. Maybe they were killed in an innocent-looking car crash while they were trying to escape. Maybe they fled to Arizona or Nevada and were killed there. The best way to cover up an assassination is to kill the assassin too."

Bird spent the better part of the hour pursuing conspiracy theories, trying to puzzle out why anyone would want to murder a useless old has-been like Charles Manson.

Finally, at the end of the hour, he turned to the last of the detectives, an older man who'd sat quietly puffing his pipe, listening to everything and saying nothing. "What do you think?" he demanded.

The old man shifted his position in his chair, tapped his pipe on the ash tray and spoke with deceptively soft words. "I think everybody's looking in the wrong place. I think the killers are already in custody," he said. "I think the LAPD picked them up on some traffic violation, found an old warrant for unpaid parking tickets and put them away for a few months. Something like that. If they're a bunch of giddy kids—and that's my guess—then they've probably told their cellmates. And I'll bet that the cellmates are too terrified to say anything. That's what I think."

The following evening, Cordwainer Bird hosted a panel of psychics to see if they could solve the murders with their metaphysical prowess.

One psychic said that the murderer had red hair. Another said that the house was the target, that the murderers were trying to avenge a crime that the house had committed. A third claimed that the murderers had a supernatural connection with their victims, a connection that could not be explained or understood within the context of Euclidean geometry—that the lives of killers and victims were tangled in a web that went beyond the context of ordinary space-time. Right.

Bird let them babble for twenty or thirty minutes before he angrily ordered them all out of the studio. Then he turned to his studio audience and delivered another of his scathing diatribes, this one about the human mind's inability to accept "I don't know" as an answer—that we will make up the most astonishing explanations and reasons and justifications, just so we don't have to live with the dreadfulness of having something in our lives feel *incomplete*.

"You supposedly intelligent human beings, educated and literate, will throw all of that rationality out of the window to become supplicants to a bunch of post-menopausal, self-important, unschooled, pretentious, posturing, posing old fools. These idiots don't know anything; they've conned themselves into believing they have some connection to the cosmic fluxes of the universe—and you idiots are so desperate to believe, you'll hang on every word, simply because you can't stand the pain of not knowing the answer.

"You wanna know the truth? When you don't know, you won't admit it. You got it hard-wired that not-knowing means you're stupid. No, you got it worse than that. You believe that not-knowing is connected to your survival. So when you don't know something, you don't put yourself into a rational investigation, an inquiry, which is what a truly intelligent being would do. No, the evidence is that when you don't know something, you make something up. All of you—and then you pass your bullshit around as if it means something. And then you have the colossal gall to wonder why you're not producing results!

"You know what I think? I think the murderers are just like you. Just smart enough to understand the difference between rational and stupid, but not smart enough to recognize which side of the line you belong on. I think that when they finally catch the bozos who did it, we'll all be amazed at how small and pitiful they really are."

He was right.

Two days later, an ABC news crew, acting on their own initiative, performed an interesting experiment.

A driver, a cameraman and two reporters started at the Manson house on Cielo Drive. They pulled out of the driveway and headed down the hill to Benedict Canyon, where they turned left to head out toward the San Fernando Valley. In the back seat, the two reporters began changing clothes. The cameraman taped the entire process.

When both reporters had completely redressed, the driver stopped the car. They were on a wide curve, overlooking a fairly steep slope. Reporting on their regularly scheduled broadcast later that night, they said, "We assumed that the murderers changed clothes in the car. We thought to recreate that drive and see what we could discover. What we discovered was the place where they threw their bloody clothes away."

Three pairs of jeans, a flannel shirt, a USC sweatshirt, a blue t-shirt and a black windbreaker were found on the hillside. Also a pair of tennis shoes and socks. All the clothes were blood-soaked.

The ABC news-team knew better than to touch the evidence, but they brought back great shots of their reporters pointing at the clothes on the hillside and the forensics team bagging the evidence and carting it away.

The USC sweatshirt provided the break in the case. It was an expensive limited-edition shirt available only to members of Tommy Trojan's Homecoming Committee. Only thirty of them had been made. Armed with a new list of suspects, the detectives fanned out again. Anyone who couldn't produce their Homecoming sweatshirt was a suspect.

The list was narrowed to ten, then six, then three.

One of the young men contacted hadn't seen his shirt in months. His ex-roommate had apparently taken it with when he'd moved out. "No, I didn't know him well at all. He was only here for a few weeks. I hardly ever saw him. He'd come in, crash for a few hours, then disappear again. A couple times he brought his doper friends around, but I wouldn't let them smoke in here, so they stopped coming. He didn't have the second month's rent, so I told him to move out. When he did, he stole a bunch of stuff. It was real annoying too. His dad was some rich director; he didn't need to steal my stuff. What's this all about anyway? Does this have something to do with those clothes they found on TV?"

A bench-warrant was issued for J. Michael Tate, also known as Joseph Tate-Polanski; the son of Sharon Tate and her ex-husband, Roman Polanski. Further investigation turned up the names of several of Tate-Polanski's frequent acquaintances: Marina Folger, Zbig Frykowski and David Sebring.

Folger and Frykowski's whereabouts were unknown; they were presumed to be in Europe somewhere. David Sebring had died of a self-induced drug overdose three days after the Manson murders. It took a while longer for the LAPD to find Joe Tate. It turned out they'd had him in custody all along.

Joe Tate had been arrested on a DUI at the end of August. It was his third offense; the judge threw the book at him; he was still incarcerated in the County Jail and would be for the next nine months.

When he was questioned by detectives, he readily admitted the killings. "It was the house, man—the house. My mom and dad lived there before the divorce. That was where I grew up. I was happy there—and then they sold it and he moved to Europe and she moved to New York, and I blame the people who bought it for breaking up our family. I wanted to get even, that's all. They had no right. I wanted to show them that they hadn't won anything at all. And I did. I don't feel sorry for them. They had it coming."

Cordwainer Bird had only a few more comments about the case. He tossed them off in his opening monologue the day after the verdict came down.

"Y'see," he said. "This was my point all along. Everyone was running around looking for grand conspiracies and strange connections. There weren't any. There never are. The universe is running by accident and God's on vacation. Stop looking for answers—even if there were any, you wouldn't understand them. Leave it be, you assholes. There just ain't no justice in this life—and that's that."

AUTHOR'S AFTERWORD:

One of the reviewers said I got my facts wrong.
No, I didn't.
Maybe one day, I'll explain.

I should have called this story The League of Giant Red-Headed Time-Travelers From Sumatra, but instead I settled for a very bad pun.

The Fan Who Molded Himself

EDITOR'S NOTE: *Seventeen copies of this manuscript were delivered to my office over a period of three weeks. Some were mailed, some arrived by courier; three were faxed, four were sent by e-mail. Several arrived by messenger. All seventeen arrived under different names and from different points of origin. I believe that more copies than seventeen were posted, but only seventeen arrived.*

The following cover letter was enclosed with every copy:

Dear Mr. Resnick,

I apologize for taking such unusual steps to bring this manuscript to your attention, but after you read it, you will understand just why I had to go to such lengths to ensure that at least one copy of this will reach your desk.

By way of explanation, I am not the author of the piece, although in the absence of other heirs to the estate, I do claim full ownership of the rights. The enclosed essay, story, letter, confession, call it what you will, came into my hands in a very curious way.

I was never very close to my father; he was a stern and rigorous man, and I moved out of his household as soon as I was old enough to make my own way in the world. I even went so far as to change my name and move to another city. For some time, I avoided all contact with my father (whom I shall not name in this manuscript); so you can imagine my surprise and annoyance to find him on my doorstep one evening. Although I felt little warmth for the man, I still felt obligated to invite him in. He carried with him a small parcel wrapped in brown paper and tied up with heavy twine.

"I have your legacy here," he said, by way of explanation. He placed the package on a side table and shrugged off his heavy wool overcoat and hung it on the rack in the hall. It was a familiar action on his part, and it jarred me to see it again in my own home. I felt very ill at ease in his presence and did not know how to respond.

"I know that you believe that I have not been a very good father to you," he said. "I did not lavish the kind of attention on you in your formative years that another parent might have. I felt that to do so would weaken you and turn you into one of those men who are less than men. Now that you are grown, I can see that I was right to do so. You have a hardness of character about you that bodes well for your ability to take care of yourself. I always felt that independence was the greatest gift I could give a son. No, don't thank me. I hope you will do the same for your child someday. Never mind that now. I don't have much time and there is much that you need to know."

He took me by the arm and led me into the parlor. It was an old house that I had taken, one that could be dated all the way back to the mid-nineteenth century. He sat down opposite me, placed his parcel on the table between us and began to speak quietly. "Perhaps you may have wondered why I have had so few friends and acquaintances over the years, and why during your childhood we kept moving to a new place every few months. Perhaps you have wondered why I have kept such distance from you for the past few years, not even trying to seek you out. All of this has been for your own protection. I did not want *him* to find you."

"After I leave, you will be free to forget me as you will; I will not trouble you again. I will leave this package with you. You may do with it as you wish. But I must caution you, that if you accept delivery of this, your life may be in terrible danger, the worst kind of danger you can imagine. No, even worse than you can imagine. You may examine the contents of the package, as I did when I was your age. You may toss it on the fire, as I was tempted to. You may choose to pass it on to your own son, someday. Or you may feel that the time is right to reveal this information. The choice will be yours, as it was mine. Perhaps I made mistakes, but…I did the best I could. If you must curse someone, curse your grandfather, because it was he who first accepted custody of this—this secret."

I had only the dimmest memories of my grandfather. He died when I was very young. He had always seemed a nervous man to me. Whatever secret my father was about to impart, he certainly had my attention now. I had never seen the man act like this before. In the space of the past few moments, he had said more words to me than he had said during the entire last year we had lived together under the same roof. Incongruously, all I could think to say was, "Would you like some tea?" I simply wanted to acknowledge his attention in some way and indicate that regardless of all else that had passed between us, he still had my grudging respect.

My father blinked at me in confusion as well as in some annoyance. His train of thought had been derailed by the question. But his features eased at the thought of my hospitality; perhaps he took it as a sign that I held some gratitude for his actions, or even affection. Perhaps I did; my own thoughts were not clear to me at that point, I was so confused by his confession. I hurried to the kitchen to put the kettle on. My face was flushed with embarrassment. My curiosity had been terribly aroused by his long preamble, and now we would both have to delay the denouement that much longer.

Shortly, however, the kettle was boiling and the tea was brewing in the ceramic pot between us, filling the room with friendly and reassuring vapors. As I placed a tray of biscuits on the table—that I had baked myself only this morning—my father resumed his narrative.

"Your grandfather," he said portentously, "was the nephew of the famous Dr. Watson—yes, *that* Dr. Watson." He paused to let that sink in.

I had known that there was some secret about our family's past, simply due to my father's reluctance to discuss it with me; but I had always assumed it was something criminal in nature. Possibly a relative who had been hung for stealing horses or some other great disgrace. "I'm afraid I don't understand you. Why should that be something to keep secret? It seems to me that we should be proud of our ancestor."

My father tapped the parcel on the table. "When you read this, you will understand. This is the *truth* about his so-called adventures. I'm going to leave this with you. It's yours now. If you want my advice, you'll toss it in the fire and be done with it. Because once you open it, once you read it, you'll never know a peaceful night again."

He finished his tea in a single swallow, glanced impatiently at his watch—more for performance, I believe, than because he had a schedule to keep—and rose immediately from his chair. "I must go now. But I'll give you one last piece of advice, perhaps the most important piece of advice I can ever give you, and you will have to take it as an acknowledgment of how much I truly do care about you and how proud I am of what you have made of yourself. Whatever you do, son, wherever you go, keep yourself secret. Keep yourself impossible to trace. Leave no record of where you may be found. It will save your life. Believe me."

And then he was gone. He slipped back into his dark old overcoat and vanished into the night as abruptly and mysteriously as he had come. The parcel remained unopened on my parlor table.

Now, at this point, perhaps I should explain a little bit about who I am. I am a single man in my late thirties; I live alone in an old house. I have never wed; I have no children, no pets, and I keep mostly to myself. I believe that this is in no small part due to the disruptive nature of my upbringing; deprived as I was of the opportunity to form attachments during my impressionable years, I have almost no social skills at all. Rather than inflict my clumsy fumblings at friendship on others, I prefer to live vicariously through the many volumes of books I have managed to collect over the years.

That my father had presented me with what was obviously an unpublished manuscript either about or by the famous Dr. Watson was an act of overwhelming generosity to me; but the manner of his presentation was so disturbing that it left me troubled and upset beyond my ability to describe. Perhaps another person would have opened the manuscript immediately, but I was in such a state from my father's visit that it was all I could do to finish my tea and wash the cups. I allowed myself the luxury of a long hot bath to calm my nerves and then went immediately to bed. I would resolve what to do about the package the following morning.

To my dismay, the package was still in the parlor the next day. I had hoped that my father's visit would have turned out to have been merely an apparition of a troubled sleep. But no such luck. Nor had anyone broken into the house and made off with the mysterious parcel either. Whatever it contained, it was still my responsibility.

After a meager breakfast of tea, toast and marmalade and a single soft-boiled egg, I sat down in the parlor and prepared to examine my "legacy." There were twenty-three handwritten pages. The writing was hurried and crabbed, as if the author was working under great stress. In some places, it was nearly indecipherable.

I worked my way slowly through the pages, reading them carefully, not going onto the next until I was fully certain I had understood everything before. When I finished, my thoughts were in greater turmoil than ever. Had I not been presented with this manuscript by the hand of my very own father, I would have been absolutely certain that this was the most elaborate literary hoax in history.

If even the smallest part of the manuscript was true, then my father was right; my life was in terrible danger. I could do nothing to validate the truth of this information without calling attention to myself and giving *him* a clue to my whereabouts as well as my *when*abouts.

After thinking about this for several days, I decided to make typescript copies of the pages, have them duplicated, and distribute them via as many channels as possible to prevent *him* from interfering with the eventual publication.

I know that most people who read these words will blithely assume that this is merely a clever piece of fiction and will casually dismiss it. However, if even one or two people who are in a position to act will take this revelation seriously, then we may be able to stop *him* before it is too late. I am sure that your curiosity is now sufficiently aroused. With that in mind, I will now get out of your way and let you read the pages of my grandfather's last story.

DR. WATSON'S TALE

Subsequent to the success of my literary efforts for the *Strand* magazine, a great deal of attention has been focused on the personal affairs of Sherlock Holmes and myself. Much of this attention has been quite unwelcome, especially those amateur analyses and salacious speculations into the nature of our relationship. I can only assume that those who waste their energies in such efforts have much too much time on their hands.

The truth is that our relationship was entirely professional in nature. Holmes and I had early entered into a partnership of convenience, which subsequently proved to be of greater mutual benefit than either of us had originally conceived. Consequently, we were stuck, as it were, with the situation as it evolved. We were holding a tiger by the tail. Neither of us could extricate himself from the partnership without the risk of considerable personal damage, and I think that neither of us really wanted to *try* to let go of the tail of this particular tiger. Together, we had both fame and fortune. Apart, who knew what we might have?

Although we shared a high regard for each other's abilities, in truth, there was little real affection between us. Mostly, we needed each other's particular abilities. Holmes had a native shrewdness and cunning which transcended his somewhat meager intellect; I had some skills, not as a reporter, but as a fabricator of tales.

Indeed, this is the substance of my confession—that Sherlock Holmes as he was known by the general public on both sides of the Atlantic *simply did not exist*. He was a total fabrication.

Let me state it clearly at the beginning that I make no claims of innocence in this accounting. I am as guilty of fraud as the man who posed as Holmes. (For simplicity's sake, I shall refer to him as Holmes throughout the rest of this manuscript.) Although most of the physical circumstances of Holmes' illustrious career were engineered by the man who was generally known as Holmes, the literary creation of Sherlock Holmes as a superlative intellect, skilled in the art of criminal deduction, was entirely a work of fiction, and that is the part of the fraud for which I must claim authorship. It greatly amused both of us to have created such a remarkable public figure as Sherlock Holmes, eminent detective.

This is not to say that Holmes did not solve the cases he did. In fact, he had the most astonishing degree of success in resolving criminal matters of any detective then or since, a fact which brought no small degree of distress to the late Inspector Lestrade. Even those incidents which were never fully described in my public writings, such as the curious affair of the Giant Rat of Sumatra, were well-known among the investigators of Scotland Yard as evidence of Holmes' incredible facility with the facts.

There was a remark I gave to Holmes in one of my stories, *The Sign of Four*: "When you have eliminated the impossible, whatever remains, however improbable, must be the truth." Holmes found this epigram so clever that after he read it in print, he began using it in his daily conversation; he was not without vanity, and on more than one occasion I literally had to drag him away from gathering admirers. This frequently annoyed him. He enjoyed the swoons of impressionable young women and the hearty congratulations of naive bystanders; but I was afraid that he might inadvertently say something so at odds with what the public believed about him that he would trigger a cascade of embarrassing questions and investigations that would leave us both destroyed. I felt then, and I still feel, that an impenetrable air of mystery would serve us both.

Even with this instruction waved so blandly in the face of the authorities, not a single one of them ever followed the thought to its natural conclusion and realized that Holmes was taunting them to figure out the real truth for his remarkable string of successes.

I must pause here to acknowledge that even at this late date I find it difficult to discuss the matter of the curious belt candidly. It seems to me a betrayal of everything that both of us worked so long and hard to create. Nevertheless, I feel compelled to impart to paper the real explanation of Holmes' skill.

The man who the public later came to know as Sherlock Holmes first approached me after the death of my beloved wife, Tess. He said he had a proposition for me. He was an American; he had that dreadful flat nasal quality in his voice that identifies the speaker as a native of that nation where the King's English has been systematically abused for generations. His name was Daniel James Eakins, and he said he was from the state of California. When I pointed out to him that California was still a territory, not yet a state, he flushed with embarrassment and begged my apology; sometimes he forgot *when* he was.

"'When?' What a curious way of phrasing," I remarked.

Then he told me a curious tale.

"Imagine," he said, "that all of time is laid out like an avenue. If we walk west along this way, we shall find ourselves in Thursday, next. But if we walk east far enough, we may travel back to last Sunday's partridge dinner. What would you do if you had such a power?"

"A fanciful conceit," I admitted. "You should try your hand at writing. Perhaps the *Strand* might be interested in such a fantasy."

"But what if I told you it were not a conceit, Dr. Watson? What if a device existed that would allow you to walk the avenues of time?"

"It strikes me as a very dangerous invention. What if you killed your grandfather before your father was born?"

"Nothing happens," he said. "I tried it. Paradoxes are impossible. He died. I remained." He then lifted up his waistcoat to reveal that he was wearing a most curious belt and harness affair. "This is a timebelt," he said. "With it I can travel anywhen I want to."

This was such an outlandish claim that I was immediately certain that the man had escaped from one of those facilities used for detaining the dangerously insane.

"I know what you're thinking," he said. "I shall give you proof. Right now." He pulled a newspaper out of his pocket, the *Evening Standard*, and placed it before me. "Look at the date," he said. The newspaper was tomorrow's evening edition. "Keep this paper. Wait twenty-four hours. Then buy a copy of the *Standard*. If the two are identical, you will have to ask yourself, how did I come by this paper before it was printed? I went forward in time and brought it back. That's how."

I examined the paper carefully. If this was a hoax, it was an elaborate one. And if it were a hoax, why invest so much time and energy in the creation of a document that could be proven false so easily?

It was at this point that my eye fell upon a small article in the lower left corner of the page. The headline said TREVOR MYSTERY RE-MAINS UNSOLVED. I pointed to that and said, "Perhaps your machine would allow you to travel backward to the day of this tragedy and prevent it?"

He took the paper from me and studied the article. "Perhaps indeed," he agreed. "I shall be back momentarily" and he stepped out the door with never a by-your-leave. He returned almost immediately, but this time he was wearing a totally different costume, something he had no doubt picked up in one of the more expensive booths at Harrods; a deerstalker cap and cane, a baroque pipe after the German fashion and a long gray fogcoat. I had seen quick-change artists in the theater before, but off the stage, such a feat of physical prowess was startling. Mister Eakins was also carrying another newspaper which he brandished at me proudly.

It was the same newspaper, only this time the headline read, PRI-VATE DETECTIVE SOLVES TREVOR MYSTERY. I read it aloud, "Mr. Sherlock Holmes of 221-B Baker street—" I looked up at him, dismayed. "Why, that's my address."

"Yes, it is," he said. "That's very astute of you, my good Watson. I had to tell the reporters something. If you don't like it, I will tell them something else. Come, the game is afoot. This is tomorrow's newspaper. If this story is to come true, we must go to the police now and tell them about the code in the mysterious message. If you read every third word in the note, you'll see that it says something quite different altogether."

I shall not repeat the details of that case here. It is fully reported in my story, *The Gloria Scott*. I wish only to establish that this was the first case in which Eakins-who-became-Holmes involved himself, much to the annoyance of the police.

As we walked, I observed a curious transformation coming over Mr. Eakins. He had somehow lost his dreadful American twang and was sounding more and more like a proper gentleman. When I remarked on this, he acknowledged that he had studied stagecraft for many years and had developed an impressive skill at adopting the speech mannerisms and dialects of others. He said he found the "English accent" charming. *Charming* indeed! Nevertheless, to give him credit, within a very short time his speech had become as clear as a native-born gentleman's.

Eakins reported the basic facts of the case to Inspector Lestrade without explaining how he had come to learn them. The good man listened politely at first, then with growing irritation. "Who are you?" he demanded. "Why should I take you seriously?"

At this point, Mr. Eakins bowed politely and introduced himself as, "Sherlock Holmes, at your service." He had a most self-satisfied expression as he did. "And this is my associate, Dr. John Watson. We are private investigators, and we are happy to make our services available to you, Inspector."

It was here that Lestrade asked the question that shaped all of our later destinies. "How did you find this out?" he demanded. "My top men have been working on this case for a week and a half."

For just a moment, Holmes-née-Eakins appeared flustered. He had not considered how he would explain how he had obtained his knowledge, and it was obvious that he did not want to reveal to anyone else the secret of his time traveling device. I felt sorry for him at that moment; he had demonstrated such power, and he did not know how to use it. That is why I came to his rescue. "Mr. Holmes has developed a methodology of criminal deduction. Over the years he has worked on his theories and philosophies about the nature of the criminal mind, and he finally feels confidant enough to put his hypotheses to the test." Both Holmes and Lestrade were looking at me curiously now. I bulled ahead.

"For instance, it is obvious even to an untrained eye like myself that you have a stain on your waistcoat, Inspector. But to Holmes' trained powers of observation, that is clearly a stain from a steak and kidney pie purchased from the stall on the other side of the mews. Indeed, as we made our way across the street, Holmes pointed the meat pies out to me and predicted that an investigation of police vests and waistcoats and ties would probably reveal the entire menu of comestibles available in a three-block radius."

Lestrade stared at me speechless. Holmes (as I was now beginning to think of him) was beaming with pride. To Lestrade, he said, "Dr. Watson is correct. Others only see, but I *observe*. That is the difference, Inspector. If you wish a full accounting of *how* I applied my deductive techniques to solve the mystery, you shall have to purchase a copy of next month's *Strand*. For Dr. Watson intends to write it for publication." And with that, we swept out.

That is how the whole affair began.

Over the years, Holmes became quite the talk of London. He used his time machine and his acting skills to whisk himself back and forth about the scene of a crime, observing everything he could. Then, taking the raw facts of his observations as grist for my literary mill, I would carefully craft about them a tale of deduction and intellect to inspire even the dullest of readers. Holmes was delighted at my invention, and I was equally pleased to be a part of such a delicious game at the expense of the authorities.

I do not ask for forgiveness. I believe that both Holmes and myself passed beyond forgiveness very early on. On more than one occasion, I asked Holmes if instead of *solving* the mystery, could he use his time machine to *prevent* the tragedy. Every time I raised the question, Holmes reacted angrily. "If we did that, there would be no mystery to solve!" He snapped in annoyance. "We would be out of business. I would have no fame and you would have no stories to write."

"Nevertheless, Holmes," I said, "you and I are taking a profit on the miseries of others, and I cannot help but feel that we are acting amorally. It is abhorrent to me."

Holmes regarded me dispassionately for a moment, as if trying to decide just what he should or shouldn't say. Abruptly, he apologized for his flash of irritation. "I am tired and I'm feeling a bit peckish. Please forgive me." Then he added, "Besides, my dear Watson, we *cannot* change the timestream. Not without serious risk to ourselves and others." He then expounded at length on matters totally incomprehensible to me; I remember only a few of the word and phrases: " ...continuity disasters, the dangers of cross-cutting, unbegun happenings...." I was not totally convinced by all of this fancy explanation, for I remembered his casual remark on the first day I met him that he had killed his grandfather, and it occurred to me, seeing his anger on the subject, that he would be equally willing to kill anyone else who opposed him. His time device gave him the power to murder with impugnity, and I often justified my participation in the whole affair by telling myself that at least this way we were serving the cause of justice.

There were, however, several who suspected that Holmes was not all he appeared to be. Moriarty for one. The affair at Reichenbach Falls caused no small amount of distress to a great many people. Afterward, Holmes told me that he knew he was never in any danger because he had observed the whole incident several times before he actually allowed himself to participate in it.

While I have elsewhere detailed the blackguardly behavior of the arch-fiend, Moriarty, I must now confess a strange admiration for the man, and in fact, on several occasions, I found myself wishing that he would actually succeed in killing Holmes and freeing me from the velvet trap in which I had found myself. But over and over again, Moriarty's intricate schemes came collapsing down around his shoulders at the hands of Holmes, until finally I realized that Holmes was toying with the villain as a cat toys with a frantic mouse. Holmes never had any intention of capturing the man and ending his crime spree once and for all. Rather, he needed Moriarty to succeed just enough so that he, Holmes, could continue to flourish as his justice-serving opponent.

It was at this point that I realized the absolute corruption of power. Holmes had developed such an arrogance toward other mortals that he no longer regarded himself as bound by their rules. And likewise, I recognized that my life depended only my ability to provide continued service to him—at least until he tired of the game.

I have realized that there is no way that I can make any of this information public. Not even after my own death, not even after Holmes'. For with his time-traveling device, he can easily travel far into the future to see how history has regarded the both of us. Should he discover the publication of any manuscript detailing the truth of our exploits, he would know that I had been ultimate source of the revelation. It would be a simple matter for him to return to our time and strangle me before these pages could even be written. My only protection, indeed the only protection for any of my heirs, is for us to keep this secret throughout all time. For I have no doubt in my mind that the man who is known as Holmes will track us down and kill us to prevent this truth becoming known.

After observing his ability to escape death over and over again, I have no choice but to assume that Holmes is effectively immortal, at least as immortal as it is possible for any man to be. If there is a way to immobilize the monster, I have not yet devised it.

But, now it is time for me to complete this piece and put it in a safe place. My next paper will detail my thoughts on how it may be possible to stop Holmes once and for all.

I shall now give this manuscript to one whom I trust and ask him to pray for us all. May God have mercy on my soul!

EDITOR'S NOTE: *The manuscript ends here. No second part has yet been found, and all attempts to contact the author or owner of the piece have met with failure. If anyone has any information on how to find the heirs of Dr. John Watson please contact me c/o this publisher.*

The reason Resnick keeps ragging on me is because he admires my ability to deliver a low-yield tactical cheap shot. Next time, he'll ask how my blood sugar is before asking me for a story.

The Feathered Mastodon

OKAY, I HEREBY PUBLICLY APOLOGIZE for pushing Mike Resnick into the La Brea Tar Pits. I did it. I'm sorry.

I won't try to excuse it by saying it was poor impulse control on my part—after all I did smack him with two feather pillows, and the fact that I'd brought the pillows along was clear proof that the ~~attack~~ stunt was premeditated. So I plead guilty for that and I apologize.

But I'm not going to give the money back. If the purchasing agent at the Page Museum was stupid enough to believe my story about having cloned a feathered mastodon, then that's his fault and his employer's responsibility.

But I do want to apologize to Bantam Books for spoiling their traditional Worldcon dinner excursion. They'd rented a big bus, filled it with beer and schlepped all of their most willing writers—those who hadn't found other obligations with other publishers—off on the science fiction version of a magical mystery tour. Tom Dupree has already told me that I'm not likely to be invited back, and that's probably punishment enough, I guess.

Tom also told me how much it cost to have the emergency vehicle called—they had to call in one of those extra-huge cranes that they use for lifting boxcars to hoist Resnick out of the sticky black oil. He looked like a giant fudgsicle—or a Godzilla turd—and while he was hanging there, all gooey and dripping and glumphing unintelligible threats, that's when I slit open the feather pillows and whacked him with them.

It was expensive, but—what the hell, even though I've apologized, I have to admit it was worth it. But Tom says they're going to take it out of my royalties. Like that's a threat. Maybe if they'd sell some books, I could get some royalties once in a while.

But I'm not worried. Even though the SFWA Defense Fund turned down my requests for legal aid, there are enough other former contributors to Resnick anthologies who have sent me generous checks—enough that I should be able to mount a credible defense. Just contributing a story to a Resnick anthology goes a long way toward proving temporary insanity.

Okay, yes, he deserved it—there's no question that he had it coming. He shouldn't have said what he said. He shouldn't have said it on camera. And most of all, he shouldn't have sent me a videotape of him saying it in front of an audience of three thousand people.

The only reason I'm apologizing now is that I didn't know about his skin condition and how when the oil and the tar seeped through his skin, that it would render him sterile and impotent—kind of a chemical castration.

While all the behind-the-back jokes about Resnick's new career as a harem guard, and how he's now in demand for the soprano lead in *La Castrata*, have been funny in their own sick way, the fact is I'm really starting to feel bad about all this. The doctors say it's unlikely that Resnick will ever grow another follicle of hair anywhere on his entire body— some kind of interaction with the pollutants in the tar—and because he has to wear those rubber pants because of the resultant incontinence problem, he looks sort of like a 300-pound baby. And they say he cries a lot too. Especially when the male nurses come to change him.

So, okay, I guess I'm not a very nice person. And this particular fraternity-level prank only proves that I'm not to be trusted out in public without a keeper. A simple pie in the face would have made the point just as easily and probably would have been a lot funnier too. But Resnick started it, so he deserves some of the blame. That remark about how "recombinant DNA splicing explains Gerrold's nose" *hurt*.

The thing is—Resnick should have known better.

It's no secret. Science fiction writers gossip. They talk about the stuff they've seen. Pournelle's been inside the space shuttle, Benford gets guided tours of particle smashers, Ben Bova got an advance peek at the—oops, not supposed to mention that one yet. But you get the idea. Where do you think we *really* get all our ideas? We hang out every year at the annual meeting of the American Association for the Advancement of Science—and hope for invitations to the real labs. And then we get drunk at the conventions and brag about what we've seen. I got invited to a tour of Intel's new fabrication plant. Ellison got to see a building demolished with a new small explosive named after him. Roddenberry once got a free tour of the whiskey museum in Edinborough.

In this case, I know that the research papers haven't been published yet, there aren't any articles yet in *Scientific American* or *Discover* magazine; only a few weird articles in the *National Enquirer* about potatoes with real eyes and hairless mice with purple mohawks. Oh, wait—there was that one thing in *Discover*, but it was in their April issue and everybody thought it was another one of their silly April Fool's jokes, like the particle the size of a bowling ball or the naked ice-borer that grabbed penguins from underneath.

But the fact is, they have been doing some serious gene-splicing work at—well, never mind. I could tell you, but then I'd have to hunt you down and kill you. Everyone who reads this. And that would seriously decimate the population of science fiction readers. Or maybe not. How many people read Resnick anthologies anyway? Not that many. The loss would hardly be noticed.

But anyway, I was invited up to a place in Marin County. It's funded by a couple of famous movie directors, you figure it out. This goes back more than fifteen years, when they first decided they wanted to do a dinosaur movie—only at that time nobody, not even Stan Winston's guys, could figure out how to coordinate all the separate machines necessary to create an illusion of real motion. That was when computers were still as big as refrigerators and cost more than Ferraris.

So that's when the dinosaur cloning project really began. They thought they'd make their movie with real dinosaurs. And maybe even open a park too—which is where they got the idea for the movie that did get made.

It wasn't done with amber—although that's sexier because it films better. It was really done by processing coal. Coal is really a compressed peat bog. And peat bogs are really good at preserving dead things—every so often somebody finds an ancient mummy in a bog. Well, sometimes they find dinosaur bones in coal—so if you process the coal immediately around the dinosaur bones, you get chains of DNA.

Most of it is damaged, of course. DNA doesn't last for eighty million years. But if you collate all the different chains, you can put them together and pretty much approximate what was there in the first place, and then you can plug them into ostrich eggs and see what you get. Mostly, you get deformed ostrich embryos. So that was pretty much a dead-end. It used up a lot of money, but the movies were paying for the research, and it was tax-deductible too, so the thing just chugged away, burning dollars and coal at the same rate.

But after a while, the guys in the lab coats decided to try something else. They thought, "Hey, why don't we back-breed from existing species of birds and reptiles until we match the dino DNA?" And so they started down that path with high hopes. That was another good way to use up millions of dollars a year. Pocket change.

Somehow, the back-breeding project took a side-turn. I think it was the time that they were trying to do all those weird fantasy movies. The Henson people were good with the puppets. The Winston people were getting better with the machines. The computers were getting smaller. But it still wasn't enough—and meanwhile, the guys in the labs had gotten a little stir-crazy—

Oh yeah, I should explain that. Because the whole thing was being done in such incredible secrecy, they had built this little city off in the hills north of the bay; the cover story was that it was a movie production facility—and they even built a real recording studio there as a kind of false front. But underneath it were the real labs. And because the work was so secret, the scientists and all the technicians were literally confined to the site. They were allowed to see their families only on Thanksgiving and Christmas. It was like being sent to Antarctica, but without the snow.

So, yeah—they got cabin fever. And they got crazy. It happens.

When I was in college—USC Film School, although I try not to admit it—one of the animation professors told us of a "tradition" at animation studios. Pornographic cartoons. Each animator would (on his own time) add a scene. The next animator would pick it up where the last guy left off. Back in the days of wild fraternity parties and pornographic movies—before VCR's—some of these animated films were floating around town. I remember one with a farmer and a donkey and...well, never mind. I also remember the instructor sighing wistfully. "Ours were good, but they were never as good as the ones coming out of Disney. Now those guys were great." I don't think any of the Disney stuff ever got off the lot though. I never saw any of it. I wonder sometimes if Walt did. I'd be surprised if he didn't.

Anyway, that's what started happening at Project Back-Breed. The DNA Team started mixing genes just to see what would happen. They weren't having any luck with anything else—they hadn't licked the viability problem, nothing lived; so they got desperate just to see if they could make *something* that would survive.

That's where the hairy chicken came from. They actually created a small flock of hairy chickens. They looked like furry bowling balls. They were hysterical to see—clucking around the yard like big fat tribbles. (That's why I got to see them. Otherwise, I'd never have been allowed near the place.) Two of them were fertile, so they were able to breed several generations by the time of my visit. All colors—blonde, brown, red, white, black, even one with a weird purplish tinge. They were pretty good eating too. They tasted like chicken. Of course.

After the hairy chicken, the DNA Team decided to try going the other way, to see if they could put feathers on a mammal. That was about the time someone had the bright idea of injecting an elephant with frozen mammoth sperm. They're always finding dead mammoths frozen in the Siberian glaciers, and it's not that hard to chip some sperm out of the ice, defrost it, do a test-tube fertilization and inject it into an unsuspecting elephant cow. The technology has been used on horses, pigs, sheep, cattle, dogs, mice, gorillas, chimps and even humans. So why not elephants? What's the worst that could happen, right?

Right. Somehow, the chicken DNA crossed the information highway.

Eventually, they tracked it back to a software error. This file and that file got crossed, so this DNA pattern got mixed with that DNA pattern—and the project was so big by that time and there was so much going on that nobody even noticed that this sample and that sample were from two different experiments, two different species—because that's what they were doing anyway, so it was just one more set of genes to be spliced—and the compatibility problem got knocked down as a matter of routine—and eventually the samples got processed and put into the pipeline and chugged along until—well, that's how they ended up with the feathered mammoth. Cute little thing.

Of course, the cow that delivered it practically died from the shock—but after a dose of prozac large enough to make New York polite, she cheered up and nursed the little guy as if he were her own calf—which he was, but he had this weird yellow down all over him. At first, everybody thought it was just normal fur, but when the first feathers started appearing six weeks later—let me tell you, there were a lot of questions asked and there were a lot of red faces too—but that could have been from the other experiment, the one about genetically redesigning already-living creatures. One of the retro-viruses had escaped, recombined, mutated and become airborne, and now half the team were evolving into Native Americans. So the red faces were normal by then.

Fortunately for everybody, there were a lot of filmic possibilities in weird animals. That was about the time Paramount was going to send Kirk and Spock to the Genesis planet, so they were looking for a cheap source of weird creatures as a way of keeping the special effects budget down, so they pumped some new money into the whole thing; two or three of the other studios also came aboard then, and in short order the guys in Marin were turning out all kinds of little monsters. Hairy chickens of all sizes—they were clumsy and unstable and a strong wind could knock them over and blow them like tumbleweeds—and that's how you saw them in *Critters*. And there was an ostrich with scales—supposed to look like a deinonychus, but ultimately unconvincing, I think the Corman people finally used it in a dog called *Carnosaur*. Carnivorous rabbits for *Lepus II*. Unmade. A green cat. (That one sold for nearly two million—but the cat died before the script went into turnaround. Pity, the merchandising on it would have been phenomenal. They were all set to breed a million green kittens in time for Christmas.)

And of course, the Feathered Mammoth. They were going to use him in something with Arnold Schwarzenegger, another Conan picture, I think, *Conan in Atlantis*, but it didn't happen either. The studio sunk it. Nobody really likes working with animals, children or Martians. They always use the Martian's best take. (But that's another story, the one about the Martians. When Resnick publishes *Alternate Martians*, I'll tell it. If they let him edit any more of these. I doubt it after this one, but who knows—they say it's good work-therapy at the outpatient clinic, so who am I to piss in his oatmeal? We all wish him a speedy recovery. Well, most of us do. Well, his family anyway. I think.)

But eventually—finally—they did manage to back-breed some real dinosaurs. Sort of.

The problem was they were working with frog and lizard and bird eggs, so the dinosaurs they got were small. Miniature. The size of Dinky toys. That's what they called them at the farm. Dinky Dinos. Stegasaurs as cute as hamsters. Hadrosaurs that looked like parakeets. A T. Rex the size of a crow. It took a lot of really skillful trick photography to make them look full size for the movie. (I hear they're going to start selling the Dinky Dinos in pet stores next year, simultaneous with the release of the sequel. That'll be interesting when Daddy brings home a little T. Rex as a birthday present for little Jill.)

What you didn't hear about—what nobody heard about—were the raptors. Three of them escaped.

At first nobody on the farm worried about it. There was a chronic problem with rats in the feedstock, so they had brought in terriers, and later on a few wild tomcats had joined the menagerie, too. That had kept the problem manageable—sort of. The cats killed as many lizards and birds as they did rats—so the guys at the farm figured the pussies and the pooches would probably kill the raptors too, thinking they were just some kind of lizard-bird. Only it didn't happen that way.

First, the rats disappeared. And the mice. And the gophers and the skunks and the badgers ("Badgers? Badgers? We don' need no steen-keen' badgers!") and the rabbits and the weasels and the foxes and the coyotes and everything else small enough to be brought down by a pack of land-piranhas. And of course, the pooches and the pussies too.

By that time, the raptors were numbering nearly thirty. They traveled in packs—five or seven to a group. At any given time there were between four and six packs of them roaming the grounds of the farm, chirruping and cooing like demented pigeons, their little heads bobbing back and forth, turning this way and that, their tails lashing frantically. They were brightly colored—the males were green or blue, with yellow flares of color down their backs and bright red stippling around their heads and forearms. The females were drab gray-green. The females traveled together; the males kept apart from them, except during mating season—then it wasn't safe to get out of your car unless you were wearing heavy boots.

It wasn't until the raptors started bringing down the newborn calves that the farm guys realized the problem was out of control; they brought in some tropical quarantine experts who laid out slabs of meat laced with poison cocktails. That got half of them; the other half got smarter. So they tried traps. And retro-viruses. And hunter-killer droids—that was another nightmare. The software mutated—remember the law of unintended consequences? The ex-terminators (formerly terminators, now just ex-terminators) shot at anything that moved—or even looked like it was thinking about moving. Finally, they cut power to the feed lines and the ex-terminators ran out of juice after two or three more weeks. Meanwhile, they still had a raptor problem.

They finally got them with pheromones. They put out lures that smelled like female raptors in heat and all the males couldn't help themselves; they came sniffing around the lures and tumbled through trap doors into little tar pits where they died like dire wolves and sa-bre-toothed cats and mastodons in prehistoric Los Angeles. (L.A. needs more tar pits. There are still too many sabre-toothed lawyers and dire agents and studio mammoths staggering around the countryside.)

That should have been the end of it, but it wasn't. By this time, the guys upstairs were so pissed they were ready to shut the whole opera-tion down. The DNA Team had to get rid of the remaining raptors, so they donated them to the San Francisco zoo. Oh, that was smart. On the one hand, there are no rats in San Francisco any more. On the other hand, there are no stray animals either. You have to keep your cat in the house, and it's not safe to walk your Chihuahua.

All of which has nothing to do with Resnick directly, except that he was supposed to be part of the solution, not part of the precipitate. In-stead, he ended up in the pits. Down in the mouth...and all his other orifices as well.

See, Resnick had been doing this whole series of anthologies—Al-ternate Nightmares, Alternate Sexes, Alternate Bicycles—whatever he thought would sell. And he had sold one called Alternate Dinosaurs or something like that. Who keeps track? And the publishers had decided that it would be fun to do some kind of tie-in with all the dinosaur mov-ies, but they couldn't afford much of a licensing fee, and the only one they could link up with was that dreadful turkey Fox was making—The Feathered Mastodon. In fact, that's what it was about—a dreadful tur-key—and the mastodon was playing the lead.

And so they sent Resnick out west to have his picture taken with the critter, and there they were, the two of them, side by side—and I was there too with my kid and my video camera, and I forgot that everything I said while taping would be heard on the tape, so when I sent Resnick a copy of the tape he could hear me saying clearly, "The family resemblance is astonishing. They both have the same birthmark in the shape of an Edsel."

I guess Resnick felt he had to get even. So there he was at the secret convention of trufans, held in Moscow, Idaho, every February, and he was still smarting over the tape I'd just sent him, and that's when he said what he said, and that's why I pushed him in the tar and smacked him with the pillows. And then, while no one was looking, also injected him with a cocktail of kangaroo, frog and lizard DNA, with a chaser of growth hormone.

Things should start hopping around the Resnick household Real Soon Now. I'd move out of the state if I were you. In the meantime, I've sold an anthology to Tor called *Alternate Resnicks*. Watch for it in the bookstores, next fall.

A deal with the devil? I'll give you a deal with the devil....

The Seminar From Hell

AFTER A MOMENT, the sad-looking woman approached the registration table. Her husband followed with visible resignation. "Is this the...seminar?" the woman asked with obvious embarrassment.

The attractive young hostess behind the table smiled warmly at the both of them. Her nametag identified her as Tia. "Yes, you're in the right place. This is the Nine Circles Corporation. Welcome to our Introduction Seminar." She slid two beige cards across the table to them, and two pencils as well. "Please fill out a guest card."

The woman hesitated. "Nobody's going to call us, are they? We don't want to be pressured."

"We don't pressure people," Tia said. "And yes, we do make one follow-up call to find out if you enjoyed the evening or have any additional questions or concerns that didn't get answered."

"We just don't want our name on some list...."

Tia's smile was warm and sincere. "You're our guests. We like to know who you are."

The woman sighed and picked up the pencil. She filled out the card slowly. Tia pushed the other card at the husband. Reluctantly, he followed his wife's lead. Both of them looked sorry and ashamed, as if by being here they were admitting all the failures of their lives. They finished filling in their names and addresses and passed the cards back.

142

Tia glanced at the tan guest cards and quickly filled out two name-tags. "Here you are, Maggie," she twinkled. Robot-like, Maggie peeled off the backing and stuck the nametag to her coat. "And here's yours, George. Thank you for being here."

"Do I have to wear a nametag?" George glowered at the invasion.

"Yes, I'm afraid so. The Seminar Leader likes to know who he's talking to."

"Who's leading the seminar?" George asked suspiciously.

"His name is Steven Keyes, and you'll find that he's absolutely the *best*. If you have any questions at all, just ask any of the assistants who are wearing gold nametags like mine." Tia indicated the badge over her heart. "I'm sure you'll have a great time tonight. The promise of this evening is that abundance is your divine right."

"*Divine?*"

"That's right," Tia said. "The Nine Circles Corporation is committed to success—*everyone's*."

"Yeah?" George grunted skeptically. "What's the catch?"

Tia's bright smile deflected George's remark as if it hadn't even been spoken. "All your questions will be answered in the seminar, I'm sure." She gestured toward the waiting door. "I hope you enjoy yourselves."

Maggie plucked at her husband's sleeve in a gesture that said more than "Let's go in." It also implied, "Please don't make a scene." In the language of husbands and wives, the shorthand was unmistakable. George allowed himself to be pulled away, and the two of them headed nervously toward the meeting room. Tia turned her attention to the next group of people waiting to sign in.

Inside, the rows of chairs were filling quickly. Maggie kept her gaze low. As curious as she was, she didn't really want anyone else to see her here. If she didn't look around, she believed, then no one else would have the right to look back at her. Nevertheless, after a moment, her curiosity won out and she began taking sly peeks at the other people in the room.

All around them, snappily dressed assistants stood at strategic intervals, smiling and eager to serve. All of the assistants looked healthy and fresh. One vigorous-looking fellow glided up and asked them to please fill up the seats toward the front. After a moment's hesitation, George and Maggie complied without argument, but they moved deeper into the room with obvious reluctance. Sitting too close to the front would make it harder to sneak out later if they got uncomfortable with what they were hearing.

"Well, they're certainly slick," George muttered resentfully as he took his seat. He folded his arms across his chest; his signal that he had brought his body here, but not his willingness.

When almost all of the chairs were filled, someone in the back began applauding. Soon, everyone was clapping excitedly. Then, as the applause reached its peak, the seminar leader came up the center aisle from the back of the room and leapt happily onto the stage—he almost bounced, he was so light on his feet. Although his hair was a graceful mane of white, he seemed ageless. He wore a light tan suit that glittered like gold. Maggie thought he looked like a movie star; George thought he looked like a Hollywood phony.

"Hello!" he called broadly. "Good evening! How are you? This isn't television—you can say hello back!" He looked out over the room, as if recognizing everyone there and acknowledging the applause of all of them. "Thank you, thank you," he said, smiling and waving at all the guests and assistants.

"Thank you all for that very warm welcome," he began when the applause finally died down. "My name is Steven Keyes, and I'm the seminar leader from Hell." He paused to acknowledge the laughter. Some of it was very nervous. "I want to thank you all for being here tonight. I know there are a lot of other places you could be. Not many people want to go to Hell. And certainly not on a school night." More laughter, this time a lot less nervous. It was all right to laugh here.

"In fact," he added, "Most people don't even want to *know* about Hell, so I have to acknowledge your courage just for coming into the room. That's right." He nodded, sharing his understanding with them.

Maggie settled herself in her seat comfortably. Whatever else he might be, Mr. Keyes was certainly charming. She had no intention of signing up for anything, but at least she could enjoy listening to what he had to say. She glanced over at George. His expression remained a resolute frown.

"Listen—" Steven Keyes held up a hand, grinning out at the crowd. "You've got to recognize the difficulty of my job here. Most people come in here, they've already got their minds made up. Hell isn't a nice place. And those of us who speak for it aren't to be trusted. Yes? Admit it—how many of you came in here tonight just a little bit afraid for your immortal souls? Hold up your hands high. That's right. Hold 'em high so everybody can see. Look around . . . ."

Despite themselves, George and Maggie slowly raised their hands. They glanced quickly around at the rest of the room and saw that most of the other people wearing guest-tags were also holding their hands up in the air.

"You see?' said Steven Keyes. "You're not alone. Okay, you can put your hands down now." His smile disappeared and he became deadly serious for a moment. "I want you to notice something here. Despite being afraid, just like you, all of these people still showed up. *You* showed up. *Why?* Because . . . despite what you've heard, despite what you think, despite what you might be afraid of, you are still *curious* enough that there might be something here—something that just might be worth your taking the time to find out *more* about it." Steven Keyes glanced around the room, shifting his gaze from person to person, and for a moment, Maggie felt he was looking straight into her heart. She glanced quickly at George, but if he had felt anything, he didn't show it.

"You want to acknowledge yourselves for that," Keyes said with almost painful directness. "Yes, you do. Because you're not letting someone else's opinion keep you from finding out for yourselves what Nine Circles really has to offer. You didn't let someone else tell you—"

Abruptly, he interrupted himself to make an additional point, gesturing with certainty and confidence. "Listen, I know how difficult it was to get here. A few years ago, I was sitting out there where you are now, wondering what kind of a con game or racket this was. And there were people in my life, too, who were telling me not to come, just like there are probably people in your life, too, who have told you that this is the wrong thing to do. They've probably said something like, 'Be careful! Don't put yourself at risk!' Am I right?" He glanced around the room. Several of the guests were nodding in agreement. He laughed; the sound was infectious. "I *am* right, aren't I?

"Well, do you want to know something?" Steven Keyes asked rhetorically. "Your friends were right. There *is* a risk here. But you've already mastered it. Just by being here, you're taking the chance that you might discover a way to be more effective and successful in your life than you have ever dreamed of before.

"You see, success—*real success*—is all about taking risks. You know that. You don't win anything by being comfortable. Comfort is a dead-end. It's a trap. Nine Circles is not about being comfortable. It's about being effective, successful and powerful—and *enjoying* every moment of it. And that means taking the biggest risk of all, *letting go of the past so you can grab hold of the future.*

"You had to take that risk to be here tonight. You had to risk being wrong in what you believed about us. You had to risk making the people around you wrong. You probably annoyed the hell out of your husbands, your wives, your family members, when you told them you were coming. Yes? I'll bet many of you have put some of your best friendships at risk just by being here. Yes? Yes?"

Maggie nodded to herself. She glanced over at George. He still had his arms folded across his chest, but he was listening.

"And you know what *else* you had to risk?" Keyes continued. "You had to risk your arrogance. That's right—*your arrogance.* Each of us, we're kind of arrogant in our lives. Yes, we are. We think we've got it all pretty well figured out. We know how to survive—and we do. We survive very well—so well in fact, that for a lot of us, mere survival looks a lot like success. Sometimes we get so good at it that we think survival *is* success.

"But, listen to me—it's all that attention on survival that keeps getting *in the way* of success. To succeed, you have to be willing to *not* know. You have to be willing to give up what you do know to find out what you don't know. And that means you have to give up your arrogance—and that's what you've done by being here. And I thank you for that. You've acknowledged that you can't afford the arrogance of not knowing something, the knowing of which might very well transform the quality *of the rest of your life.*"

Maggie's forehead creased in puzzlement. She wasn't sure she understood exactly what he was saying. Some of it sounded like pyschobabble, techno-jargon to her; but she was sure that Steven Keyes understood it, and if she just listened hard enough, perhaps she would get it too. Beside her, George was also frowning again.

"Look," said Steven Keyes, as if he was responding directly to her thoughts. "This isn't weird. It isn't mysterious. It's really very simple. What we're offering is the possibility that there's another whole way to *be.* It's the chance to have everything you've ever wanted, right here, right now. You shouldn't have to wait for your rewards. You're entitled to them *now.* You've earned them. It's just that simple."

He held up a hand as if to stop himself. "I'm not stupid. You're not stupid. We *all* know that you can't get something for nothing. That's the way the universe works. The Nine Circles Corporation is offering a service here—and you want to know what it's going to cost you.

"I know what the *other side* has said about us. So do you. The other side says that we're trying to trick you out of your immortal soul…." He looked around the room expectantly, smiling and nodding. "Yes?" he asked. "Isn't that what they say?" He held up his hands again, spreading them wide and open. "But did you ever stop to ask yourself what is the other side *trying* to do? *What do they want?*"

Keyes waited a moment, letting his audience consider the answer to that question. He looked around the room, studying their faces, watching to see if his words had had the desired effect. They had. Some of the faces looked angry, others looked amused, still others were worried at the implication of the thought.

Maggie had never considered this thought before. It troubled her. She slipped her hand sideways, into George's. He let her put her hand in his, but she could tell he was too preoccupied with his own thoughts to acknowledge the gesture.

"Listen," Steven Keyes was saying. "You don't need me to tell you. You've heard it all your life what *they want* from you—not what they're going to do for you, but what you have to do for them. They want you to forego the pleasures and rewards of this world. In return, they promise you the *unspecified* pleasures and rewards of the next world. They want you to live a life of deprivation and sacrifice, they want you to live in guilt and shame for all of your days, confessing and repenting your sins, begging their forgiveness, so you can attain worthiness—*but in exchange for what?* Just what are the rewards of the next world? Have you ever noticed that they never tell you!"

Keyes sounded angry, as if raging at a colossal betrayal. His anger resonated throughout the room. Maggie glanced around nervously. Other people looked equally unhappy with this news. She didn't know how she felt about it. She felt torn and confused.

"I'll tell you what they want," said Keyes. "They want the same thing we do. They *want* your immortal soul! That's right—*they* want your souls too." He stepped forward to the edge of the podium, leaning out toward his audience. "And they don't even have the honesty to offer you something in exchange for it. *They* just keep saying, 'Trust me!' Well, you're big boys and girls. You know what 'trust me' means in the real world. You've been there. Would you trust anyone who isn't willing to sign a contract? Would you buy a car that way? Or a house? Why would you trust your immortal soul to someone who says, 'Trust me?' We offer you signed contracts. Do they? No—but they'll give you all the *faith* you want. Try spending *that* at the supermarket."

Keyes was clearly warming to his subject now. He'd let his temper flash, just enough to be interesting. Now, he allowed his good-natured geniality to surface again. He unbuttoned his gold jacket; he hitched his thumbs into his waist band, stepped down off the podium and began pacing up and down the aisles like a high school math teacher drilling his students. He looked directly into people's eyes and spoke to them like old friends. Maggie put her fist to her chin and chewed worriedly on a nail. She didn't like this part.

"Let me tell you something," Steven Keyes said. "This is a business. I get paid for doing these talks. But even if I didn't get paid, I'd still do it, because I love the chance to work with people like you, people who care about themselves and their families and their futures. I have a family too. And a future. And I came to an event like this six years ago, just as worried as you about the direction my life was going. I'd lost my faith in the product offered by the *other side*. I'd tried it their way for nearly forty years and it didn't work. That's right. I'm forty-five years old. And no, I don't look it, do I? I've been invigorated. And you can be invigorated too. Listen—I was desperate. My life was a mess.

"Oh, my life looked ideal to those who didn't know. My wife and I had kids and dogs and two cars and a swimming pool and a house in the suburbs—but we weren't *happy*. We weren't having fun. The joy had leached out of our marriage and our lives. And one morning, I found myself standing in front of the mirror, thinking about work, thinking about family, thinking about bills and problems and all the little things that kept going wrong, thinking about gray hairs and gray days stretching out in front of me until I dropped dead either of a coronary or cirrhosis of the liver, thinking and thinking and holding my razor and wondering whether I should shave or slash my wrists—and that's when I knew I needed to *do something*.

"What I did was this—" He pointed to the floor where he stood. "I accepted an invitation to come to one of these seminars. And I came here just as skeptical and worried and fearful as each and every one of you probably is right now. I had just as many questions and concerns. And yes, I was just as apprehensive as you are now about being conned one more time—especially this time, when the stakes look to be so high. So I know what you want to hear, what you *need* to hear. Because I've been there myself.

"Let me start at the beginning. This used to be a protected market, this little rock we're living on. Six thousand years ago, nobody believed that human beings represented much of a commodity, certainly not a worthwhile market. Most of the services offered here in the far past were mom-and-pop operations, strictly local, strictly small-time. It wasn't until the Yahweh Corporation was granted a license for development that real growth became possible.

"Now, look. I'm not going to say bad things about them—that's not good business, in any case. And the fact is, they did a great job in elevating this market to a whole new standard of productivity in a very short time—only six thousand years. Look around. We're not shepherds anymore. We're a major industrial world. And that's the point. This market is now large enough and successful enough to support free competition. You deserve it. You've earned it. You have a right to a fair choice. That's what this is.

"They've had their monopoly long enough. They've made their money back, a long time ago. Now it's time to open up this arena. Over a thousand years ago, the Nine Circles Corporation began petitioning to have this market expanded. We've had to work very hard to prove ourselves—we've had to run a lot of pilot projects, but we've finally been granted full license to compete here. And that's put a real scare into the Yahweh people. So they're saying a lot of bad things about us, hoping to keep you so scared about who we are and what we represent that you won't even consider our services.

"Listen—they've had sole custody of the market for nearly six thousand years. Do you know what's happened to them? They've forgotten how to play on a level field. They've gotten complacent, lazy and arrogant...and worst of all, they aren't delivering the services they're promising. And that's not fair to you, because you have no other supplier—*until now.*"

Keyes still paced around the room. He stopped and looked directly at George and Maggie, startling them both in their chairs. "I know what you're thinking. No—not because I read minds. I don't. I know it because I've been there myself. You're asking yourself, the same way I did, six years ago, 'What is this wonderful product anyway?'" George shifted uncomfortably in his seat. Maggie felt flattered at the personal attention.

"Well, I'm going to tell you." Keyes said. "The product is something so intangible that when I tell you, you won't really hear me. You won't hear what I'm saying—you'll hear what you want to hear, or what you're afraid to hear, or what you think you hear. It won't get through your filter. You'll shrug it off. You'll dismiss it. You'll disregard it as trivial. Maybe, you'll even be annoyed that I've spent so much time talking about something so simple. Or maybe you'll say, 'Oh, hell, Steven, I already knew that.' Yes, you will. This isn't the first time I've delivered this talk—and the truth is, you aren't unique. That's the bad news. The good news is that our product works. It works better than you imagine. It works better than you *can* imagine. And best of all, it works *a hell of a lot better than theirs*. Pun intended!" Keyes grinned broadly, nodding and looking around the room, once again meeting the eyes of all of the guests. "So, here's what you've got to do," he said. "You've got to listen to me as if the quality your life depended on it—because it does!" He continued looking and nodding, waiting until the room was absolutely silent and every eye was fixed directly on him.

"What is our product?" he asked again, rhetorically. "Very simple. What we're selling here is *a whole other way to be*. Let me say that again. We are offering you an opportunity to change your way of *being*. You will stop being the way you have been, the way that doesn't produce the results you want, and take on instead a *new* way to be, a way that *does* produce the results you want. It's that simple.

"You know—" Keyes interrupted himself again, dropping back into his friendly conversational tone. "I read in a book once a very interesting definition of what it is to be crazy. Do you know what being crazy is? It's doing the same thing over and over and over, but each time expecting a different result. Well, that's what the other side is telling you to do. That's the product that the other side offering you. Have faith. Trust. Pray. Sacrifice. Be patient. And you'll get what you want. Someday. Not now, though. No matter what you ask for, that's their answer. And they expect that same answer to produce different results each time! That's crazy!

"Let's face it! Their way of being doesn't work!" Keyes accused, suddenly and angrily stabbing the air with his finger. "If it did, you wouldn't be here—not even out of curiosity!" He began moving about the room again, weaving his way up one aisle and down the next, pausing only to touch people on the shoulder or pat them reassuringly. "Look, I know it's tough out there. You know what everybody says, you've heard it, you've probably said it yourself: '*Life is hard. Then you die. Then they throw dirt in your face. Then the worms eat you. Be grateful it happens in that order.*'" He laughed along with the rest of the room. "Yeah, we laugh. It's funny. If we didn't laugh, we'd have to cry. Like that's something to be grateful for—right?

"If their way is so wonderful, how come so many of us are out of work? How come so many of us are going to bed hungry? How come so many of us have no place to live? If their way is so wonderful, how come there's so much evil in the world? Have you ever asked yourself that? Sure you have. Have you ever come up with a satisfactory answer?

"I know what *their* answer is—they blame us. They say it's *our* fault. That's their answer for everything—to blame the opposition. Notice that they *never* take responsibility for their own way of being!"

Steven Keyes stepped back up to the dais at the front of the room and allowed his raw anger to show again. "The truth is, we've all been conned, dominated, manipulated, cheated, beaten up, beaten down and used until we're all used up. And after a while, we think that's normal. Well, it isn't. It isn't normal. It isn't natural. *It isn't right!*"

Keyes was nearly shouting now. "And all it takes to change it is you being willing to make the commitment to change it. You've got to say, 'I'm sick and tired of being sick and tired.' You've got to say, 'I'm mad as hell and I won't take it any more.' You've got to say, 'I won't have it!' You've got to say, 'I deserve a fair share! I deserve the best!'

"That's right. You do. And I'm going to tell you how to have it." He stepped over to the podium and lifted up a single sheet of paper with a crisp black writing on it, easily readable. "See this? This is our contract. We're willing to put it all in writing. It's a legally binding document. When you read it, you'll see that it compels us to produce specific measurable results, a tangible change in your situation for the better, resulting in your personal satisfaction. If you're not satisfied—and you're the *only* arbiter of whether or not you are satisfied—but if you're not satisfied, then the contract is null and void.

"If we do satisfy you, then all we ask you to do is share this work with your friends. Ten friends. Twenty. As many as you want. Don't worry—once you're successful, you're going to have a lot of friends, and they're all going to want to know how you got so successful and effective and happy. Bring them to one of our seminars. We have seminars every week. We'll give them the same opportunity as you.

"Listen, you can have your lawyer look at this contract. You can have a hundred lawyers look at it. I promise you, it'll stand up in court. It's legal and binding and it compels the Nine Circles Corporation to produce results. When was the last time you signed a contract with this kind of a guarantee? Think about it. Not in this lifetime, right? *Right?*"

Around the room, people were nodding. Even George grunted a reluctant assent. Maggie glanced at him in surprise.

"And what do we get in return? What's the catch?" Steven Keyes asked the question with a sudden quiet solemnity that startled the room back into intense silence. "*They* tell you that we want your immortal soul. That's what *they* tell you. But *they* want your soul too. So the real catch is that we're offering you a choice and they're telling you that you have *no choice*. How does that make you feel? Angry? Yes? That's how it made me feel too. Well, I'm telling you that you *do* have a choice.

"You see, the *real* question is not who wants your soul—but *what* are they going to do with it once they get it?"

"They don't tell you that, do they? Just what are they going to do with your immortal soul that's so wonderful? I mean, there's this whole wonderful mythology about heaven and how great it's supposed to be, but just ask one of its representatives what heaven is really like and listen to what he or she says. Do you believe those stories? I don't. Is that the kind of place *you* want to spend eternity? I don't.

"Now, let's be honest with each other. Let's get past the mythology and the fairy tales and the glittering generalities and duck-billed platitudes. Let's talk specifics.

"There's no such place as Hell. Not like they tell you. There're no fires. No devils. No damnation. No eternal torment. I promise you that. I've been there. I've seen it. It's actually a very nice place. By the way, there's no such place as Heaven either. That's just as big a lie.

"Now, you've probably been told by your friends not to believe me; that I'll probably lie about Hell just to trick you. But I want you to stop a moment and think. Really *think* about the concept of Hell that they keep insisting is the truth. It's a pretty sick idea, isn't it? Can you imagine a just and compassionate deity plunging his children forever into the fires of eternal damnation just for making a mistake? Would you treat *your* children that way? Of course not. No *sane* person would. So why would a god, who's supposed to be omniscient and omnipresent, all-knowing and all-wise and all-loving, behave like a psychotic thug? That doesn't make sense, does it?

"You want to know what's really going on—both Heaven *and* Hell? I'll tell you."

Steven Keyes stepped down from the dais and began walking through the room again. Once more he touched the people he spoke to. He held their hands, he patted their shoulders, he held one woman's cheek. He dropped to his knees beside George and Maggie. "Listen to me. The whole point of this is to experience the adventure of yourself to the *fullest*—to live passionately! Your job is to look and listen and smell and touch and feel! Your job is to be alive and do all the things that people do when they are fully and completely alive! Roar with anger, weep with fear, laugh with joy, cry with sorrow—build, fight, love, plan, enjoy! The whole point of being alive is to experience yourself as a piece of the universe, to learn something about what it means to be a human being...*so you can bring that lesson back to the godhead.*

"The Yahweh company—they want you to believe what they tell you to believe, because they want to redesign the godhead in their own image. We don't agree with that. The Nine Circles Corporation wants you to have the most successful and powerful life you can. We want you to love the life you're living. We want you to be effective and masterful and satisfied. We want you to learn as much about the way the universe works as possible. And then...when it's time to fulfill the contract, we want you to bring that knowledge and joy into the godhead that we represent. We want to make you powerful, so you can bring your power back to us when you've mastered it. We want to make you wise, so you can bring that wisdom back to us when you've gained it. We want to have you satisfied, so you can add the wealth of your satisfaction to the larger satisfactions of our company. We want to make you strong, so you can incorporate your strengths into our body of thought. We want to make you stronger and wiser and happier, so that you can help make the Nine Circles Corporation stronger and wiser and happier. That's the deal. It's that simple."

Steven Keyes went back to the front of the room. "Now, here's what it's going to take," he said. He held up the contract again. "In a minute, we're going to have an opportunity for you to sign one of our contracts. There are tables at the back of the room. There are tables at the sides of the room. Our assistants—the good-looking young men and women in the gold nametags—are there to answer your questions and help you fill in your contract. All you have to do is list what you want out of life and then sign your name at the bottom. Be specific. Demand miracles. You'll get them. I promise you.

"But, remember, you're going to have to put yourself at risk," Keyes said directly. "And risk is scary. Especially *this* risk. Let me tell you something about risk. No matter what you do, it's all the *same* risk. You're stepping off into the unknown. It *always* feels like you're stepping off the top of a building. But *not* taking the risk is to stay stuck where you are. Is that where you want to be? So let me tell you what happens after you step off the top of the building. Most people just scream—all the way down. But, here's what happens when you step off the top of *our* building—*you get to look in all the windows!*

"That's right. You're still going to end up at the bottom—a big red splotch on the sidewalk—but the difference is that you're going to have much more fun on the way down." Keyes stopped himself. He held up his hand. He became serious again. "Listen, you took one big step just being here tonight. You took the risk that maybe—just *maybe*—there might be something to this. This is the opportunity to take the other half of that risk…to make the commitment to be the person you've always wanted to be. But what you have to give up is the person you think you are now.

"Let me say that again. It's important. You have to give up who you think you are so that you can discover who you're going to become. You're going to have to give up the past to grab hold of the future.

"Now, I know where you are with this. You're probably in one of three places. Some of you in this room are ready to jump. And when we take the break, you'll go right back to the table and sign up. Some of you may never be ready, and you're not going to sign up. And that's okay too. Thank you for being here. Thanks for coming to find out what we're up to. And last, some of you are poised on the edge, not quite ready to go, not quite ready to say no, because you think you want to think about it a little bit longer. If you're in that place, I just want to say one thing to you. I want to ask you one question. How much jogging do you get done thinking about jogging? You have to seize the moment—or the moment passes without you.

"So, here's how to know if you should sign up. Ask yourself what you most want out of life. Ask yourself if you're getting it. Ask yourself if you can expect to get it if you keep on doing what you're doing now. If the answer is no, then you had better start thinking about doing something else, hadn't you? That's right.

"So here's something else to do. Go to one of the tables. Pick up a copy of our contract. Read it. Read it carefully. Even if you're not planning to sign up tonight, read one of our contracts so you can satisfy yourself as to our integrity. If there's anything you don't understand—*anything* at all—then have one of our assistants explain it to you. Don't worry. Our assistants won't let you sign anything until you fully understand *exactly* what it is you're signing. And then…when you're ready, *sign it.* Yes, an ordinary ball-point pen is sufficient." Steven Keyes flashed one last genial grin. "All right, thank you again for being here. Let's do it now—all those who want to go to Hell with me, come to the tables and sign your contracts." He waited until the last of the applause died down and then he stepped down off the dais and headed up the aisle to the tables at the back of the room.

A buzz of excited noise began. People stood up, some of them stretching, some of them heading straight for the tables. Maggie turned and looked to George. "I want to do it," she said quietly.

George's hands had fallen to his lap. They were old and rough and battered-looking. He seemed to be studying them, but Maggie knew better. He had withdrawn into thoughts. She'd seen him do this before. Whenever he felt pressured, he disappeared inside himself. He simply wouldn't respond.

"George," she said insistently, refusing to be ignored this time. "I want to be happy. I want you to be happy. I'm going to sign up." She reached over and put her hand on his shoulder. "I want you to sign up with me."

Slowly, he lifted his gaze. He turned heavily to look at her. His eyes were rheumy and shaded with years of unspoken sadness. When he spoke his voice was barely audible. "I can't," he said. "I—I'm afraid."

She was astonished by his honesty. "There's nothing to be afraid of," she tried to reassure him. "These people won't hurt us—"

"No," he shook his head. "I'm not afraid of dying. I've been dying all my life...." For a moment, Maggie thought he was through speaking, but then he managed to croak out the last of the thought. "I'm afraid...of living."

Maggie let the words hang in the air between them while she studied his face. "Fine," she said, finally. "I'll do it without you then." After a moment more of waiting, she got up and headed for the table at the back of the room.

George watched her go, his eyes filling up with years of shame and failure.

If you get too close to my keyboard, you get written into a story. The funny thing is, shortly after this story was published, the neighbors did calm down....

The Spell

PART ONE:

My next-door neighbors have six children. This is not enough reason to hate them, but it's a good start.

The smallest one, Tali, is ambulatory, but still pre-verbal. She is not a problem. She can stay. We will leave her name off the eviction notice.

Next up is Nolan. He has been retarded at the age of three for four years now. Nolan is an interesting social experiment. What do you get if you allow a child to raise himself without any parental involvement at all?

He breaks things. He takes things. He denies accountability. He starts fires. He blames other children. He screams. He goes into other people's yards, and he climbs up onto the roofs of houses—usually his own, but occasionally the roof of a neighbor as well. He throws things over the fence into my yard, oftentimes aiming for the pool. A half-eaten Taco Bell burrito must be retrieved within the first thirty minutes or you can plan on having the filter cleaned again.

Wait, there's someone at the door—

(on paper the pauses don't show)

—it was Nolan. I can't even write this down without one of the little monsters knocking on the door. They have been sent to bedevil me.

Next up are Jason and Jabed, hovering somewhere in age between eleven and juvenile hall. Jason and Jabed are the coming attractions for Nolan's adolescence. They specialize in noise and attitude. They have no manners. They have no courtesy. They have no conception of consideration for others.

My life was quiet and peaceful once. I work at home. I take my time to think things out. I sit in my office and think and write. I sit in my living room and read and listen to classical music; Bach, Vivaldi, occasionally a Shostakovitch string quartet—nothing too strenuous. I open all the doors and all the windows, and the cross breeze keeps the house pleasant and sweet-smelling. I would love to be able to do that again. Last year, I paid six thousand dollars to install a 4000 BTU air conditioner on the roof so I could close all the doors and windows and still keep working. The noise from the fan drowns out the softer strains of Debussy.

In the afternoon, they play touch football and baseball across three lawns. Mine is in the middle. Even the judicious planting of large amounts of purple Wandering Jew has not deterred them. They leap over it...sometimes. They scream, they shout, they claim the ball in mid-air. "It's mine—mine!" Their voices are atonal and dissonant, precisely mistuned to jar with whatever music is on the turntable.

In the evenings, they play basketball in the back yard. I used to go to bed at eleven. But they play basketball until one in the ayem, shouting and jabbering. The basketball hoop is opposite my bedroom window. It serves as the perfect acoustic focus aimed at my headboard. I am not making this up. A specialist in theatrical sound systems came out to my house, took some measurements and ran them through the computer.

Jabed and Jason like to climb roofs, too. Last January, they climbed up on the roof of the auto parts store behind the alley and plugged up its storm drains, just for the fun of it. When the big rains came in February, the water puddled on the roof. The weight of the water brought the whole ceiling crashing in, causing over a half-million dollars worth of damage to the store. The police refused to arrest the boys because of insufficient evidence. In August, they were accused of stealing 120 dollars from a neighbor's wallet and spent the night in juvenile hall. The next day, they were swimming at the same neighbor's house. How do they get away with it? What magic are they working?

Then there's Vanessa. She's another sweetheart. I think she's eighteen.

She takes care of the kids while Mom's at work. No, check that. She's *supposed* to take care of the kids while Mom's at work. What she does is have parties. One of her friends once took forty bucks from Mom's purse—but Mom and Dad blamed every other child on the street for the theft, and when the truth came out, didn't bother to apologize.

I'm not the only one who feels this way. The neighbor on the other side of Hell House has developed an ulcer. The neighbors across the street have put their house up for sale. Half the parents on the block have forbidden their children to play with the demonic brood. This is validation. It's not me. It's *them.*

Mom and Dad. Lyn and Bryce. He's a former minister, she's a former cheerleader who never aspired to anything more than the right shade of blonde. She hasn't yet noticed that her tits are working their way south and her ass is spreading faster than the crab-grass on their lawn. I gave up on my lawn this year. There's no point in it, while the crab-grass sod farm next door is so aggressive.

Their philosophy of childrearing is non-existent. They daydream their way through life, drifting from one day to the next, oblivious to the fact that they are loathed by all of their neighbors. No, check that. They are loathed by all of the neighbors who live close enough to know who they are.

Oh—I almost skipped Damien. He's the one I like. He moved out and went to college four hundred miles away. We only see him on holidays. He has manners and courtesy and is obviously a changeling, not a real part of the family. He wants to major in art. Maybe he's gay. I hope so. I'd like to see the look on their faces when he comes home with a boyfriend. Idle fantasies of revenge are rapidly becoming an obsession over here.

I like to believe I'm smarter than they are; but I still haven't been able to plot the perfect crime—one that would allow me to chop their bones into fragments, burn their house down and salt the earth into toxic uninhabitability, without anyone ever suspecting that I was the agent responsible. In some matters, anonymity is preferable to acknowledgment. Revenge is one of them.

It bothers me, because I am supposed to be a specialist in revenge. Writers, as a class, are the research-and-development team for the whole human race in the domain of revenge. We ennoble it, we glorify it; we earn our livings inventing wonderful and exotic ways to justify the delicious deed of puncturing the pompous who make our lives miserable. We create virtual daydreams for the masses in which the mighty are humiliated for their misdeeds of oppression against those who are still climbing the evolutionary ladder. It is our job to tend the flames of mythic vision, creating the cultural context in which the arrogant are accurately mirrored and drawn, so that all will know who they are. It is our job to prepare the ground so that the thieves of joy can be reduced to craven, whimpering, pitiful objects of scorn and abuse.

And...the fact that I remain unable to find a way to drive these people screaming from their house frustrates me beyond words, because it implies that I am not yet a master of my trade. If anyone should be able to envision a suitable revenge here, it should be me. Through a delightfully Machiavellian bit of timing, innuendo and legal maneuvering, I once engineered the enforced exit off the Paramount lot of a particularly leechsome lawyer; studio security officers arrived with boxes, and physically escorted him off the premises—so abusing a few troublesome neighbors should be easy. Shouldn't it?

The problem is Grandma. Theirs, not mine. Grandma is a space-case. Not of this world. She exists in her own reality of hydrangeas and luncheons and Cadillacs. Life is pleasant, life is good, there are no problems. Let's all be nice to each other and everything will work out fine. She sees and hears only what she chooses to. Grandma owns the house and Mom and Dad and all the little Mansons live in it rent-free. They couldn't afford to live in this neighborhood otherwise. There is no way they're ever going to move out. Ever try to pull a tick off a dog? Grandma is the problem—

(narrative interrupted again)

—that one used up the rest of my evening. While I admit that it gave me no small amount of satisfaction to see three police cars pulled up in front of *that* house, it did not bring me any joy. I appreciate the validation; I do not appreciate losing half a day of working time.

This time, Jason was chasing Damien with a knife, threatening him. Damien socked him with a frying pan in self-defense. Damien got arrested. He'll end up with a charge of child-abuse on his record. These people have a way of getting *other* people in trouble and coming out unscathed themselves. It's a talent.

PART TWO:

That was six months ago.

The day after I wrote that, I ran into my friend, Sara McNealy. Sara is a witch.

I had stopped in at Dangerous Visions bookstore in Sherman Oaks to deliver my monthly box of books that I would rather not have in the house and to select a few volumes in return that would enhance my bookshelves. Given the fact that most publishers seem to have given up the publication of real books in favor of the production of commodity products, the task of reinvigorating the sleeping sense of wonder becomes harder and harder every year. Nothing destroys a person's enjoyment of a subject as fast as becoming obsessive about it. Never mind.

Sara was standing at the counter, chatting with Lydia Marano, the store owner. There were two other customers in the back of the store, browsing through the non-readers' section, looking for the latest *Star Trek* novel.

Sara doesn't look like a witch. She does not have flaming red hair. She does not have green eyes. She does not dress in flowing capes with unicorn embroidery.

Sara is short, not quite dumpy but almost, and she has little tight black curls framing her pie-shaped face. She is given to flowing dresses and little round spectacles that look like windows into her dark gray eyes. She looks like a yenta-in-training, but without the guilt attached. She is obscenely calm and unruffled.

Sara never talks about the goddess; she is not given to feminist rhetoric and rarely reads fiction. She created her own job, managing the computers for a major theatrical booking-chain. She is the first stop for technical support for a very small and very exclusive group of science-fiction, fantasy and horror writers. She is equally conversant with nano-technology, transhuman chickens, selfish genes, disturbed universes, dancing Wu-Li masters, motorcycle maintenance (with or without the zen), virology (both human and silicon strains), paleontology, biblical history and several mutant strains of buddhist discourse. She can quote from Sun Tzu's *Art of War* as easily as from *The Watchmen*.

She does not cast spells herself. She works only as a consultant, serving as the midwife at the spellcasting sessions of others. She was telling Lydia, behind the counter, about her experiences breaking up a fannish coven, trying to grow hair on Patrick Stewart. "Finally, I just flat out told them, 'Witchcraft is potent stuff. Every spell you cast uses up part of your life force. If you assume that every spell you cast takes a year off your life expectancy, you don't do it casually. You save it for things that matter.'"

I looked up from the copy of *Locus* I was browsing through. They hadn't reviewed a book of mine in years—not since I'd requested that the reviewers read the books before writing about them. "Hey, Sara, didn't you say there were ways to rebuild your life force?"

"Oh, yes." She smiled sweetly as she said it. "Creativity. Haven't you ever noticed that a disproportionate share of conductors, writers, musicians, directors, et al, live well into their nineties? The act of creation is very powerful. When you bring something into existence out of nothing, it becomes a focus for energy. If you create positive energy, you get invigorated. If you create negative energy, you diminish yourself. You can't afford the luxury of nastiness."

"You're right, *I* can't—but what if you don't have a choice in the matter?"

"You *always* have a choice," she said.

"You don't know my next-door neighbors."

She raised an eyebrow at me. A raised eyebrow from Sara McNealy is enough to curdle milk.

I refused to be intimidated. "My next door neighbors are destroying my life," I said. "They're noisy and intrusive. They've upset my whole life. My writing is suffering. And I can't afford to move."

Sara scratched her nose. "Negativism starts by blaming the other person. It's a way of avoiding personal responsibility."

"I'm not avoiding personal responsibility," I said. "I just don't know what to do."

"What result do you want to produce?" Sara asked.

"I want them to move away. Very far away."

She nodded. She was thinking. Lydia studied us both. Sara was turning over ideas in her mind. She said, "You could invite an evil spirit to move in with them. But that's dangerous. Sometimes the spirit decides it would rather move in with *you*."

"No, no spirits, thank you. Is there some other way?"

"Are you willing to pay the price—time off your life?"

"I'll earn it back with increased writing time. Won't I?"

Sara didn't answer that. At the same moment, we both noticed that there were suddenly other customers waiting—*and listening*. Sara put down the copy of *Chaos Theory* she had been browsing through and drew me carefully aside, leaving Lydia to ring up another large royalty for Stephen King.

"Listen to me," Sara said softly. "Witchcraft is a very specialized form of magic—you're trying to control the physical universe with experiential forces. That means that you need to create a specific context and appropriate symbology with which to control those forces. I prefer to do it with symbolic magic rather than calling on spirits. Sometimes when no spirit responds to your call, new ones are created out of nothingness, and that can be extremely dangerous. Young spirits are…well, they're like kittens and puppies. They leave puddles."

"Can't I just animate the life force of their property or something?"

"It doesn't work that way." She frowned. "You're going to have to give me the whole story if you want me to advise you."

I took Sara by the arm and led her to the specialty-coffee shop next door. She had hazelnut coffee with bay leaves. I had fruit-tea. I can't stomach caffeine. I told her about the Partridge Family from Hell; I didn't leave anything out. I even told her about Princess, the unfettered cocker spaniel who never missed a chance to run up onto my porch and bark *into* my house.

Sara listened intently to the whole story without comment. Her dark eyes looked sorrowful. I could understand why she was such a good witch. Most of it was good listening. When I finished, she said, "You have a great deal of negative energy bound up in these people. That's a very expensive burden you are carrying. It needs to be released." She made a decision. "I'll help you."

"How much will it cost?" I asked.

She shook her head. "Witches don't work for money. Prostitutes do. Witches take…*favors*."

"Okay, I'll read your manuscript," I said with real resignation.

"Sorry, I have no interest in writing a novel."

"Thank God."

"Don't worry," she said. "I don't want your soul. Writers' souls are usually very small anyway, and not good eating. Too much gristle." She reached over and patted my hand warmly. "We'll talk about your first-born later, all right?"

I assumed she was joking.

PART THREE:

Sara showed up seven o'clock, carrying two shopping bags.

"Ahh," I said, thinking I was being funny. "Did you bring the right eye of a left-handed newt? The first menstrual blood of the seventh virginal daughter?"

"This is California," she said. "There are no virgins. No, I brought pasta, mushrooms, bell peppers, tomato sauce, olives, garlic bread, salad and a bottle of wine. Let's eat first, then we'll plan. Did you get the Cherry Garcia like I asked?"

"Of course, I did." I took the bags from her. "But I really have to say I miss the old traditions of witchcraft."

"Do you want to dance naked around a bonfire at midnight?"

"Not particularly."

"Neither do I. Open the wine."

After dinner, we cleared the table and spread out our plans. "First of all," Sara said, "You have to decide what power you want to invoke. Who are you calling on to do the deed?" She handed me a printout. "You don't want to invoke the powers of Satan, whatever you do. Dealing with demons is also dangerous; for the most part, the demons are only facets of Satan anyway. You don't want to do anything that puts your immortal soul in danger. I'm just showing you this to give you some sense of what you're going to be dealing with.

"Lower down, you have the lesser spirits and the spirits of the dead. Also not recommended. Spirits usually have their own agendas. They're very hard to control and almost never grant requests. Spirits are deranged."

I scanned the lists with very little interest, then passed her back the printout. "Let's stick to white magic, okay?"

"Right." She passed me another set of pages. "See, the thing is, you have to invoke *some* power to energize the spell. Otherwise, it's like a new Corvette, all shiny and beautiful, but without an engine it isn't going anywhere."

"Yeah, I just hate it when that happens."

She ignored my flippant interjection. "The problem with western magic is that as a result of the pernicious influence of Christian theology, westernized magic has anthropomorphized everything; we've given personalities to supernatural forces. It gives them *attitude*. It makes them impossible to deal with. But when we go back to the eastern disciplines, we're operating in a whole other context. The truth is that the flows of paranormal influence are directly linked to the yin-yang flow of solidity and nothingness, of creation and destruction, of beingness and non-being. Real magic happens when you align yourself with the flows of chaos and order. When you ride the avalanche, you need only a nudge to steer it. If you want to have a profound effect on the course of events in the physical universe, without running the risk of a serious causal backwash of energy, you have to create a spells that are in harmony with what the universe already wants to do. From what you've been telling me, it seems to me that the universe already *wants* to do something about these people next door. All you need to do is give it a focus."

I wasn't sure I understood anything of what she said, but I nodded as if I did.

Sara wasn't fooled. "Listen to me. Remember what I said about negative energy? You can't afford it. You are a fountain of creative power. You can't risk having your spring contaminated. You have to act now before you are permanently polluted. But whatever you do—you have to make sure that you don't do *greater* harm to yourself."

"What are you recommending?" I asked. She sounded so serious.

"Think of the peacock," she said.

"Pretty. Loud. Pretty loud." I free-associated.

"Do you know what a peacock eats?"

I shook my head.

"It eats the poisonous berries. It thrives on all the toxics that other birds won't touch. And it turns them into beautiful peacock feathers. That's the peacock—it takes nastiness and turns it into beauty. That's your job. Find a way to take all that stuff about the neighbors and turn it into something useful and rewarding and enlightening."

"A nice bonfire is the first thing that comes to mind. We could dance naked around it."

"It's time to stop being silly," Sara said. "You asked for my help. That's why I'm here. What kind of spell do you want to cast and what power do you want to invoke?"

"I want a spell that's quiet and unobtrusive. Inconspicuous. It shouldn't call attention to itself. No fireworks. No explosions. No ectoplasm, no manifestations, no mysterious cold spots. Just something that makes them *go away*."

"That's the best kind," Sara said.

I was looking at the list. "Let's invoke the power of the universe," I said.

"Huh?"

I pointed at the organization chart. "Look, all the power flows from the top. Let's go to the source. Let's call upon the universe to activate the spell."

Sara thought about it. "It might be overkill."

"There's no such thing as overkill," I said. "Dead is dead."

"How big an impact crater are you willing to live with?" she asked. "Remember, your house is well within the blast radius."

"We're going for gentleness, aren't we?"

"Gentleness is not delivered with a firehose," Sara said.

"Good point. We'll have to be careful."

"There could be side effects. You're probably going to get hit with some of them. Are you sure you want to do this?"

I nodded. A thought had been lurking at the back of my mind for three days. Ever since Sara had first begun coaching me. Now it was ready to blossom forth as a full-blown idea. I handed her my notes. forty-three ideas. Forty-two of them had been crossed off. Only one remained.

Sara looked at it. She frowned. She narrowed her eyes. Her eyebrows squinched together. Her lips pursed. All of the separate parts of her face squinched up for a second, then relaxed, morph-like, into a big happy grin. "I think you may have real talent in this area," she said.

She took her pen and underlined my note. *__Love-bomb the bastards!__*

PART FOUR:

At a quarter to midnight, we began. I went out to the back yard and flipped off every circuit-breaker. There was no electrical power at all to the house. There would be no contaminating fields of magnetic resonance. The computers had all been unplugged. The batteries had been removed from every radio and flashlight.

Sara gave me a diagram, and I began to lay out a complex pattern of thirty-nine votive candles. As I went around the room, lighting them, I recited a simple prayer of absolution. "May this light give me guidance. Help me align myself with the flows of universal power."

When I finished, I began unwinding a long yellow cord around the room, putting a loop around each candle as I strung a spiral pattern leading to an empty plate in the center. I sat down at the outside of the spiral and held the other end of the cord. I began winding it around the fingers of my left hand. The power would flow from my heart to the empty plate. And back again.

I looked to Sara. She nodded. I hadn't forgotten anything.

"Hello," I said.

I waited a moment. If the universe was listening, it hadn't given me any evidence. But then again, the universe never gives evidence of its involvement. It's just there—the ultimate in passive aggressive.

I took three deep breaths. I closed my eyes and took three more. I waited until I thought I could see the candle flames through my closed eyelids. Then I waited until I was certain we were no longer alone.

"Hello," I repeated. "Thank you. I apologize for any intrusion this action of mine might represent. I only wish to serve the flows of the universe, not to impede them. And I hope that the universe will let me be a part of its grander plans."

I waited. This time I got the feeling that some*thing* was waiting for me.

"My neighbors," I said. "The people who live in the house next-door. Particularly Bryce, Lyn, Vanessa, Jabed, Jason and Nolan. I believe that they have been impeding the natural rise toward godliness. Perhaps it is through no fault of their own. Perhaps it is because they have been seduced by the darker flows of nature. Perhaps there are reasons for which I have no language. Whatever forces are at work, I believe that they are at odds with the natural flow of universal power and goodness."

I glanced over to Sara. She was watching me intently. She nodded and smiled.

"I believe that somehow they have become separated from their own abilities to connect with others and feel compassion. I believe that are unable to know the effects they have on the people around them. I believe that they do not see the pain they leave in their wake."

With my right hand, I placed a bowl on the empty plate in the center of the room. I poured red wine into the bowl, then I placed a single rose-blossom in the wine. "I offer you this gift," I said. "I do so freely and with no thought of personal reward or gain. I ask nothing for myself, nor for anyone close to me. I ask only that you grant my neighbors an opportunity to join your larger purposes, to swim in the flow of universal spirit that heads inevitably toward the light and glory of enlighten-ment. Please help direct their energies toward goodness and joy."

I bowed my head. "Thank you," I said. "Thank you for listening. Thank you for being here. Thank you for letting me serve you to-night."

And—maybe it was the sudden breeze from the door—but every single candle in the room went out simultaneously.

"Nicely done," said Sara, after a long startled silence. "*Very* nicely done."

EPILOGUE:

The next morning, I felt rather silly for having gone through the whole silly ritual. But I made up my mind to wait a week. Or two. Or even six.

Nothing happened at first.

Then, one horrible weekend, *everything* happened. Lyn and Bryce were out somewhere. Vanessa had invited 500 close friends to a backyard bash, with 600 decibels of heavy metal rock music and illegal fireworks. Jabed and Jason were sitting on the roof of the garage throwing cherry bombs into the dancers, which triggered a spate of angry gunfire between members of two rival gangs who were trying to crash the party from the alley-side of the yard. In the ensuing panic, several automobiles were smashed into each other as people tried to flee—a dead-end street does not lend itself to an orderly evacuation. In the confusion, Nolan found the box of fireworks and managed to light both them *and the house* on fire. By the time the police and the fire department arrived, the structure was sending fifty foot flames into the air and I was hosing down my roof and praying that the overhanging tree wouldn't catch. The fire crew couldn't get through the mass of cars to the fire hydrant, and even if they could have, it wouldn't have done any good because someone had crashed into it, knocking it off, sending a high-pressure fountain spraying high into the air where it made an impressive, but otherwise useless, display of un-contained aquatic energy. They ended up taking one of the units around to the alley side and backing it into my backyard so they could pump the water out of my pool and onto the neighbor's roof. It took them twenty minutes to knock down the blaze, leaving the house a charred and wa-terlogged mess. By the time they were through, there were over twenty police vehicles on the block, three ambulances and four news vans.

In the aftermath, four stolen cars were recovered from joy-riding gang-bangers, seventeen people were arrested for possession and dealing of illegal substances, twelve illegal weapons were confiscated and twenty-six of the party-goers spent the night in jail for being drunk and disorderly. Fourteen outstanding warrants were served for offenses as varied as unpaid parking tickets and felony armed robbery. Vanessa's friends were an assorted lot.

The following Monday, Lyn and Bryce were investigated by the Department of Social Services.

And I called Sara and asked what went wrong. She told me not to worry. Everything was fine. Just be patient.

She was right. It took a while for everything to get sorted out, but eventually, it did.

The judge ordered three years of family-counseling for the whole clan. Vanessa was put on probation, conditional on her remaining in Alcoholics Anonymous. Jabed and Jason were put into a special education program to help them recover from prolonged emotional abuse and also to prevent them from drifting into patterns of juvenile delinquency. Nolan was identified as suffering from a serious learning disability and is now in full-time therapy. Tali is in pre-school. Damien is president of the local Queer-Nation chapter. Grandma had to sell the house to help Lynn and Bryce cover the legal expenses. They all live with her now.

The insurance company leveled the remains of the house and sold the land to the city for use as a pocket park. It wasn't cost-effective to rebuild.

To paraphrase my favorite moose, sometimes I don't know my own strength.

For a while, both Sara and I were concerned about the backwash from the spell. We'd love-bombed the entire family, and they were all definitely much better off than they had been before. But Sara was afraid that there would be serious side-effects to the spell that might affect both of us. If there have been any, we haven't noticed them yet. But then again, we've been much too busy. Sara's planning to move in with me next month, and I've applied to adopt a little boy. And I expect to get back to my writing Real Soon Now.

AUTHOR'S AFTERWORD:

Next up, the money spell. . . .

The seed for this story was an actual anecdote I'd read many years ago and saved in my idea file—something about archaeologists and blind spots and how much does a Grecian urn?

Digging In Gehenna

DADDY WAS ARGUING WITH DR. BLOM AGAIN, so Mom told me to stay away from the dig for awhile, at least until tempers cooled off. That was the only thing likely to cool off anytime soon. Spring was rising, and so were the daytime temperatures. We would be heading back south to the more comfortable polar zones as soon as the last trucks were loaded and the skywhale arrived tomorrow morning. Twenty-four months would pass before the sand would be cool enough to stand on again, but nobody knew if we would be coming back.

"They're arguing about the horn again, aren't they?"

Mom nodded. "It's their favorite argument."

"Do you think Daddy's right? Or Dr. Blom?"

"Actually, I hope they're both wrong." Mom looked up from the fabber she was disassembling. "Pray that we never find out what the damn thing was really used for. If either one of them is proven right, they'll never be able to work together again."

"They'll just find something else to argue about."

"No, this is one of those arguments that people don't forget. If you're wrong, it's a career-killer. The only hope for resolution is for them to

170

be equally embarrassed by the facts. And don't tell Daddy I said this. It would hurt his feelings enormously."

"I didn't think anyone could hurt Daddy's feelings."

"Only people he cares about." She closed the lid of the machine and handed me the used cartridges for the recycler. "Just because he doesn't show his feelings doesn't mean he doesn't have any."

There were over two hundred people on the dig. We weren't the only family here. There were twenty others who'd brought their children. We were a whole village. We had sixteen acre-tents and at least a hundred equipment and storage tents scattered around. Three of the acre-tents were habitats, with hanging rugs to give each family-group some privacy.

We had offworlders here too. The dig was big news all the way back to Earth; the first alien civilization ever discovered. And because the actual site was habitable only four out of twenty-eight months, this was a precious opportunity, especially for the Ph.D. candidates, like Hank, the big goofy guy who called me "swee'pea" and "short stuff" and "Little Darlin'" until Mom gave him *the glare*. So of course, I wanted to see more of him.

Actually, she's my stepmom, and according to the rule-books, I'm supposed to resent her, but mostly she and I are good friends. Probably because she's only twelve years older than me, so she feels more like a big sister than a stepmom, but I call her Mom anyway. I'm almost seventeen, old enough to get married; but Mom has this rule that nobody gets married until they finish college. She refused to marry Daddy for three years until she finished her doctorate.

Mom said that Hank was too old for me anyway. I respectfully did not point out that Hank was only five years older than me while Daddy was fifteen years her senior. I didn't need to start that fight. And besides, she was twenty-four when she married him.

Hank was one of the offworlders who had trouble adapting to Gehenna's seventy-two-hour day, but eventually he found his rhythm. The others settled in too. Everyone does. Daddy says that twelve hours on and twelve hours off mimics Earth time almost perfectly—despite the fact that the sunlight doesn't match.

I'd been allowed to come on the dig because Mom and Dad were team leaders. There were another dozen college students who'd been brought along for grunt-work and experience, so I was lumped in with them.

We all had class in the morning and chores in the afternoon. Then class in the evening and chores again in the early morning. Interspersed with sleep, of course.

I was part of the toddler-team; we took care of the little ones while the various moms went off to work. There were only five of them, but they were a handful. I don't think we ever had five dry diapers at a time. We solved the problem by putting one person on diaper-duty each shift.

There's this about changing diapers—it keeps you from biting your nails. My private goal was to potty-train the little monsters as quickly as possible. We'd made real progress with the other four, but my little brother, Zakky, had so far resisted all inducements toward sanitary behavior. Despite that, I still thought he was cute. Mom said that my attitude would change as soon as Zakky learned how to say no. Once he learned how to argue, he'd be just like his daddy.

Daddy was famous for his arguments. Of maybe infamous. He wasn't loud or aggressive. I'd never even seen him raise his voice. He was painfully polite. He would make his points carefully, exquisitely, elegantly reasoned, making connections so obvious you could slap your forehead for not seeing them yourself. And when he was done, he had assembled a framework of logic as marvelous as a Chinese tapestry—so beautiful and compelling and overwhelming in its construction you were left with no place to stand. You just wanted to find a great big club and whack him across the head with it for being so damnably, blandly, patiently, *right*. Again.

Daddy's brain never stopped working. The universe was a giant puzzle to him, and he felt it was his personal responsibility to fit the pieces together. When I was little, I was afraid of him; but now that I understood better, I admired him. I used to wonder why Mom had married him, but most times I envied her for the adventure.

But Daddy could get so preoccupied with solving the puzzles of the universe that sometimes he forgot everything else. Sometimes we had to drag him physically away from the dig just to get him to eat, and even then we could have put a slice of shale between two pieces of bread and he wouldn't have noticed, he'd be so busy talking about what he had found and what he had to do next and what it might mean. Of course, that led to a lot of arguments with the other diggers, about what each new discovery *meant*. They were all on new ground here. Nobody knew for sure what any of it really was, so everything was still just opinion.

The one thing we knew about the tripods—that's what we called them—was that we didn't know anything about them at all. We had no idea how they had lived, what they ate, what they believed in, what kind of culture they had or even how many sexes they had. Every new fragment suggested as many possibilities as it disproved.

Daddy wasn't the only one arguing, of course. Everyone argued with everyone. Mom said that was because -ology didn't mean "the study of" as much as it meant "the argument about." But Daddy *liked* to argue. He said that arguing was the highest exercise of intelligence at work, measuring, testing and challenging ideas. He said that it was the passion of the argument that ultimately revealed the true self. Of course, Daddy would argue with the weather if he could. Failing that, he had argued for extending our stay onsite by an extra two weeks. He'd won half that argument. We were a week past our original departure date and already the temperatures were half-past unbearable.

But Daddy wasn't the only one who wanted to stay. Almost everybody on the team was so excited at what they were pulling out of the ground that nobody wanted to quit, even if it meant working in 110-degree weather. What if we were only half an hour away from finding the tripod Rosetta Stone? There might not be another expedition like this one in our lifetime. Gehenna's weather wasn't exactly friendly.

The tripod village had only been discovered six years ago, when one of the radar-mapping satellites discovered patterns underneath the sand. Detailed scanning showed eleven separate buildings embedded in the soft shale. The access team had trucked in huge sand-dredges and digging machines and cut a ramp down to the target layers. Only then could the archeology teams start working.

Once we'd finally gotten down to the roofs of the domes, and gotten inside a few, we began discovering the first artifacts of an entire civilization. Dr. Blom said this village was less than a hundred thousand years old. On a geological scale, we'd just missed them. Of course, having their star flare up might have had something to do with that too.

Daddy's team had put a three-acre tent over the site. That got everybody out of the direct sun, and it brought the temperature down at least ten degrees; but mostly it kept the sand from covering the dig. The long nights brought hot roaring winds that could dry out your skin in an hour, leaving you itchy and cranky and desperate. Thirty-six hours later, when the sun crept over the sharp horizon again, there would be

orange dust covering everything, sometimes as much as thirty centime-
ters. Everything had to be tented, or you might as well abandon it.

Mom's team kept busy cataloguing the artifacts, scanning and decon-
structing them, then test-fabbing duplicates and comparing them to the
originals. When the dupe was accurate to the limits of the measuring
equipment, Mom would finalize it and make it available in the catalog.
Then, anyone could log on and fab a copy.

Some of the artifacts were easy, because they were mostly complete.
A knife. A basket. A bowl. A jar of dessicated grain. A stool. But some of
the items were impossible to figure out. Not just because they were fragments, but because nobody had any idea what kind of people the tripods
might have been. Like the hairbrush thing with two handles—what was
that for? A toothbrush? A backscratcher? An envelope holder?

Even the word "people" was cause for argument. Dr. Blom was an
alienist. She said that alien meant *gaijin*. Different. Therefore, human
paradigms couldn't apply. Just using the word "people" created an anthropomorphic mind-set.

So of course, Daddy took the anthropomorphic position—that life
is messy everywhere, but it isn't infinite. The physics of the situation
define what's possible. Life occurs as an expression of opportunity. And
the same evolutionary imperatives are at work everywhere, regardless of
the DNA coding; Gehenna had oxygen and water and a mobile temper-
ate zone conducive to the carbon cycle, etc. etc., therefore, knowing the
circumstances of the environment, we know the limits of what kind of
life is possible. Therefore, therefore…ad infinitum. Rumor had it that
Dr. Blom had actually asked one of her assistants to fab a club….

Eventually, the whole camp was arguing the point—if the tripods
were so alien as to be beyond our comprehension, and this dig repre-
sents an insoluble puzzle to humankind, then why are we even bothering to dig anything up and study it? Wasn't the whole point of any "-ol-
ogy" to increase our understanding, not our befuddlement?

None of which solved the problem of the *thing*, which along the way
had become the focus of the whole argument. Dr. Blom had found it in
one of the broken domes. It was some kind of ceramic, so it was obviously manufactured for a purpose. But what purpose? She and Daddy
had been arguing about it from the very first day.

Complicating the argument, the thing wasn't a complete thing. Mostly, it was a tray fragments. Mom had spent a week scanning them, ma-

nipulating the pieces around, extrapolating what the thing might have looked like when it was whole. That was a month's worth of squabble, right there—how did the fragments fit together?—with Daddy and Dr. Blom fussing over asymmetry, polarity and even which end was up.

What they finally agreed to was that in size and shape, the thing could have been some kind of table vessel. Like a punch bowl or a centerpiece or a coffee pot. One end of the thing was a bowl-shaped flare, like the horn of a trumpet; it narrowed into a hollow pedestal. The thing could have stood on the large end or the small, but it was obviously more stable resting on the large end.

Dr. Blom had initially suggested that it had a ceremonial function, like a wine-glass or a chalice, except that the thing had three scooped-out openings in the sides of the flared end. The openings were supposed to be there; they were sculpted in. Daddy suggested that the sculpting suggested that another object was to be placed in the horn, perhaps a triangular bowl, or even a symbolic representation of the tripodal makers.

So then Dr. Blom decided that they were looking at it upside-down. The horn-end was the bottom and the pedestal was a support for something else. Maybe it was a flower-holder, or a vase. Then she decided that it had a ceremonial function and was used for lustral rites. Some kind of purification ritual.

Whenever she said this, Daddy rolled his eyes in exasperation and began muttering about Occam's chainsaw—whatever was the simplest, most obvious explanation had to be the right one. Finally, in frustration, Mom fabbed a couple dozen replicas of the thing and passed them out like party favors. Very quickly it became the symbol of everything we didn't know about the tripods. If it had been half a size larger, we could have worn it as a dunce cap.

If only there had been wall-markings in the domes or illustrations on the side of jars or something like that. But there weren't any. Apparently, the tripods didn't make images of themselves. And that was good for another whole area of argument—that maybe something about the way their eyes worked, or their brains, they didn't have visual symbology.

That could have been an even bigger disagreement than the argument about the *thing*, except by that time we'd found the first skeletons, and that's when the real excitement began. Everything before that was just a warm-up.

Hank was on the exo-biology team, so I heard about lots of stuff before it was presented, and some stuff that wasn't presented at all, because it was still only speculation. Most of the skeletons were complete and fairly well-preserved; carbon-dating and iridium-scanning showed that this village had died when the sun flared up.

Hank had a lot of ideas about that. His team had fabbed copies of three skeletons, two adults and a juvenile, and now they were working on the nature of the tripod musculature. As bad as the arguments were about *the thing*, the arguments about tripod biology were even worse.

First off, the tripod brain case was too small. It was a dorsal hump opposite what was assumed to be the rear leg. Channels in the bone suggested routes for optic nerves. Other structures might have been a nasal chamber, which would indicate an "anterior" as opposed to "posterior." But there was also the suggestion of some kind of a collagenous snout, like an elephant's trunk, only it seemed to serve as a mouth, not as a nose. But nobody wanted to say for certain in case it turned out to be something else, and then they'd be embarrassed for guessing wrong; so for the moment everything everybody said about the tripods was prefaced with "suggests," "could be," "possible," "might serve as" and even an occasional "probable." But the size of the brain case was clearly insufficient for sentience.

A full-grown tripod was only waist-high. Not much more than a meter tall. The exo-biology team estimated that it would mass no more than eighty kilograms. So that would make it the size of a large dog, or a small ape; but the estimated size of the brain wasn't large enough even for that size a creature. The exo-biology team estimated that the tripods maybe had the intelligence of a cocker spaniel—just smart enough to pee outside. So that was another mystery.

And then there was the business of the fingers. They were short and stubby, more of a splayed paw than a hand, and not really suitable for grasping large or heavy objects. The simulations showed that if a tripod squatted on its hind leg, the two forward paws could be used to manipulate simple objects, but that was about the limit. The tripods would not have been very good typists. That is, if they had anything to type.

Dr. Blom said that intelligent creatures needed the ability to handle objects, not just as tools, but more importantly because the ability to understand an object was directly related to the ability to touch, feel and manipulate it. "Fingers are the extension of the mind," she said.

Wisely, Daddy did not disagree with her on that one. Instead, he took a gentler tack, pointing out that dolphins and other cetaceans had demonstrated sophisticated language and intelligence skills without any grasping limbs at all; so clearly there was something else at work here. But dolphins and whales have very large brains, and tripods didn't—so that just brought us back to the problem of the too-small brain case.

But those were only sidebar discussions. The main event was much more serious.

Hank explained it to me at dinner in the mess tent. Nowhere else in the universe—not in simulation, and not in the laboratory, and not on any other life-bearing planet—had nature produced a three-legged creature. The asymmetry of the species was unprecedented, and Hank said that it was going to cause a major upheaval in both biological and evolutionary thinking. There was no way it couldn't. This was the real issue: whatever the tripods had been, they were so far outside the realm of what we had previously known or believed to be possible, that they represented a massive breakdown in biological science. That's what was so exciting; this was a real opportunity for genius to prove itself by re-inventing the paradigm.

After dinner, most folks gathered in the rec-area for news and gossip and mail. Sometimes we'd see a movie, sometimes we'd have a dance or celebrate someone's birthday. Some of the folks played instruments, so we had a makeshift band. And the bar was open for two hours if people wanted to have a drink.

But not everybody wanted to be sociable all the time. Some folks had to be alone for a while. They'd go outside and sit under the stars or maybe walk out to one of the boundary markers. It was hard to get lost in the desert. The camp gave off a bright glow, and if that weren't enough, the housekeeping team had installed three bright red lasers pointing up into the sky. They were visible for kilometers, so anyone who ventured too far out only needed to head for the light at the edge of the world. Folks who wanted a bit of solitude sometimes planned midnight picnics and hiked a few kilometers out to sleep on the warm sand. And no, sleeping wasn't all they did.

I wanted to go out on a midnight picnic with Hank, but Mom wouldn't allow it; she wouldn't even let me appeal to Daddy and said we didn't need that fight in the camp. So the most I could do with Hank was walk around the big tent once in a while, mostly when Mom wanted to be alone with Daddy. Some of the girls on the toddler-team went out for a midnight picnic once, I went with them, but all we did was giggle about the boys we liked and make lewd guesses of what we thought they looked like naked. Maybe that's fun when you're fifteen, but I was too old for that now. I wanted something more than embarrassed giggling.

And, there was that other thing too. I didn't want to be the *last* one in the group. I didn't want to be the only one who didn't know what the others were giggling about. Though sometimes it seemed so silly I couldn't imagine any serious person wanting to do it at all, sometimes I couldn't think about anything else. I wondered if it was that way for anybody else. I wanted to ask Mom about it, but she was so busy she never had time; the one time I brought the subject up, she asked me to wait until we got back home so she and I could spend some serious time talking about it. But when your insides are fizzing like a chocolate soda there's no such thing as patience.

So that night, when Hank put his arm around my shoulder and I pulled me close against him, he smelled so good kissing him just felt like the right thing to do. The thing about kissing someone you like kissing—once you start, it's hard to stop. And I didn't want to stop, I just wanted to keep going. But then Zakky's diaper-monitor chimed and Hank pulled away gently and said, "Come'on, Swee'pea, I'll walk you home," as if that was all there was to it, and I wondered how he could be like that. Didn't he have any normal feelings?

And that's the other thing about changing diapers. Mom says that they're punctuation marks in the paragraphs of life. Whatever thoughts you might have been working on, they end up in the diaper pail with all the rest of the crap. And that night, I understood exactly. Whatever fizzy feelings I might have had inside of me, they were all fizzed out by the time Zakky's messy bottom was clean again.

So when some of the team members said to me stuff like, "You can't understand how frustrating it is to be this close," I just smiled weakly and said, "Yeah, I guess so." They were the ones who didn't understand.

After a couple weeks of tinkering, Hank's team fabbed a walking tripod, just to see if they could build one that could walk, run, squat or even mount another for mating; the only thing it couldn't do was lift a leg to pee on a lamp post.

The team went through several iterations until they hit the right combination of musculature and autonomic intelligence; then they fabbed a bunch more for everyone else to play with or experiment on. The bots weren't very big; the largest was the size of Zakky. Some of them had scales, some had fur, some had feathers, some had naked skin; and they were all different colors. At this point, the team was still guessing. It was kind of like having a pack of three-legged dogs from the rainbow planet running around the camp, but Hank said it was necessary for us to observe these things in action to get some sense of what the real tripods might have been like. I wasn't exactly sneaking out to see him behind Mom's back, but I did make sure that my regular chores took me through the bio-tent during his shifts. Mom certainly couldn't complain about me doing my regular duties. Of course, she didn't have to know why I had traded shifts with Marlena Rigby either.

Hank liked my visits. He gave me one of the robots, and even programmed it to follow Zakky around like a baby-monitor, so we would always know where he was. Zakky decided the tripod was a chicken and called it "Fuffy." I thought it looked more like a yellow cat with a limp.

When I said that, Hank admitted that getting the creature to walk right had been his biggest problem. He had started by studying the algorithms for three-legged industrial robots, but plastic autonomy is different from biological, and there are a lot of different ways a three-legged creature can walk. It can move one leg at a time, each one in turn, which means it sort of scuttles or zig-zags or walks in circles. Or it can alternate moving its two front two legs with its single rear leg in a crippled imitation of a four-legged creature. That was was faster but it created musculature issues that weren't resolved in the actual skeletons.

Hank finally resolved it by not programming the tripod at all. Instead, he gave it a neural network and let it teach itself to walk. What it came up with was—well, it was just weird, but efficient. But it still looked like a yellow cat with a limp.

As a joke, Hank taught the tripod to squat on Zakky's potty chair. That made me laugh, and for a moment I thought Zakky might take the hint, but the devil-baby was actively disinterested. Instead, he put a plastic bucket on his head and banged it with a spoon, and laughed delightedly at being inside the noise.

On the last full day before the skywhale arrived, I was helping Mom disassemble the last three fabbers. We wrapped all the pieces in plastic and packed them in stiff boxes. Nobody knew if the Institute would authorize a second expedition. There was a lot of disappointment that we hadn't found more—no books or wall carvings or statues—so the folks who passed out the money had lost some of their enthusiasm. Despite their effusive praise at a job well done, despite their protestations of support, it was no secret that this expedition was considered only a partial success, which is a polite way of saying "an ambitious failure."

Some of the more aggressive members of Daddy's team were arguing for mothballing the entire site as a way of forcing the issue. With all of the equipment still in place, the Institute would have a financial investment in returning; but Daddy shook his head. If a return were guaranteed, then storing the hardware onsite made financial sense; but if the Institute decided not to fund a return, they would write off the machinery, and then it wouldn't be available for any other enterprise anywhere else, and that would hurt everybody. Daddy was right, of course.

Some of the folks were eager to head back home—like Hank; he said he had enough material to fund a dozen years of study, and he could hardly wait to get the skeletons back to the lab and begin micro-scanning and DNA-reconstruction; it was his hunch that the DNA sequences were too short for a creature this size.

But most folks were sad that the adventure was ending so abruptly, and without a real resolution. That was how I felt. Hank was going back to wherever, and I'd probably never see him again. So, I'd sort of made up my mind that I was ready to sneak away from tonight's party with him for an hour or two.

We finished packing the last fabber, and then the toolkits, and we were done. Mom sat down on a bench and sighed. "This was fun."

"Are you going to miss it?"

"Not at all," she said. "Once we get back home, I'll have so much work to do just sorting everything out, I won't have time to miss anything." And then her hand flew up to her mouth. "Oh, sweetheart, I'm sorry. I promised you that we would find some time together, just for us."

"It's all right, Mom—"

"No, it isn't all right. There are things you need to talk about."

I shrugged, embarrassed. "I'm okay now."

"Mm." She didn't look convinced. "All right, let me give you the speech anyway. I know you already know this, but I have to say it anyway, because if I don't say it, you'll think that I don't know it. Come here, sit down next to me."

She put her arm around my shoulder, pulled me close, and lowered her voice almost conspiratorially. "Look, Hank is a real nice boy—" she began.

"He's a *man*, Mom."

"He's a big boy on a big adventure," she corrected. "He won't be a man until he starts thinking like one. And you won't be a woman until you stop thinking like a teenager."

"What is that supposed to mean?"

"What it means is that sometimes, it isn't about *now*. It isn't always about what you want, what you think you need, what you think you have to have. Sometimes, it's about who you're going to be when it all works out, and your responsibility to that moment outweighs whatever you think you want now."

I didn't say anything to that. I could already see where she was headed.

"Sweetheart, here's the question I want you to ask yourself. What kind of a person do you want to be? Whenever you have a big choice in front of you, that's what you have to ask yourself. Is this the kind of thing that the person I want to be would do? What kind of memory will this be? A good one or an embarrassing one or a terrible regret?"

I stared at my knees. Whenever I sat, they looked bony. Knees were such ugly parts of the body. Knees and elbows. Why couldn't somebody design joints that didn't make you look like a chicken? Like the tripods. They had nice joints. They could swivel better than human joints—

"Are you listening to me?"

"Yes, Mom."

"What did I just say?"

"You said that I shouldn't do things that I'll regret."

"What I said was that life is about building a collection of good memories. As you go through life, you need to choose what kinds of memories you want to collect. Because your memories determine who you are."

"Oh."

"All right," she said, patting me on the shoulder in a gesture that was as much resignation as it was completion. "I can see that there are some mistakes you're going to have to make for yourself. Maybe that's the only way you're ever really learn where anything is—by tripping over it in the dark." She sighed. "Go ahead. Go get cleaned up for the party."

There wasn't much left to do. Most of the camp had already been packed up and loaded onto the trucks. So folks just stood around waiting, listening to the tent poles groaning in the wind. Overhead the lights swung back and forth on their wires. We waited in an uneven island of brightness. Only the generator, the mess tent, the hospitality tent and the shower tents were left. Almost everything else had disappeared, or was in the process of disappearing under a fresh layer of sand and dust.

Zakky was asleep in the hospitality tent. His diaper was clean, so I decided not to wake him; Marlena would handle it. She was on diaper-duty tonight. I headed back out to the party.

The mess team had prepared a grand smorgasbord; we had to finish the last of the perishables, so it looked like more food in one place than I'd ever seen in my entire life. The bar was open too. It seemed like an invitation to pig out and drink yourself silly. After all, you'd have twelve hours on the skywhale to sleep it off. But the disciplines of the past four months were too ingrained. The party was more subdued than usual. People were tired, and a lot of folks seemed depressed as well.

The band played everybody's favorite songs, and all of the team leaders made speeches about how hard their folks had worked and how grateful they were and what a successful expedition this had been. And everybody made jokes about the thing and the tripods and offered bawdy speculations about where the thing might really fit and how the tripods made baby tripods, and so on. But it felt forced. I guessed the simmering resentments were still simmering.

I found Hank near the bar, chatting with the other offworlders and a couple of the interns. He saw me coming and excused himself. He took me by the hand and led me out of the tent, out of the island of light, out toward the soft red sand.

"There's something—" I started.

"—I have to tell you," he finished.

"You first."

"No, you."

We played a couple of rounds of that for a bit, laughing at our mutual silliness, until finally, I just blurted it out, "I really like you, Hank," and he said, "I'm engaged to a girl back home" at the same time.

And then I choked on my tongue and said, "What?" and he started to repeat it, and I cut him off. "I heard you the first time." And meanwhile, my heart was in free fall, while my brain was saying, "Thank Ghu, you didn't give say anything stupid—" and my fingers wanted to reach into his chest and shred his heart for not telling me this before.

He held me by the shoulders and made what he must have thought were compassionate noises: "—I just wanted to tell you that you're really sweet, and I'm sure you're going to find the right guy, and I hope you'll have a happy life because you deserve it—oh, look, here comes the skywhale!"

I turned to look, not because I didn't want to see it, but because I didn't want Hank to see the tears running down my cheeks. The big ship came majestically over the ridge, all her lights blazing, a vast platform in the sky. She floated toward us, passing directly over the camp, while everyone came pouring out of the mess tent, cheering and waving. The skywhale dropped anchor half a klick past the camp and began pulling herself down, like a grand gleaming dream come to rest.

The camp speakers came alive with fanfare and trumpets and everyone shouted themselves silly, hugging and kissing each other in celebration. It looked like the party was finally starting; but actually it was ending. This was just the final beat. We had ninety minutes to load and be away, if we wanted to beat the heat of the morning. There wasn't a lot of slippage on that; most of the tents and air-cooling gear had already been collapsed and packed. If we didn't get out on time, we could be in serious trouble.

I threaded my way around the edges of the crowd, looking for Mom. I wanted to tell her that I was going to grab Zakky and his diaper bag, my duffel too, and just go on aboard and curl up in a bunk somewhere. And not have to talk to anybody. There wasn't anything I wanted down here anymore. But Hank came following behind me and grabbed my arm. "Hey, Swee'pea, are you all right?"

"I'm fine, thank you! And I'm not your Swee'pea. You already have a Swee'pea." I pulled free and stormed away, not really caring which direction I headed, so I ended up smack in the middle of the party, and that meant that I had to hug everyone goodbye, even though I'd be seeing most of them on the skywhale, and back home too.

—Until I bumped into Marlena Rigby. "What are you doing here?"

"What do you mean?" she asked, bewildered.

"Who's taking care of Zakky?"

"You're supposed to—he's your brother."

"We traded shifts, remember?"

"No, we didn't—I told you I wasn't going to miss the party."

"Oh, good grief. You are such a stupid airhead! We made this deal a week ago. Oh, never mind—" I headed off to the hospitality tent.

Zakky was gone.

Okay, Mom had come and gotten him.

Except the diaper bag was still there.

Mom wouldn't have collected the baby without gathering his things. I unclipped my phone from my belt. "Mom?"

I waited while it rang on the other end. After a moment, "Yes, sweetheart?" Her voice founded funny—like she'd been interrupted in the middle of a mouthful.

"Where are you?"

"I'm with Daddy, down by the dig. We're … um, saying goodbye. What do you need?"

"Is Zakky with you?"

"Isn't he with you?"

"He's not in the crib."

"When did you see him last—"

"I checked on him thirty minutes ago. I thought Marlena was watching him. We had a deal. But she went to the party anyway." I was already outside, circling the hospitality tent. "He couldn't have gone far—"

She made an exasperated noise. The sound was muffled for a moment, while she explained the situation to Daddy. Then she came back. "We're on our way. You start looking."

Everybody I passed, I grabbed them, "Have you seen Zakky? He's missing—" Nobody had seen him. And nobody had time to help me search either. They were all hurrying to gather their things and board the dirigible. In frustration, I just stopped where I was and started screaming. "My little brother is missing! He's somewhere out there!! Doesn't anybody care?!"

The problem was, the skywhale had to leave whether everybody was aboard or not. She wasn't rigged to withstand the heat of the day. And most of the camp had been dismantled and was already on its way south on the trucks, so there weren't the resources on the ground to support more than a few people anyway.

Thirty seconds of screaming was more than enough. It wasn't going to produce any useful result, and Daddy always said, "Save your upset for afterward. Do what's in front of you, first."

But the screaming did make people aware there was a problem. By the time I finished circling the camp, calling for Zakky everywhere, Dr. Blom was already organizing a real search. She came barreling through like a tank, snapping out orders and mobilizing her dig team like a general at war.

She had a phone in each hand, one for incoming, one for outgoing. "No, you're not getting on the whale," she barked at one of them. "We're not going home until we find that child. We'll ride back in the trucks if we have to." I was beginning to understand why Daddy had invited her along. She was good at organization. And no one argued with Dr. Blom. Except Daddy, of course.

She marched into the mess tent and started drawing on one of the plastic table cloths, quickly dividing the camp and its environs into sectors, assigning teams of three to each sector. "Take flashlights, water, blankets, a first-aid kit, and at least one phone for each person. With a working GPS, dammit!" To the other phone: "Well, unpack the flying remotes then! I don't care. We've still got twenty hours before infra-red is useless."

Dr. Blom didn't stop talking until Mom and Dad came rushing into the mess tent. She looked up only long enough to say, "I need another thirty people to cover the south and west. Pull as many members of your team off the dirigible as you can."

Daddy opened his mouth to say something, then realized how absolutely stupid it was to object. He unclipped his phone and started talking into it. Mom did the same. In less than a minute, the skywhale started disgorging people, running for the mess tent. Other people began pulling crates off the trucks, cracking them and pulling out equipment. I'd never seen so many people move so fast. It was all I could do to keep out of the way. I felt useless and stupid. But it wasn't my fault, was it? I mean, stupid Marlena was the one who screwed up, not me—

Daddy came striding over; his face was red with fury. "Go get your stuff and get aboard the whale. Now." I'd never seen him so angry.

"But I have to stay and help with the search."

"No, you will not. You've done enough already."

"Daddy—"

"We'll talk about this later. If there is a later. Right now, the only thing I want you to do is get onboard and keep out of the way—"

I didn't wait to hear the rest. I sobbed and ran. All the way to the gangplank and up into the whale, where I threw myself into the first empty seat I could find; half of them were filled with duffels and back-packs. Everything was all screwed up. I wanted to die. And I was so angry, I wanted to scream. If only—

Except there wasn't any "if only." There was only me. Stupidly chasing Hank. Stupidly not checking Zakky. Stupidly acting like a stupid little spoiled brat.

Suddenly, I stopped and sat up. Wait a minute. I bounced out of my seat and went looking for Hank. He was on the upper deck, already sacked out in a bunk. I shook him awake, hard. "Come on, I need your help."

"Huh, what—?" He rubbed his eyes. "Look, if you're going to yell at me some more, can't it wait until tomorrow?"

"Zakky's missing. You can track him."

"Huh? What?"

"Would you two take that somewhere else? People are trying to sleep here."

I said something very unpolite. But I pulled Hank out of his bunk. I grabbed his clipboard and dragged him out. "The tripod you gave me for Zakky. You can track it!"

"Well, yeah," He said, still rubbing his eyes. "Only all the equipment is packed up."

"Well, unpack it then!"

"The truck has already left," he said. "We sent it off an hour ago."

"Can we call it back?"

"No, wait—" He closed his eyes for a moment, thinking. He looked like he had gone back to sleep. "Yeah, that'll work." We headed down to the communications room of the whale. It was his turn to drag me. The communications officer looked annoyed at the interruption. I knew her from back home. The kids called her Ironballs, but her real name was Lila Brock. She was a wiry little woman with a hard expression and her hair tied back in a bun.

I didn't understand half of what Hank said to her; most of it was in another language, techno-babble; but even before he finished, she was already turning to her displays and typing in codes. The screens started to fill with overlaid patterns and colors. She frowned. "Wait a minute, let me see what I can read from the satellites." More typing. More colors, more patterns. "Okay, I've got probables." She tapped the big display. "Here, here, and here—"

Hank copied the feed to his clipboard and overlaid it on a map of the camp. "Okay, that first one is the truck," said Hank, eliminating the one that was moving too fast. "And this one is the lounge of the whale—"

"And the last one is in the center of the dig," I said. I recognized the spider-shaped pattern of the excavation. "Come on!" I was already out the door.

"Call the camp! Tell them!" Hank shouted back to Brock, and followed me down the gangplank at a run. The whale was closer to the dig than the mess-tent, but there were rolling dunes in the way—it's not easy to run in sand of any kind. Hank made me slow down, lest I exhaust myself. He kept referring to the updated scans on his clipboard, steering us toward the west end of the dig, where the first big ramp had been carved into the shale. "Down there," he pointed.

I was already calling, "Zakky! Zakky! Where are you?" Off to the left, I could see the first few searchers rolling out of the camp on sand-scooters, and then a sledge carrying Mom and Dad. But we were already heading down the ramp. They were still a few minutes away.

At first it was too dark to see anything, but then the whole night lit up—as if a great white star had been switched on above us. It was startling. At first I didn't understand; we'd already packed most of our fly-beams; but Hank said curtly, "Satellite. False-white laser. Good idea. Somebody was thinking."

It wasn't quite as bright as daylight; in fact, it wasn't even twilight; but it was a hundred times better than the silky darkness. At the bottom of the ramp, there wasn't much to see. The important stuff had been covered with plastic sheets. Most of the open domes had been sealed. All except one.

Hank and I climbed down into it, peering into the different chambers. One still had an inflatable bed in it. The blankets were rumpled. Okay, that explained that. Zakky hadn't been down this way. But Hank wouldn't let me go into any of the tunnels "We have to wait for the others. They'll have lights."

I called into each of the passages, "Zakky, want a cookie? Zakky?" We both listened, but there was no reply. "Zakky? Come on, sweety. It's cookie-time." Nothing. "That doesn't mean anything," I said. "Zakky has selective hearing. If he doesn't want to hear…."

Hank put his hand on my shoulder. "We'll find him. The tripod is down that one."

And then Dr. Blom arrived, scrambling down the steps into the dome, followed by Dad and then Mom and three of the folks from the closest search teams. Suddenly, there were lights flashing everywhere. I grabbed one and headed into the passage Hank had pointed. "Zakky!"

The passage led into the next dome over. Zakky was sitting on the floor playing with three discarded replicas of the famous unknown *thing*. One of the replicas had been shoved point-first into the sand, and Zakky's toy tripod was squatting up and down on it. Its three legs fit perfectly into the openings in the sides of the bowl. "Go potty, Fuffy," Zakky said insistently. "Go potty. Do faw momma."

Daddy and Hank came scrambling into the dome after me. Then Mom and Dr. Blom. I pointed my light at the tripod and everybody just stared for a moment.

I couldn't help it. I started laughing. It was too silly. Then Hank started chortling. And then Mom. And Dr. Blom. And finally, Daddy.

"Well, I guess that answers that," said Dr. Blom. To her phone, she said, "We've got him."

Daddy shook his head. "How are we going to write this up?"

"With a straight face," said Mom, scooping up Zakky. He cooed at her; she cooed back at him, then turned to Daddy and Dr. Blom. "It's not everybody who discovers an alien potty chair. You realize, of course, that a potty chair will get you a lot more headlines than a lustral chalice."

"Yes, there is that," Dr. Blom agreed.

I cleared my throat. "It's not a potty chair."

"But of course it is," said Daddy. "Look at the way the tripod fits. Look at the way—" He stopped. "Why not?"

"There's a hole in the point. Whatever the tripod poops into the bowl is supposed to come out the bottom."

"Well, yes—" said Dr. Blom. "That makes it easier to bury the waste in the sand. It's a portable toilet."

"Yes, it's a toilet," I agreed. "But it's not a potty chair. It's a kitty-box. Sort of."

They all looked at me. "Huh—?"

I poked Hank. "Tell them."

"Tell them what?"

"What you haven't told anyone else yet—that the tripods didn't build these domes."

Everybody looked at him. *Oh, really?* Hank looked embarrassed.

"Um, I didn't want to say anything yet. Because I wanted to be sure. I wanted to run more tests at the university. But, well, yes. Their brains were too small, and their DNA sequences are too short. Too well-ordered. These things weren't sentient. And in fact, it's my guess that they weren't even natural. I think they were genetically designed by the beings who really built these domes. These things...well, they're just the equivalent of farm animals. Like pigs or chickens."

Daddy nodded, considering it. "It almost makes sense. This wasn't a village. It was a farm, and these are a bunch of kennels or coops and storage sheds. The tripods would wander around the crops, eating bugs and insects and little crawling things, whatever. But the horns...?"

Dr. Blom looked annoyed, that same look she always got when Daddy was right. Had she just spent four months excavating a chicken coop? But to her credit, she tried on the idea to see if it fit. "We know that chickens can be designer-trained. We've done it ourselves. If you can train chickens to use a toilet, you don't have to shovel the poop. So why not put out the horns and let them fertilize the field for you."

Mom chimed in then. "Wait a minute. You're not going far enough. Remember that jar of seeds you found? It's part of the process. The farmer puts out horns and scatters seeds in the field. The chickens roam the field, eating the seeds. Some of the seeds get digested, but some don't; they pass right through the chickens. The chickens poop in the horns, and the seeds get planted in their own personal package of fertilizer. Then the farmer picks up the horns and moves them to the next part of the field and starts again the next day. He's planted his crop *and* fertilized it."

They all looked at each other, surprised. It fit. In a bizarre kind of way.

"That's the only explanation so far that fits all the available facts," Daddy said slowly.

Dr. Blom held up a hand. "Wait a minute. Not so fast. Answer one question. Why would any rational being deliberately design a *three-legged* chicken?"

"Isn't it obvious?" I said. They all turned to me, surprised that I even had an opinion. "A three-legged chicken gives you an extra drumstick." I took Zakky from Mom; his diaper was full. "Yick. Come on, baby. The skywhale is waiting."

Out in the asteroid belt, the mountains fly. They tumble and roll silently. Distant sparkles break the darkness. Someday we'll get out there, we'll catch the mountains, we'll break them into kibble to get at the good parts. We'll find out if the centers are nougat or truffle. And some of us—some of us will even become comet-tossers, throwing the mountains around like gods.

Riding Janis

If we had wings
where would we fly?
Would you choose the safety of the ground
or touch the sky
if we had wings?
—Janis Ian & Bill Lloyd

THE THING ABOUT PUBERTY is that once you've done it, you're stuck. You can't go back.

It's like what Voltaire said about learning Russian. He said that you wouldn't know if learning Russian would be a good thing or not unless you actually learned the language—except that after you learned Russian, would the process of learning it have turned you into a person who believes it's a good thing? So how could you know? Puberty is like that—I think. It changes you, the way you think and what you think about. And from what I can tell, it's a lot harder than Russian. Especially the conjugations.

You can only delay puberty for so long. After that you start to get some permanent physiological effects. But there's no point in going through puberty when the closest eligible breeding partners are on the other side of the solar system. I didn't mind being nineteen and unfinished. It was the only life I knew. What I minded was not having a choice. Sometimes I felt like just another asteroid in the belt, tumbling forever around the solar furnace, too far away to be warmed, but still too close to be truly alone. Waiting for someone to grab me and hurl me toward Luna.

See, that's what Mom and Jill do. They toss comets. Mostly small ones, wrapped so they don't burn off. There's not a lot of ice in the belt, only a couple of percentage points, if that; but when you figure there are a couple billion rocks out here, that's still a few million that are locally useful. Our job is finding them. There's no shortage of customers for big fat oxygen atoms with a couple of smaller hydrogens attached. Luna and Mercury, in particular, and eventually Venus, when they start cooling her down.

But this was the biggest job we'd ever contracted, and it wasn't about ice as much as it was about ice-burning. Hundreds of tons per hour. Six hundred and fifty million kilometers of tail, streaming outward from the sun, driven by the ferocious solar wind. Comet Janis. In fifty-two months the spray of ice and dye would appear as a bright red, white and blue streak across the Earth's summer sky—the Summer Olympics Comet.

Mom and Jill were hammering every number out to the umpteenth decimal place. This was a zero-tolerance nightmare. We had to install triple-triple safeguards on the safeguards. They only wanted a flyby, not a direct hit. That would void the contract, as well as the planet.

The bigger the rock, the farther out you could aim and still make a streak that covers half the sky. The problem with aiming is that comets have minds of their own—all that volatile outgassing pushes them this way and that, and even if you've wrapped the rock with reflectors, you still don't get any kind of precision. But the bigger the rock, the harder it is to wrap it and toss it. And we didn't have a lot of wiggle room on the timeline.

Janis was big and dark until we lit it up. We unfolded three arrays of LEDs, hit it with a dozen megawatts from ten klicks, and the whole thing sparkled like the star on top of a Christmas tree. All that dirty ice, thirty kilometers of it, reflecting light every which way—depending on your orientation when you looked out the port, it was a fairy landscape, a shimmering wall or a glimmering ceiling. A trillion tons of sparkly mud, all packed up in nice dense sheets so it wouldn't come apart.

It was beautiful. And not just because it was pretty to look at, and not just because it meant a couple gazillion serious dollars in the bank either. It was beautiful for another reason.

See, here's the thing about living in space. Everything is Newtonian. It moves until you stop it or change its direction. So every time you move something, you have to think about where it's going to go, how fast it's going to get there and where it will eventually end up. And we're not just talking about large sparkly rocks, we're talking about bottles of soda, dirty underwear, big green boogers or even the ship's cat. Everything moves, bounces and moves some more. And that includes people too. So you learn to think in vectors and trajectories and consequences. Jill calls it "extrapolatory thinking."

And that's why the rock was beautiful, because it wasn't just a rock here and now. It was a rock with a future. Neither Mom nor Jill had said anything yet; they were too busy studying the gravitational ripple charts, but they didn't have to say anything. It was obvious. We were going to have to ride it in, because if that thing started outgassing, it would push itself off course. Somebody had to be there to create a compensating thrust. Folks on the Big Blue Marble were touchy about extinction-level events.

Finding the right rock is only the *second*-hardest part of comet-tossing. Dirtsiders think the belt is full of rocks, you just go and get one; but most of the rocks are the wrong kind; too much rock, not enough ice—and the average distance between them is fifteen million klicks. And most of them are just dumb rock. Once in a while, you find one that's rich with nickel or iron, and as useful as that might be, if you're not looking for nickel or iron right then, it might as well be more dumb rock. But if somebody else is looking for it, you can lease or sell it to them.

So Mom is continually dropping bots. We fab them up in batches. Every time we change our trajectory, Mom opens a window and tosses a dozen paper planes out.

A paper plane doesn't need speed or sophistication, just brute functionality, so we print the necessary circuitry on sheets of stiff polymer.

(We fab that too.) It's a simple configuration of multi-sensors, dumb-processors, lotsa-memory, soft-transmitters, long-batteries, carbon-nanotube solar cells, ion-reservoirs and even a few micro-rockets. The printer rolls out the circuitry on a long sheet of polymer, laying down thirty-six to forty-eight layers of material in a single pass. Each side. At a resolution of $3,600^2$ dpi, that's tight enough to make a fairly respectable, self-powered paper robot. Not smart enough to play with its own tautology, but certainly good enough to sniff a passing asteroid.

We print out as much and as many as we want, we break the polymer at the perforations; three quick folds to give it a wing shape, and it's done. Toss a dozen of these things overboard, they sail along on the solar wind, steering themselves by changing colors and occasional micro-bursts. Make one wing black and the other white and the plane eventually turns itself; there's no hurry, there's no shortage of either time or space in the belt. Every few days, the bot wakes up and looks around. Whenever it detects a mass of any kind, it scans the lump, scans it again, scans it a dozen times until it's sure, notes the orbit, takes a picture, analyzes the composition, prepares a report, files a claim and sends a message home. Bots relay messages for each other until the message finally gets inserted into the real network. After that, it's just a matter of finding the publisher and forwarding the mail. Average time is fourteen hours.

Any rock one of your paper planes sniffs and tags, if you're the first then you've got first dibsies on it. Most rocks are dumb and worthless—and usually when your bots turn up a rock that's useful, by then you're almost always too far away to use it. Anything farther than five or ten degrees of arc isn't usually worth the time or fuel to go back after. Figure fifty million kilometers per degree of arc. It's easier to auction off the rock, let whoever is closest do the actual work, and you collect a percentage. If you've tagged enough useful rocks, theoretically you could retire on the royalties. *Theoretically.* Jill hates that word.

But if finding the right rock is the second-hardest part of the job, then the *first*-hardest part is finding the *other* rock, the one you use at the *other* end of the whip. If you want to throw something at Earth (and lots of people do), you have to throw something the same size in the opposite direction. Finding and delivering the right ballast rock to the site was always a logistic nightmare. Most of the time it was just difficult, sometimes it was impossible, and once in a while it was even worse than that.

We got lucky. We had found the right ballast rock, and it was in just the right place for us. In fact, it was uncommonly close—only a few hundred thousand kilometers behind Janis. Most asteroids are several million klicks away from their closest neighbor. FBK-9047 was small, but it was heavy. This was a nickel-rich lump about ten klicks across. While not immediately useful, it would *someday* be worth a helluva lot more than the comet we were tossing—five to ten billion, depending on how it assayed out.

Our problem was that it belonged to someone else. The FlyBy Knights. And they weren't too particularly keen on having us throw it out of the system so we could launch Comet Janis.

Their problem was that this particular ten billion-dollar payday wasn't on anyone's calendar. Most of the contractors had their next twenty-five years of mining already planned out—you have to plan that far in advance when the mountains you want to mine are constantly in motion. And it wasn't likely anyone was going to put it on their menu for at least a century; there were just too many other asteroids worth twenty or fifty or a hundred billion floating around the belt. So while this rock wasn't exactly worthless in principle, it was worthless in actuality—until someone actually needed it.

Mom says that comet tossing is an art. What you do is you lasso two rocks, put each in a sling, and run a long tether between them, fifty kilometers or more. Then you apply some force to each one and start them whirling around each other. With comet ice, you have to do it slowly to give the snowball a chance to compact. When you've got them up to speed, you cut the tether. One rock goes the way you want, the other goes in the opposite direction. If you've done your math right, the ballast rock flies off into the outbeyond, and the other—the money rock—goes arcing around the solar system and comes in for a close approach to the target body—Luna, Earth, L4, wherever. This is a lot more cost-effective than installing engines on an asteroid and driving it home. A *lot* more.

Most of the time, the flying mountain takes up station as a temporary moon orbiting whatever planet we throw it at, and it's up to the locals to mine it at their leisure. But this time we were only arranging a flyby—a close approach for the Summer Olympics, so the folks in the Republic of Texas could have a sixty-degree swath of light across the sky for twelve days. And that was a whole other set of problems—because the comet's appearance had to be timed for perfect synchronicity with the event. There wasn't any wiggle room in the schedule. And everybody knew it.

All of which meant that we really needed this rock, or we weren't going to be able to toss the comet. And everybody knew that too, so we weren't in the best bargaining position. If we wanted to use 9047, we were going to have to cut the FlyBy Knights in for a percentage of Janis, which Jill didn't really want to do because what they called "suitable recompense for the loss of projected earnings" (if we threw their rock away) was so high that we would end up losing money on the whole deal.

We knew we'd make a deal eventually—but the advantage was on their side because the longer they could stall us, the more desperate we'd become and more willing to accept their terms. And meanwhile, Mom was scanning for any useful rock or combination of rocks in the local neighborhood—approximately five million klicks in any direction. So we were juggling time, money and fuel against our ability to go without sleep. Mom and Jill had to sort out a nightmare of orbital mechanics, economic concerns and assorted political domains that stretched from here to Mercury.

Mom says that in space the normal condition of life is patience; Jill says it's frustration. Myself...I had nothing to compare it with. Except the puberty thing, of course. What good is puberty if there's no one around to have puberty with? Like kissing, for instance. And holding hands. What's all that stuff about?

I was up early because I wanted to make fresh bread. In free fall, bread doesn't rise, it expands in a sphere—which is pretty enough, and fun for tourists, but not really practical because you end up with some slices too large and others too small. Better to roll it into a cigar and let it expand in a cylindrical baking frame. We had stopped the centrifuge because the torque was interfering with our navigation around Janis; it complicated turning the ship. We'd probably be ten or twelve days without. We could handle that with vitamins and exercise, but if we went too much longer, we'd start to pay for it with muscle and bone and heart atrophy, and it takes three times as long to rebuild as it does to lose. Once the bread was safely rising—well, expanding—I drifted forward.

"Jill?"

She looked up. Well, *over*. We were at right angles to each other. "What?" A polite *what*. She kept her fingers on the keyboard.

"I've been thinking—"

"That's nice."

"—we're going to have to ride this one in, aren't we?"

She stopped what she was doing, lifted her hands away from the keys, turned her music down and swiveled her couch to face me. "How do you figure that?"

"Any comet heading that close to Earth, they'll want the contractor to ride it. Just in case course corrections have to be made. It's obvious."

"It'll be a long trip—"

"I read the contract. Our expenses are covered, both inbound and out. Plus ancillary coverage."

"That's standard boilerplate. Our presence isn't mandatory. We'll have lots of bots on the rock. They can manage any necessary corrections."

"It's not the same as having a ship onsite," I said. "Besides, Mom says we're overdue for a trip to the marble. Everyone should visit the home world at least once."

"I've been there. It's no big thing."

"But *I* haven't—"

"It's not cost-effective," Jill said. That was her answer to everything she didn't want to do.

"Oh, come on, Jill. With the money we'll make off of Comet Janis, we could add three new pods to this ship. And bigger engines. And larger fabricators. We could make ourselves a lot more competitive. We could—"

Her face did that thing it does when she doesn't want you to know what she really feels. She was still smiling, but the smile was now a mask. "Yes, we could do a lot of things. But that decision has to be made by the senior officers of the Lemrel Corporation, kidlet." Translation: *Your opinion is irrelevant. Your mother and I will argue about this. And I'm against it.*

One thing about living in a ship, you learn real fast when to shut up and go away. There isn't any real privacy. If you hold perfectly still, close your eyes and just listen, eventually—just from the ship noises—you can tell where everyone is and what they're doing—sleeping, eating, bathing, defecating, masturbating, whatever. In space, *everyone* can hear you scream. So you learn to speak softly. Even in an argument. Especially in an argument. The only real privacy is inside your head, and you learn to recognize when others are going there, and you go somewhere else. With Jill…well, you learned faster than real fast.

She turned back to her screens. A dismissal. She plucked her mug off the bulkhead and sipped at the built-in straw. "I think you should talk this over with your mom." A further dismissal.

"But Mom's asleep, and you're not. You're here." For some reason, I wasn't willing to let it go this time.

"You already have my opinion. And I don't want to talk about it anymore." She turned her music up to underline the point.

I went back to the galley to check on my bread. I opened the plastic bag and sniffed. It was warm and yeasty and puffy, just right for kneading, so I sealed it up again, put it up against a blank bulkhead and began pummeling it. You have to knead bread in a non-stick bag because you don't want micro-particles in the air-filtration system. It's like punching a pillow. It's good exercise and an even better way to work out a shitload of frustration.

As near as I could tell, puberty was mostly an overrated experience of hormonal storms, unexplainable rebellion, uncontrollable insecurity and serious self-esteem issues, all resulting in a near-terminal state of wild paranoid anguish that caused the sufferer to behave bizarrely, taking on strange affectations of speech and appearance. Oh yeah, and weird body stuff where you spend a lot of time rubbing yourself for no apparent reason.

Lotsa kids in the belt postponed puberty. And for good reason. It doesn't make sense to have your body readying itself for breeding when there are no appropriate mates to pick from. And there's more than enough history to demonstrate that human intelligence goes into remission until at least five years after the puberty issues resolve. A person should finish her basic education without interruption, get a little life experience, before letting her juices start to flow. At least, that was the theory.

But if I didn't start puberty soon, I'd never be able to and I'd end up sexless. You can only postpone it for so long before the postponement becomes permanent. Which might not be a bad idea, considering how crazy all that sex stuff makes people.

And besides, yes, I was curious about all that sex stuff—masturbation and orgasms and nipples and thighs, stuff like that—but not morbidly so. I wanted to finish my *real* education first. Intercourse is supposed to be something marvelous and desirable, but all the pictures I'd ever seen made it look like an icky imposition for *both* partners.

Why did anyone want to do *that?* Either there was something wrong with the videos, or maybe there was something wrong with me that I just didn't get it.

So it only made sense that I should start puberty now, so I'd be ready for mating when we got to Earth. And it made sense that we should go to Earth with Comet Janis. And why didn't Jill see that?

Mom stuck her head into the galley then. "I think that bread surrendered twenty minutes ago, sweetheart. You can stop beating it up now."

"Huh? What? Oh, I'm sorry. I was thinking about some stuff. I guess I lost track. Did I wake you?"

"Whatever you were thinking about, it must have been pretty exciting. The whole ship was thumping like a subwoofer. This boat is noisy enough without fresh-baked bread, honey. You should have used the bread machine." She reached past me and rescued the bag of dough; she began stuffing it into a baking cylinder.

"It's not the same," I said.

"You're right. It's quieter."

The arguments about the differences between free fall bread and gravity bread had been going on since Commander Jarles Ferris had announced that bread doesn't fall butter-side down in space. I decided not to pursue that argument. But I was still in an arguing mood.

"Mom?"

"What, honey?"

"Jill doesn't want to go to Earth."

"I know."

"Well, you're the captain. It's *your* decision."

"Honey, Jill is my partner."

"Mom, I have to start puberty soon!"

"There'll be other chances."

"For puberty?"

"For Earth."

"When? How? If this isn't my best chance, there'll never be a better one." I grabbed her by the arms and turned her so we were both oriented the same way and looked her straight in the eyes. "Mom, you know the drill. They're not going to allow you to throw anything that big across Earth's orbit unless you're riding it. We have to ride that comet in. You've known that from the beginning."

Mom started to answer, then stopped herself. That's another thing about spaceships. After a while, everybody knows all the sides of every argument. You don't have to recycle the exposition. Janis was big money. Four-plus years of extra-hazardous duty allotment, fuel and delta-vee recovery costs, plus bonuses for successful delivery. So, Jill's argument about cost-effectiveness wasn't valid. Mom knew it. And so did I. And so did Jill. So why were we arguing?

Mom leapt ahead to the punch line. "So what's this really about?" she asked.

I hesitated. It was hard to say. "I—I think I want to be a boy. And if we don't go to Earth, I won't be able to."

"Sweetheart, you know how Jill feels about males."

"Mom, that's *her* problem. It doesn't have to be mine. I like boys. Some of my best online friends are boys. Boys have a lot of fun together—at least, it always looks that way from here. I want to try it. If I don't like it, I don't have to stay that way." Even as I said it, I was abruptly aware that what had only been mild curiosity a few moments ago was now becoming a genuine resolve. The more Mom and Jill made it an issue, the more it was an issue of control, and the more important it was for me to win. So I argued for it, not because I wanted it as much as I needed to win. Because it wasn't about winning, it was about who was in charge of my life.

Mom stopped the argument abruptly. She pulled me around to orient us face to face and lowered her voice to a whisper, her way of saying *this is serious*. "All right, dear, if that's what you really want. It has to be your choice. You'll have a lot of time to think about it before you have to commit. But I don't want you talking about it in front of Jill anymore."

Oh. Of course. Mom hadn't just wandered into the galley because of the bread. Jill must have buzzed her awake. The argument wasn't over. It was just beginning.

"Mom, she's going to fight this."

"I know." Mom realized she was still holding the baking cylinder. She turned and put the bread back into the oven. She set it to warm for two hours, then bake. Finally she floated back to me. She put her hands on my shoulders. "Let me handle Jill."

"When?"

"First let's see if we can get the rock we need." She swam forward. I followed.

Jill was glowering at her display and muttering epithets under her breath.

"The Flyby Knights?" Mom asked.

Jill grunted. "They're still saying, 'Take it or leave it.'"

Mom thought for a moment. "Okay. Send them a message. Tell them we found another rock."

"We have?"

"No, we haven't. But they don't know that. Tell them thanks a lot, but we won't need their asteroid after all. We don't have time to negotiate anymore. Instead, we'll cut Janis in half."

"And what if they say that's fine with them? Then what?"

"Then we'll cut Janis in half."

Jill made that noise she makes, deep in her throat. "It's all slush, you can't cut it in half. If we have to go crawling back, what's to keep them from raising their price? This is a lie. They're not stupid. They'll figure it out. We can't do it. We have a reputation."

"That's what I'm counting on—that they'll believe our reputation—that you'd rather cut your money rock in half than make a deal with a *man*."

Jill gave Mom one of those sideways looks that always meant a lot more than anything she could put into words, and certainly not when I was around.

"Send the signal," Mom said. "You'll see. It doesn't matter how much nickel is in that lump; it just isn't cost-effective for them to mine it. So it's effectively worthless. The only way they're going to get any value out of it in their lifetimes is to let us throw it away. From their point of view, it's free money, whatever they get. They'll be happy to take half a percent if they can get it."

Jill straightened her arms against the console and stretched herself out while she thought it out. "If it doesn't work, they won't give us any bargaining room."

"They're not giving us any bargaining room now."

Jill sighed and shrugged, as much agreement as she ever gave. She turned it over in her head a couple of times, then pressed for *record*. After the signal was sent, she glanced over at Mom and said, "I hope you know what you're doing."

"Half the rock is still more than enough. We can print up some reflectors and burn it in half in four months. That'll put us two months ahead of schedule, and we'll have the slings and tether already in place."

Jill considered it. "You won't get as big a burnoff. The tail won't be as long or as bright."

Mom wasn't worried. "We can compensate for that. We'll drill light pipes into the ice, fractioning the rock and increasing the effective surface area. We'll burn out the center. As long as we burn off fifty tons of ice per hour, it doesn't matter how big the comet's head is. We'll still get an impressive tail."

"So why didn't we plan that from the beginning?"

"Because I was hoping to deliver the head of the comet to Luna and sell the remaining ice. We still might be able to do that. It just won't be as big a payday." Mom turned to me.

"The braking problem on that will be horrendous." Jill closed her eyes and did some math in her head. "Not really cost-effective. We'll be throwing away more than two-thirds of the remaining mass. And if you've already cut it in half—"

"It's not the profit. It's the publicity. We'd generate a lot of new business. We could even go public."

Jill frowned. "You've already made up your mind, haven't you?"

Mom swam around to face Jill. "Sweetheart, our child is ready to be a grownup."

"She wants to be a boy." So Jill had figured it out too. But the way she said it, it was an accusation.

"So what? Are you going to stop loving her?"

Jill didn't answer. Her face tightened.

In that moment, something crystallized—all the vague unformed feelings of a lifetime suddenly snapped into focus with an enhanced clarity. Everything is tethered to everything else. With people, it isn't gravity or cables—it's money, promises, blood and feelings. The tethers are all the words we use to tie each other down. Or up. And then we whirl around and around, just like asteroids cabled together.

We think the tethers mean something. They have to. Because if we cut them, we go flying off into the deep dark unknown. But if we don't cut them…we just stay in one place, twirling around forever. We don't go anywhere.

I could see how Mom and Jill were tethered by an ancient promise. Mom and I were tethered by blood. Jill and I were tethered by jealousy. We resented each other's claim on Mom. She had something I couldn't understand. And I had something she couldn't share.

I wondered how much Mom understood. Probably everything. She was caught in the middle between two whirling bodies. Someone was going to have to cut the tether. That's why she'd accepted this contract—so we could go to the marble. She'd known it from the beginning. We were going to ride Janis all the way to Earth.

And somewhere west of the terminator, as we entered our braking arc, I'd cash out my shares and cut the tethers. I'd be off on my own course then—and Mom and Jill would fly apart, too. No longer bound to me, they'd whirl out and away on their own inevitable trajectories. I wondered which of them would be a comet streaked across Earth's black sky.

> *Take me to the light*
> *Take me to the mystery of life*
> *Take me to the light*
> *Let me see the edges of the night*
> —Janis Ian

Printed in the United States
by Baker & Taylor Publisher Services